TRY ME

ADRIANA LOCKE

UMBRELLA
PUBLISHING INC.

BOOKS BY ADRIANA LOCKE

My Amazon Store

Purchase Signed Copies

Play Me Series

Play Me | Try Me | Show Me

Brewer Family Series

The Proposal | The Arrangement | The Invitation | The Merger |
The Situation

Carmichael Family Series

Flirt | Fling | Fluke | Flaunt | Flame

Landry Family Series

Sway | Swing | Switch | Swear | Swink | Sweet

Landry Family Security Series

Pulse

Gibson Boys Series

Crank | Craft | Cross | Crave | Crazy

The Mason Family Series

Restraint | The Relationship Pact | Reputation | Reckless |
Relentless | Resolution

The Peachwood Falls Series

Tempt | Truly

The Exception Series

The Exception | The Perception

CAST OF CHARACTERS

Gianna Bardot

Drake Bennett

Audrey Van

Renn Brewer

Gray Adler

Astrid Lawsen

Brooks Dempsey

Hartley Adler

PLAYLIST

<u>Playlist</u>

"Touch Me Like a Gangster" by Jessie Murph
"Actually Romantic" by Taylor Swift
"Worst Way" by Riley Green
"Hard" by Hayley Williams
"I Think I'm In Love" by Kat Dahlia

For full playlist, go here.

SYNOPSIS

"Try me."

That's what Drake Bennett said when I declared on my live podcast that **no man could make me fall in love**. The former pro football star turned sportscaster didn't just laugh—he challenged my entire brand.

Gianna Knows Things is built on the idea that love is a choice. Drake says it's a feeling—a magical, uncontrollable, world-shifting experience.

I call BS. He says I'm scared.

The audacity.

So we make a bet. Six weeks of dating … in front of millions of listeners. If I don't fall for him, I win. If I do … don't worry. Not going to happen.

I expected **spicy nights and viral ratings**. What I didn't expect was thoughtful surprises, spontaneous affection, and moments that make my heart do strange things.

Drake isn't who I thought he was, and I can't tell what scares me more: that **he's been playing me all along or that I'm wrong**

about love. Either way, someone's about to get hurt—and I hope it's not me.

CHAPTER
ONE

Gianna

"My sweet friend Audrey likes to say that revenge isn't necessary," I say, adjusting my headphones. "Whoever hurt you has to live with their rotten self, and that's punishment enough."

Roxie, a name I'm positive she chose just before calling into my live-streamed podcast, sighs in abject disappointment.

I smirk. "I wholeheartedly disagree with Audrey."

"*You do?*"

"Of course, I do." I lean toward my bright pink microphone, wondering if Roxie has ever listened to my advice before today. "Sometimes revenge is necessary. Imagine if you take the option of revenge off the table. What happens then? What discourages assholes from being assholes? It's not like they're going to suddenly turn empathetic."

"This is what I've been telling my friends, but they keep telling me that I have to move on. To let it go—to forget what my ex did to me."

"Well, that probably *is* the healthier option. But if you aren't there emotionally and need to check this chump, and the only way for you to take your power back is to toss those cheese slices wrapped in thin plastic on his windshield on a particularly hot day, then do it." I bite my bottom lip, grinning. "*Or,* depending on your definition of revenge, you could find out if his dad is hot and then do with that information what you will."

Roxie's laughter is quick, singing through the recording studio in satisfied, if not amused, notes.

I'm always curious about how seriously my callers take my opinions. I'm even more interested in whether any of them follow through with my *controversial suggestions*, as the head of Canoodle Media calls them. But, as my producer, Francine, always reminds me, I'm probably better off not knowing if they do or don't—plausible deniability and all.

Francine holds up a finger and twirls it from the sound booth, indicating one more caller, and then we'll wrap up the episode.

"Now is a good time to remind everyone that the opinions expressed on *Gianna Knows Things* are my own and not necessarily shared by Canoodle Media or its sponsors," I say, reading the script off the screen in front of me. "The information shared on this podcast is for entertainment purposes only and should, in no way, be considered professional advice. We recommend consulting a professional regarding your specific situation. Now that's out of the way, we have time for one more caller." I scan the screen and find their name. "Hi, Hannah. What do you need to know?"

"I'd love to know why I apparently hate myself," Hannah says with a tight laugh. "Can you answer that?"

We gotta find a way to put notes next to the caller's name so I know what I'm getting into. "No, but I can refer you to a great therapist."

"I'm just kidding. Thanks for taking my call, Gianna. I'm a huge fan."

Francine rolls her eyes, making me laugh.

"Here's what I really need to know," Hannah says. "How do

I know if the guy I've been seeing is serious or if I'm just a friend giving him benefits that he doesn't deserve?"

Here we go …

I managed to answer nine questions—seven call-ins and two online submissions—in this episode without coming across one like this. These are my least favorite situations for a litany of reasons. These inquiries seem crystal clear to me, but my answers always seem to portray *me* as the bad guy. One thing I've learned in this role is that not everyone who asks a question wants the truth. Or my version of it, anyway.

"Before I answer, I want you to be sure you really want the answer," I say.

"Yeah, of course, I do."

"Okay," I say, gritting my teeth. Something in her voice—the hope in her tone—kills me. I'm about to break this poor girl's heart. *Hell, maybe I am the bad guy, after all.* "Hannah, I'm sorry to have to tell you this. He's not serious about you."

Silence.

"If you have to wonder if he's committed to you, then he isn't," I say with as much empathy as I can muster. "Guys put a lot of effort into the things they want. It's that simple."

"Do you really think so?" Her words are nearly a whisper. "He *has* been swamped at work and with family obligations. Maybe I'm being unfair to question his intentions."

"How long has he been this swamped?"

"For a while." She groans. "Actually, it's been months since we've had any real time together. I keep thinking that life will calm down, but it doesn't."

I sigh, carefully adjusting the mic in front of me. "I'm going to go out on a limb and say that I think you agree with me. I think you know down deep that he's not into you anymore. That's why you called me, because you know I'll tell you the truth. I think you're probably sitting around, *waiting*, in his absence, and the needs he doesn't meet are becoming glaringly obvious."

Hannah either whispers that she agrees with me or sniffles. I can't tell which, so I press on.

"No woman who feels loved and valued asks this question. Right?" I ask.

"Yeah," she says softly. "But ... Gianna, I love him."

Of course, you do.

I try so hard not to roll my eyes.

When Francine pitched the idea of segueing my viral advice column, *Just Between Friends*, into a podcast titled *Gianna Knows Things* for Canoodle Media, it wasn't scalability that nearly killed the deal. Our concept wasn't too niche, nor were the production costs too high to almost keep me off the air. The executives could handle my unfiltered takes, and they welcomed my unapologetic opinions with open arms. Pushing the envelope is good for ratings, and at the end of the day, solid ratings pay the bills. But what nearly cost me the deal was my refusal to water down my stance on love, the dirtiest four-letter word in the English language.

The execs thought my take on the idea of coupledom in the modern era, namely that love is a choice rather than a magical chemical reaction, was too countercultural. There was concern of social media backlash. *Would my refusal to believe in love at first sight alienate me from the very demographic I champion?*

It was Francine who convinced Canoodle Media that people, namely women, are tired of having recycled garbage shoved down their throats, and that they crave an authentic voice offering a space that challenges societal norms.

I was in the top trending podcast on most major platforms across all media in two weeks.

"Hannah, I know it feels like you love him," I say. "But love isn't an emotion. It's a decision. It's a choice that you make. You need to set aside your feelings and decide if this relationship is healthy, if it meets *your* needs, and if it's a situation that you want to be in ... as it stands in the real world. Not in your hopes and dreams."

"Wow. Okay." Hannah clears her throat. "You've given me a lot to think about."

"I wish you the best of luck."

The outro music plays as Francine gives me a thumbs-up.

"And that's it for this week's episode of *Gianna Knows Things*," I say. "Tune in next week for more hot takes and cold truths. Bye, everyone."

A prerecorded reel of me thanking our sponsors plays as I peel off my headphones.

The expected rush of weightlessness that I feel at the end of each episode washes over me instantly. It's satisfaction and awe—a flutter of disbelief and delight that I get to talk to people for a living. *People pay me for this.* Never in my wildest dreams did I think this was possible, and not a day goes by that I'm not utterly grateful.

I lug my bag off the chair beside me and haul it onto my lap. Before I can start the search for my keys, my phone lights up next to the computer.

Astrid: Are we still on for tonight?

Audrey: The last I heard, we were meeting at Stupey's tonight at seven. Please tell me we're still on. I miss you guys.

Astrid: We saw you on Monday.

Audrey: And now it's Friday. I don't have a life, okay?

I pick up the device, smiling as I look at my two best friends' names on the screen.

Me: I keep telling you, Auddie. I can help you get a life. Just ask.

Audrey: I'm not brave enough for that kind of life. But thanks.

Me: One of these days …

Astrid: Speaking of days, tonight? Stupey's at seven?

Me: I'll be there.

Astrid: See you guys then.

Audrey: xoxo

I lock the screen, then begin the plunge into the abyss of my new navy tote. Paintbrushes, a package of tissues, and my earbuds are on top. My knuckles swipe against the side of a water bottle as I descend farther into the mess. I find my wallet, the smartwatch I thought I lost, and more candy wrappers than a sweets shop has in stock.

"Why don't they make fobs bigger so I can find them easier?" I groan.

"Hey, Gianna," Francine says, popping into the room. Her hair, the color of ripe cherries—golden with a hint of blush— shines beneath the LED lights. "Am I interrupting something? You look so serious."

I huff a breath. "Why do I buy bags this size when I know damn good and well that I'm going to be pissed off the first time I actually have to use it?"

"I don't know, but that bag is super cute."

"It is, isn't it?" I hold it by the handles and dangle it in the air. "It came with a gaggle of charms that I promptly removed and gave to a friend because I can't handle the jingling all the time. I felt like a cat wearing a bell."

Francine laughs. "Well, we know that you don't need a bell to announce your arrival."

"What's that supposed to mean?" I ask, laughing, too.

"Chaos—the good kind, but chaos nonetheless—both precedes and follows you."

Memories flood my brain of my arrival this morning. My bag and keys were in my left hand, and a latte was nestled carefully in the crook of my left elbow. My right palm held a little orange kitten that I found next to a trash bin in the office parking lot.

Then I stepped inside the building, and all hell broke loose. The kitten went spastic and leaped from my hands like a circus performer. Its claws, which felt more like talons, dug through the sleeves of my shirt and kissed my skin. Super Kitty ripped around the lobby, knocking over plants and a jar of candy off Juni's reception desk. Finally, in a heroic effort by my now-favorite intern, the kitten was captured in a dramatic scene that included a piece of ham, a bit of blood, and more than a little urine on the shirt of the intern ... who will probably never speak to me again.

"Yeah, I guess you're right," I say with a shrug.

"So let's talk about today's episode. How did you feel about it?"

She's leading me somewhere. I can hear it in her tone.

"I feel great about it," I say, sussing her out. "Unless there's a reason that I shouldn't ..."

Her lips press together in a firm line before she shakes her head. "You killed it, Gianna. Our live metrics far exceeded our expectations and nearly broke Canoodle's one-day record. With these numbers, I don't see how you won't get the Thursday evening slot."

The Thursday evening slot? My jaw smashes against the floor. *No freaking way.* "Seriously?"

"Oh my gosh, yes." Her affable smile, the one that helps seal any deal she's after, shines on me as she enters the room. "There was a meeting this morning with Spaulding and the other

Canoodle executives, and your name was brought up repeatedly."

I rise to meet Francine eye to eye … and so I don't fall out of my chair.

The Thursday evening slot is currently held by a true crime podcast that's ending next month, and every podcaster at Canoodle is frothing at the mouth for the opportunity to fill it. Not only is it prime listening time but it also attracts the most sponsorships and has the greatest potential for organic growth.

Scoring that slot is akin to swiping right on a guy who also matches with you—and isn't a creep.

I've imagined owning that hour, but never truly considered that I would be in the running for it. Sure, I've had dreams of making this into a forever type of gig, and I've had delusions of becoming a household name. Never having to go back to serving customers at The Swill because I'm financially set, doing something I absolutely love? *Yes, please!* But that hour will surely go to someone with more experience and a heftier brand … *right?*

"I don't know what to say," I say, brows raised and mouth still agape. "I mean, I know my numbers are great. But *Gianna Knows Things* has only been a thing for six months. We're still growing."

"You're growing right into the Thursday slot if I have anything to do with it."

"Do you really think I have a chance? You're not just hyping me up to make me feel good?" Bubbles of excitement begin bursting inside me, and a giggle passes my lips. "If you are, I love that you'd do that for me, but help me balance my expectations, please."

Her fingertip trails the edge of the table. "I'd say it's between you and Drake Bennett, and that man is a power in his own right."

I hum, hoping it hides the smirk tickling the corners of my lips. "I can handle Drake Bennett, Francine. That's not a problem."

"That sounds like a challenge I'd be more than happy to accept," someone, distinctly *not* Francine, says from the doorway.

I lift my gaze over Francine's shoulder as a ribbon of fire licks through my veins and feast my eyes on the man leaning casually against the doorframe.

Damn.

CHAPTER
TWO

Drake nods subtly toward Francine, politely acknowledging her presence, but his eyes—wild sapphires rimmed with the darkest lashes—are glued to me.

"I don't know about accepting that challenge so quickly," Francine says, teasing him. "Gianna's quite a force to be reckoned with."

"I didn't say that I'd win," Drake says, his grin digging deeper. "I just said I'd be happy to give Gianna a chance to handle me. Sounds fun."

My teeth bite into my bottom lip to keep from smiling too wide. It's also a futile attempt at redirecting my attention away from thoughts of *handling* Drake Bennett, which is easier said than done.

Drake's physical appearance alone could unravel even the strongest woman's inhibitions. Squarish jaw. Thick neck. Corded forearms that scream capability and strength. His body was deliciously sculpted by years as an elite athlete, culminating in a Hall of Fame football career as a tight end. He's hot enough to make your knees weak, but so handsome he steals your breath.

The truly confounding thing about Drake—the piece of him that could seduce even the holiest saint—is his magnetism. Women return his smile without realizing it. Men clamor to be in his circle because his mere presence gives them social proof. He has a way of making everyone feel as if they share a secret with him.

It's almost criminal.

Drake slides one hand into his pocket and moves closer. "How's our resident dream crusher today, anyway?"

I lift a brow in amusement. "Dream crusher?"

"The office plays our podcasts live through the building, you know. I couldn't help but listen to you crush dreams left and right today."

"You're so dramatic."

"And you're so mean," he says playfully. "You're like the Grinch who killed Cupid."

I laugh as he comes closer and the notes of his cologne drift through the air. They're subtle yet intentional—spicy but with discipline. It feels like an assurance that he's a gentleman, but also a promise that he will have no problem being a bad boy if I ask nicely.

My arms cross over my chest, creating a nice view of my cleavage. If Drake happens to notice … oops.

"I like to think of myself more like the female version of Dr. House," I say. "But without the PhD and a much better fashion sense."

"Wasn't he known for his terrible bedside manner?" Drake smirks.

"Only to weak individuals incapable of taking it." I smirk right back. "And I can assure you that I've never heard any complaints about my bedside manner."

His brows shoot up just before a wicked grin curves the edges of his lips. "And I assure you that I can take it."

Now that's *a challenge I'd like to accept.*

My pulse quickens as his confidence gives way to curiosity—

and maybe a little admiration of my ability to give it as good as I get it. It's the cornerstone of our friendship, a push and pull that straddles the line of professionalism in the workplace. But it's okay because it's just for fun. As much as I would like to take him home for a night, I won't.

Francine clears her throat, reminding us that we aren't alone. My head whips to hers just in time to catch a cheeky smile.

"I need to be going," she says. "I promised my husband that I'd be home while it's still daylight outside. But if I could squeeze in just a moment to mention that Mercy Malone's publicist got back with me just before you went on air. She's apparently a huge fan of yours."

"Did you hear that?" I ask Drake smugly. "Mercy Malone, the drummer for Wildfire, is a fan."

If he rolled his eyes any harder, they'd fall out of his head.

"We're trying to work together to get her on your show," Francine says, adjusting her shirt collar. "I'm cautiously optimistic, but there's always a chance that it'll fall through. If it does come together, it might be a quick turnaround. You may want to start putting together some questions. Just in case."

"Absolutely," I say. "I'll get a list to you for approval by Monday."

"They're chill and said nothing's off the table. So have fun with it. Put your famous Gianna spin on it, and it'll be magic, I'm sure." She glances at her phone. "That's it for me. You two can return to your verbal pickleball. Gianna, great work today. And Drake … behave."

I snort. *Come on, Francine. Where's the fun in that?*

"It's a pleasure to see you, as always," he says, flashing her a smile that could kill lesser women. Francine, however, has worked with Drake longer than I have. She's not exactly immune to his charm, but doesn't trip over herself, either.

With a final wave, she leaves and shuts the door behind her. It closes with a crispness that punctuates her departure.

I take a deep, steady breath and blow it out with the same

rhythm. My heart drums in my chest in wild strokes. *The Thursday slot* and *Mercy Malone? Wow.*

"Well, I didn't expect to get confirmation of *that* today," Drake says, stroking his chin. "And I'm rather surprised to get it from Francine …"

"What are you talking about?"

He drops his hand, his eyes twinkling. "When you spin on it, it's magic."

"Like there was any doubt." I mock him with a smile. "How did your show go this afternoon?"

"This is such an imbalanced friendship. Do you know that?"

I roll my eyes. "You only listened to mine because you were here."

"You don't know that. Maybe I listen to yours every week."

"Oh, I'm sure you do," I say sarcastically as I return to the search for my keys. "But even if I were a …" I lift my gaze to his. "What sports season is it right now?"

"Baseball."

I nod before diving back into my tote. "Even if I were a baseball fan, I spent the late morning up to my knees in a dumpster. That reminds me—I need to check to see when my tetanus shot expires. *Ah ha*!" I pull my keys out from under a tampon and dangle them in the air. "I knew they were in there."

"Can we back up to the part about you in a dumpster?"

"Sure. What do you want to know?"

"Let's start with *why*."

Drake half leans, half sits on the edge of the table, rolling up his shirtsleeves. Inch by inch, he exposes his forearms in a casually cool kind of way. I'd think he doesn't know what he's doing —giving great forearm—if it weren't for the way the corners of his lip quirk toward the ceiling.

"Why?" I repeat. "Well, I was doomscrolling the other night and saw someone cutting butterflies out of cans. And I had an idea to take this one weird wall in my kitchen and fill it with butterflies made from different-colored cans. I think it would look beautiful, and it's basically free if I can use discarded material. Then, if I ever get tired of it, I can pull them down and recycle them." I beam. "Smart, huh?"

"Yeah. Great. Now, what about the tetanus part?"

I run a hand absentmindedly over my calf. "I got scratched by something while rummaging. A piece of glass, I think."

"How deep?" he asks, his brows pulling together. His words are absent from the breeziness of before. "Do you know what the glass was from?"

"It's a little hard to tell what touches you when everything shifts each time you move. Have you never been in a dumpster?"

He cocks his head to the side, as if he's uncertain whether to laugh or have me committed. "No, Gianna. I've never been in a dumpster."

"Well, you're missing out. I mean, you have to pick the right one, but you can find fascinating things in there."

"I bet," he deadpans. "Now, where did it slice you?"

"My leg. But really, it's fine. It barely got me."

He lifts off the table and pats the place he just vacated. "Grab a seat."

"I'm good, but thanks."

He sighs, squeezing his eyes closed. "Humor me."

"*It's fine.*"

"Sit." His eyes open, jaw ticking, and his gaze narrows. "Now."

Damn, that's hot. I should push back and not let him anywhere near me when he's bossy like this—a side of him that I've gotten occasional glimpses of before. But who am I to refuse kindness? People say you get out of the world what you put into it, and I've put a lot of nice vibes out there. If the universe is trying to repay me with Drake Bennett's hands on my skin, I can't really turn that down. That would be rude.

And such a missed opportunity.

"You really need to work on your bedside manner." I make a

face as I round the corner of the table. He, however, isn't amused. "Seriously, relax. I have a friend who's a doctor. I'll send her a picture of the cut when I get home."

"Your friend is a doctor?" He steps back as I hop onto the table and pull my knee up to my chest. "A real one?"

"You say that like you're surprised that a doctor would be friends with me."

He arches a brow. "You didn't answer my question, which makes me more doubtful."

"*Yes, she's a doctor*," I say with mock exasperation. "In philosophy but she's a doctor nonetheless." I hike my pant leg up to expose the little cut on the side of my lower leg. It's crimson and jagged—decidedly not pretty. But it doesn't look infected. "See? It's not bad."

He takes the back of my leg with his large hand, bringing the small red line closer to him. His palm is warm, and his fingers press into my skin. His touch is tender, but his skin is rough, and if he notices my goose bumps, he doesn't show it. It's this juxtaposition mixed with his genuine concern that has me struggling not to pant.

For a girl who lives for physical touch? This is big, *big* trouble.

"I think it's superficial," he says, setting my leg down carefully. His eyes don't meet mine. "And it doesn't look angry." He backs away as I tug my pant leg back down. "Do you dumpster dive often?"

"No. Not often. I don't actually enjoy sorting through trash, but it's a necessary part of the hobby sometimes."

"And that hobby might be ..."

I hop off the table. "I like to make art out of things people toss away, like cans, newspapers, and buttons. One of my favorite pieces is a fountain that I made from a urinal. It's so fun."

"That sounds ..." He pauses. "Gross."

I laugh at his reaction, and his chuckle joins mine. Together, it fills the recording booth with an easiness that's hard to find with men. That's one of the reasons Drake and I get along. Beyond his sittable face and fuckable body, he's a pretty likable guy.

"What about you?" I ask, standing beside him. He's a good six inches taller than me, and I have to look up to see him. "What are your hobbies outside of armchair quarterbacking sports teams?"

"I don't armchair quarterback sports teams."

"You decide whether it was a good call or a bad one after the fact. That's the literal definition of armchair quarterback."

He shakes his head, but his half smile erases the sarcasm. "I analyze players and games, discuss sports news and culture." He taps the tip of my nose. "If you listened to an episode, you'd know that."

"How do you know that I haven't listened to an episode?"

He shrugs. "Just a hunch."

"I know you think I'm just a pretty face, but I played volley-ball in middle school. I know a thing or two about sports."

His chuckle rumbles through me. "I didn't realize I was standing next to one of my peers."

"See?" I grin. "You don't know me as well as you think you do."

I return to the other side of the table and retrieve my purse, phone, and keys. Drake checks his phone, chuckling at something on the screen. I'm curious about what he's seeing and who sent it. I really don't know much about him. *Who are his friends? Where does he live? What does he do for fun?*

Is he a good fuck?

"So what are you doing this weekend?" he asks as I hoist my tote onto my shoulder. "Any big plans?"

"I'm meeting my friends for dinner tonight. And I'm supposed to have a date tomorrow night, but we'll see."

"Hopefully, you've met your dream-crushing quota for the week, and he'll be spared from your wrath."

"You're hilarious." I stand next to him again. "Matthew and I have gone out a few times. It's nothing new."

"So *Matthew* understands he could be crushed at any given time?"

I bump Drake with my shoulder. He humors me by pretending to be knocked off balance.

"We're not serious," I say, thinking about how just un-serious my thing with Matthew really is—which is why it works out perfectly. I glance down at my phone and spot a text from Astrid. "I need to get out of here. I have a few errands to run before I meet my friends for dinner."

Drake opens the door and waits for me to exit first. Once in the hallway, we face each other. His smile lifts mine as Juni makes her way around us, muttering something under her breath that has her shaking her head.

"Don't forget to check your tetanus shot records," he says.

"Yes, Daddy."

His blue eyes darken, resembling a raging storm.

I give him a sweet, innocent smile and leave with the upper hand.

CHAPTER
THREE

Gianna

"Have I ever told you two how much I appreciate that you're not completely unhinged?" I slide into my usual seat beside Audrey. "Because if I haven't, let me do it now."

"Bad day?" Astrid asks from across the table.

I plunk my tote next to her purse on the empty chair to my left. "No, I had a great day, actually, and we can get into that later. But I've just spent an hour and a half haggling with a woman online about the price of an old coat tree. I need a stiff drink." I sigh. "A stiff cock wouldn't hurt, either."

Audrey's cheeks match the color of her blush-pink cardigan.

I settle in my seat, attempting to let go of the stress saddling my shoulders, and listen to their banter about the music playing overhead. It's opera, so I have nothing to add to the conversation. The only music I understand usually includes cowboy boots. When we first discovered Stupey's, I found their switch to opera music in the evenings to be a bit disturbing. Like … *what the heck?* Now, though, I kind of like it. I pretend I'm the main character in an action movie and the bad guys are about to come in … and I save the day.

Naturally.

Kim, our favorite server, slides up to the table and hands me a fruit-laden sangria. "Hey, Gianna! The girls said you were coming, so I figured you'd want your usual."

"You know me so well," I say, taking the drink from her.

"Sorry that this took a second, Astrid," Kim says, handing her a beer. "Do you mind if I come back and get your order? I have a table being a giant pain in my ass, and they're over there signaling for me again."

"Go do what you need to do," Audrey says. "We're just catching up. We're in no rush."

Kim's shoulders sag. "Thank you. I'll be right back."

"A beer?" I point a freshly manicured nail at Astrid as Kim scurries away. "Are you kidding me right now?"

"Shut up," she says, taking a sip.

"You've spent far too much time in Sugar Creek if you're ordering a beer," I joke. "The next thing you know, you'll be hunting wild game for dinner."

"I can't help it. It's all the guys drink on the ranch, and it's the only thing the bar in Sugar Creek always has in stock. I love it out of necessity."

Astrid happily munches on a piece of bread like she hasn't a care in the world. Funny what a good dick can do for a girl.

Her relationship with rugby pro Gray Adler has been an interesting study—and it proves my theory on love. They utterly despised each other when they first met. I actually considered that I might have to bail Astrid out of jail a few times. It got so bad that I even threatened the guy with a Taser while sitting in this exact chair, coincidentally. But somewhere down the line, they worked through their differences—and they *chose* to commit. They weren't sprinkled with fairy dust that turned their pupils into flashing hearts. They decided to love each other.

If more people realized that was how this works, the world would be a better place.

"Are you still liking it on the ranch?" Audrey asks.

"We finally got settled in the cabin on Wednesday," Astrid says. "Now I'm trying to get my home office set up, ignore the revolving door of people coming in and out every day, and learn how to deal with the locals."

"What do you mean?" I ask, sipping my drink. The wine is perfectly mellowed by the sweetness of the strawberries and the zing of the citrus fruit. It's liquid happiness.

"Oh, just that there are expectations in Sugar Creek. There are town hall meetings and charity events that require your presence. If someone dies, you contribute to a flower fund by adding dollars to an envelope that a kid on a bike passes around." She flinches as if this still hasn't fully processed in her brain. "If you go to the farmers' market once, you must then go every week. If not, someone will come knocking on your door with soup, assuming you're sick. Ask me how I know."

I laugh at the look on Astrid's freckled face.

She sighs with a smile. "But, yes, Auddie. I'm still liking it there. I'm really, *really* happy. It's a different way of life—slower and quieter. But I love it, and I think I'll miss it when we come back to Nashville when the rugby season starts in January."

"I love this for you," Audrey says. "Gianna and I would love to come visit you."

"As soon as I get settled, I'm having you come out for a weekend," Astrid says, grinning. "We'll go line dancing and play with the chickens. It'll be fun."

We've officially lost Astrid to a life of chickens and flannel. It was good while it lasted.

"How's the new house?" Audrey asks. "Did you finally decide what mural you're going to paint in the sun room?"

"Hear me out ..." I laugh as Audrey and Astrid exchange a look. "I saw this thing online a couple of days ago, where you take pennies and lay them over the floor and then cover it in a clear epoxy. It's so gorgeous, and it fits my aesthetic because no one uses pennies anymore ... although I don't know if it's legal to use pennies like that." I start to think that through, then stop myself. "I just don't know how to find that many pennies."

Astrid shrugs. "If anyone can find them, you will."

"Damn right," I say as Kim arrives at the table. I make my order quickly. As my friends decide what they want to eat, I check my texts.

> Francine: It's a go on Mercy! 🐷 Finalized it a few minutes ago.

My fingers fly across the keys as I bite back a yelp of excitement.

> Me: OMG. Can I tease it?

> Francine: Yes. Let's not give out her name and just hype up that someone very cool will be joining you on Friday. That should push our live stream numbers, and then we'll get a surge in playbacks once word gets out that it was Mercy.

> Me: I'm just … 😭 Thank you for making this happen!

> Francine: It wasn't me. It was teamwork. Now go celebrate.

I glance up, but Audrey is trading book recommendations with Astrid and Kim. So I hop to my Social account, find a suitable picture of me looking like I have a secret, and type out a caption.

@giannaknowsthingspod: I know something you don't know … but I'll share it with you. Soon. 😉

Almost immediately, my notifications pop off. The number climbs higher and higher. My inbox number grows until the count maxes out, and my text alerts ping my phone. I could sit in this moment and absorb this reaction forever. But before I close my screen, I notice one comment that piques my interest.

@drakestakepod: The options with you are endless.

I laugh to myself, imagining the little grin cracking his cheeks and the tease in his voice if he were saying this aloud. I give his comment a heart and then respond.

@giannaknowsthingspod: I like to keep things interesting.
@drakestakepod: I don't think you need to try so hard.
@giannaknowsthingspod: Can't help it. It just comes naturally.

The replies to our exchange are a wildfire, an assault of marriage proposals to Drake, and a nice mixture of comments to me suggesting that I'm either the greatest podcaster ever or that I should off myself for daring to breathe. But then there are the other, far more entertaining comments suggesting that Drake and I have dated, are dating, or should date. *Gotta love social media.*

Kim is gone when I lift my gaze to my friends. Astrid and Audrey are engaged in a conversation that has Audrey biting her lip. I set my phone face down on the table and lock in.

"I agreed to teach a couple of online philosophy classes next semester," she says. "I hope it's enough to get my juices flowing again."

"I've told you," I say, smirking. "I know people who could have your juices flowing in ten minutes tops."

Astrid stifles a laugh as Audrey looks slightly horrified.

In some respects, it's altogether amazing that Audrey has

reached the age of twenty-seven without being sullied. She has been friends with Astrid and me since high school, after all. But Audrey has held tight to her convictions. As much as I tease her about introducing her to the wilder side of life, namely, enjoying a sex life without feeling guilt or remorse, I respect her choices. I'd probably die if she ever took me up on one of my offers.

But that doesn't mean that I don't try—especially because Audrey has seemed a bit down since the beginning of summer. She spent months finding ways to hang out around "her crush" and had finally talked herself into shooting her shot … only to discover that he's engaged. *I'm still heartbroken for her.*

"I'm joking, but I'm also not," I say. "Maybe it's time to throw a little caution to the wind, Auddie. Let your hair down. Have some fun."

"While I appreciate your concern, I'm not sure our definitions of fun in this context match very well," she says sweetly.

"Maybe not. But I don't think we're as far apart as you might think."

Astrid groans. "I can't wait to see where you're taking this one, Gianna."

"Patience, grasshopper," I say, laughing before returning my focus to Audrey. "Isn't it true that Socrates believed that the more you know, the better choices you can make to find true happiness?"

"Yes," she says, curiosity thick in her tone. "How do you know that?"

I throw up my hands. "Why does everyone today seem surprised that I have smart friends?"

"Gianna must be fucking a philosopher," Astrid whispers to Audrey just loud enough for me to hear.

"Fucking a philosopher?" I gasp. "*I would never.* Take that back. No offense, Auddie. Your philosophy doctorate is super hot. I'm just not sure it would be on a guy. I mean, the only visuals we get of that sort of thing are busts of serious-looking men with no glasses."

Astrid shakes her head, grinning.

"Glasses would help." I shrug. "Think about it."

We pause our conversation to chitchat with Kim as she doles out our dinner. The asshole customer finally left just moments before Kim lost her cool. We try to distract her with tales of our week until another server calls her away.

Astrid waves at someone across the room. "Excuse me for just a second. I need to say hello to someone."

"Sure," Audrey says as Astrid stands.

We watch as she approaches a *very* handsome man standing at the front of the restaurant. He's much taller than Astrid, with sandy brown hair and a solid jaw. He carries himself with a sexy confidence that reminds me of someone else I know.

"I didn't say that I'd win. I just said I'd be happy to give Gianna a chance to handle me. Sounds fun."

A smile tickles my lips. *That it does, Drake.*

"Who the heck is that?" Audrey asks. "He looks vaguely familiar, but his name eludes me."

I refocus on the man conversing with our friend. "Don't know. I've never seen him before. I'd remember that face."

Astrid gives a final smile and then returns to her seat.

"Hello?" I ask as her ass hits her chair. "Who in the hell was *that*? You have two very single friends sitting right here."

"Jason Brewer!" Audrey shakes her head. "I knew I recognized him. He's Renn's brother, right?"

Well, that makes sense. Those Brewer men, especially the youngest one, Tate, are *stun-ning*. I have no idea how Astrid works with them without a bib to catch her drool.

Astrid returns her napkin to her lap. "Yes, that's him. Jason owns Brewer Air, which is convenient when I'm trying to schedule a family vacation for their entire freaking family. Having an airline at my disposal makes things infinitely easier."

"Who has an airline at their disposal?" I laugh before taking a large drink. "It must be nice to live in their world."

"They don't complain much," she says, smiling. "But can we

get back to the fight you were having over a coat tree? What in the world was that about?"

"What's a coat tree, anyway?" Audrey asks. "Or is that a euphemism I'm not aware of?"

I chuckle. "It's a tall wooden pole, kind of, with hooks on it. People put them in foyers and hang their coats and hats on them."

Audrey nods, adjusting the ribbon in her hair. "Oh, yeah. I know what you're talking about. My parents have one. I've only ever heard them called a hall tree, though."

"Are you getting into coats all of a sudden?" Astrid asks, scooping rice up with her fork. "Or is this another project?"

"Project, of course."

My friends exchange a glance that can easily be read as *here she goes*—the *she* meaning *me*—and that's fair. I'm always getting myself into one project or four hundred. Luckily, my friends understand my artistic quirks and indulge my big ideas … even though they probably think I've lost my mind most of the time.

"But my vision may or may not come to fruition because the woman who has the perfect coat tree has decided it's worth a small fortune." I huff. "It's in a backyard barn. She's not even using it, yet she won't sell it to me at a reasonable price. Hell, if I pay her what she wants, I won't have a house to put it in. It'll be me and the perfect coat tree living in my car. So sad."

"It may hold sentimental value," Audrey says as if getting attached to a piece of pine is normal behavior. "Maybe it was her grandmother's, or her late husband hung his cap there every night after work."

"Yeah, or she might be trying to get rich off me, Auddie."

Astrid snorts. "There's only one type of pole that you can get rich on, and I don't think it's an antique hall tree."

"I'll have to take a turn on that pole to afford this one if she doesn't cut me a deal," I say, groaning.

Audrey takes a drink of her Arnold Palmer. "You could

always keep searching until you find a more affordable option. I'm sure there are others out there that will work just as well."

"Audrey," I say, giving her a pointed look that makes her smile. "I love you. Endlessly, really. But this isn't a moment when I need you to be sweet and reasonable. I need you to ask me whose car we're taking to go steal that coat tree tonight."

"Let's change the subject." She shakes her head as if she doesn't know whether to laugh or be scared. "How is the podcast going? Today's episode was fantastic."

I beam. "Thank you." A bubble of excitement gathers in my stomach, making it hard to sit still. "So two fabulous things happened today. The first is that Mercy Marlow, drummer for Wildfire, accepted our request for an interview."

"No way!" Astrid says, covering her mouth.

"Gianna, this is incredible. I can't wait to listen," Audrey says.

Astrid laughs. "Can you ask anything you want? Because I have a few questions I'd like to throw in the mix."

"They said anything goes, so, yeah. I have open access to her." I giggle, still stunned. "I still can't believe this is happening."

"Believe it." Audrey places her hand over mine, her eyes shining with pride. "You deserve this, my friend."

Gosh, I love how supportive my friends are. They are truly the best thing that has ever happened to me.

My eyes begin to grow foggy, but I'm not about to cry. I'm no sap.

"And the other very cool thing is that my producer told me that I'm in the running for the Thursday slot," I say, dancing in my seat. I'm too pumped not to move, and I don't care who is watching. The movement also helps segue the sappy feelings to more celebratory ones. "That's like prime time for podcasts, guys. The big leagues."

Astrid smiles. "I can't say I'm surprised."

"Really?" I ask, laughing. "Because I am."

"No. You've found your niche, and anyone with eyeballs can see that you're perfect for this," Astrid says. "Who are you running against?"

I take a breath and lick my lips. "It's apparently between me and *Sports Take* with Drake Bennett."

An amused grin slips across my cheeks. Even the man's name is a vibe, leaving a taste on my tongue after it passes my lips. It's too bad that he isn't my type.

Astrid leans forward, her eyes crinkling in the corners. "Drake Bennett, huh? Gray listens to his podcast all the time. He says that Drake's the only sports guy worth listening to because he really knows his stuff."

"I will never tell Drake that," I say, laughing.

"Why?" Audrey slices her chicken breast. "That's a nice thing. He'd probably like to hear it."

"Of course, he would, which is precisely why I won't tell him." I shrug, dusting a strand of hair off my shoulder. "He's the kind of guy who doesn't need his ego stroked, okay? He's hot as hell. I think his show is the most popular sports podcast in the world—if not, it's close. And he's also a reasonably nice guy." I lift a brow before taking a sip of my drink to cool myself down. "See what I mean?"

"Oh, I see what you're saying," Astrid says, grinning.

Audrey giggles. "Me, too. Is he your next victim?"

"Absolutely not." I shove a forkful of salmon into my mouth. "And I can't decide whether I'm offended by your use of the word *victim* to describe the men I sleep with, or if I'm proud of it."

Astrid sets her fork down and lifts her glass, swaying it back and forth in the air. The smugness of her grin piques my interest.

"What?" I ask.

"Why did you say *absolutely not* in response to Audrey's question? He seems right up your alley."

I snort. "Of course, he's right up my alley. I can't imagine a female who wouldn't want him up their alley." Turning to

Audrey, I wink. "That was a euphemism in case you didn't catch on."

"Believe it or not, I do get them sometimes," she says, shaking her head.

Our laughter floats through the air, attracting glances and smiles from patrons nearby. A woman not far from us lifts a glass in a toast. *To what?* I don't know. Maybe she's just acknowledging our friendship. But I respect the sentiment and lift mine back to her.

Kim drops by to check on our table, and I use the opportunity to segue our conversation from Drake to Kim's new puppy because the last thing I want to delve into tonight is my coworker. While *delving into him* would undoubtedly be a memorable experience, it's also undoubtedly even better in my head.

And that's where it'll stay.

CHAPTER
FOUR

DRAKE

The back door springs stretch, pinging like metal does when it's old and begging to break. I can't remember a time when they didn't sound like this. I've offered to replace the door many times, but every time, the offer is quickly refused.

"Mom," I call out. I step across the threshold and breathe in the scent of freshly baked blueberry muffins. "It's me."

I listen for her to shout back or for her footsteps against the hardwood, but the only thing I hear is a sports show Dad has on in the living room. Despite the pang in my chest, I smile.

Mom and I have always been close. My sisters were Daddy's girls, which meant that my mom and I formed a special bond. Still, up until just a few years ago, Dad would be the one meeting me at the door. He wanted to hear all about my life, fascinated by a world he had always dreamed of living in, but married too young and had kids too soon to see if he could make it as a pro athlete. My sisters were his pride and joy, but I was the one who carried his dreams across the goal line.

I know he's proud of me, even on the days he doesn't remember who I am.

"Hey, you," Mom says, taking me by surprise. Her blue eyes, the same color as mine, brighten as they settle on me. "I didn't think you were coming today."

I pull her into a hug, letting her hold on to me for a few extra seconds. "I was going to stay home and get some work done, but your daughters called me last night." I pause to roll my eyes for effect. "They told me they were coming here this evening, and I couldn't let those two heathens win any favoritism points."

Her laughter is as breezy as it gets these days. "*My daughters*? You mean *your sisters*?"

"I prefer to think of them as your daughters, but yes. Elodie and Evie. Your spawn." I widen my eyes before I laugh, too. "What time are they supposed to be here?"

"With those girls? Who knows. They'll get here when they get here." She shrugs as if she's as helpless when it comes to my sisters as the rest of the world. "They're going to entertain your father so that I can have a few minutes with my friends. I'm gonna see if I still know how to drink a martini."

I flash her a reassuring smile. She doesn't leave Dad much anymore—out of love, sure, but there's some misplaced guilt in there, too. This is all still so new, and we're walking a tightrope about how to handle this reality. Especially Mom.

"Well, if you need help remembering how to do that, let me know," I joke. "My skills are razor sharp."

She laughs, leading me into the kitchen. "I bet they are. Hungry?"

"Is that a serious question?"

Her smile spreads from ear to ear. I'm not about to tell her that I hit a drive-thru in Nashville before I left the city and downed two breakfast sandwiches and a hashbrown. At Mom's house, I'm always hungry even when I'm not.

I don't make the rules. I just live by them.

"Let me fix you a sandwich." Mom turns toward the refrigerator, gesturing to a basket on the table. "I made some muffins this morning if you want one while you wait."

"Do you know one of the things I love most about you ... besides the fact that I'm your favorite child?" I ask, reaching for a blueberry-dotted piece of heaven. "It's that you have an appetizer on hand for every occasion."

"Bacon or sausage for your sandwich?" she asks, poking around the inside of the fridge.

I hum as I consider my choices. "Bacon."

"Good. I bought a package of applewood smoked bacon at the grocery and I've been wanting a reason to fry it. Your dad has been on a sausage kick and I can't fry bacon just for me. It's too much work."

I lean against the counter, peeling the wrapper from my muffin like I've done a million times over the past thirty-two years. Despite not having lived here since I left for college at eighteen, it still feels like home. The door is always open for my sisters and me. We could swing by and grocery shop from Mom's pantry and it would somehow delight her. She gets a thrill when we bring dirty laundry with us.

There's a sense of peace inside these walls. Growing up, my friends would often comment on it—how our home felt different from everyone else's. Everyone was welcomed with open arms. Everyone left with a full stomach. As life has gone on, I realize how special it really is to have a home like this to fall back on. My biggest dream, more than any Hall of Fame jackets or podcast numbers, is replicating this.

So far, it's the only failure to my name.

"Evie got a new boyfriend," Mom says over the sizzle of the bacon. "Did she tell you?"

"Yeah."

"What do you think about him?"

I shrug, popping a chunk of muffin into my mouth. *Damn, that's delicious.* "I haven't met him yet, so I don't know." *If he's secured Elodie's approval, he's probably all right.*

"Just based on what she's told you, what do you think?"

"What do *you* think about him based on what she's told *you*?" I ask, chuckling.

She looks at me over her shoulder. "I know I get an edited version. I might be getting old, but I'm not naive."

"I'm not either, which means that I know *I* also get an edited version."

Her brows pull together. "Why?"

I take another bite of my muffin. "Because Evie knows that if she tells me he steps a toe out of line, that I'm going to show up. Remember Tony Rosedale?"

Mom nods with her back to me. I know she remembers Tony Fucking Rosedale. I also know that Tony Fucking Rosedale remembers me and won't ever come within ten miles of either of my sisters again. *I won't get within five hundred feet of him either just in case the restraining order is still in effect, but that's beside the point.*

"If you want the truth, you need to ask your daughters. I'd start with Elodie," I say. "She's the oldest. Aren't the oldest children supposed to be the most responsible and honest?"

"Oh, like she's going to tell me the truth." Mom snorts. "Those two girls are as thick as thieves."

"Well, you raised them this way."

"You're damn right I did." She fiddles with the flame on the stove, turning it down as the bacon starts to pop. "I told Evie to bring him for dinner next Sunday. Maybe we can figure him out together."

I swallow and toss the wrapper in the trash. "Sounds good." I pause, licking the remnants of the snack off my lips. Then I clear my throat and try to keep my voice as nonchalant as possible. "So how's Dad?"

Mom exhales a long, deep breath. Her shoulders fall with the weight my question just lumped on them—and I hate it.

My fists curl into balls at my side as I watch her wrestle with the topic that has always brought us so much happiness and safety but now is associated with pain. *And dread.* Fire licks at the back of my throat as I, too, fight the emotions creeping inside me. There's nothing fair, or fixable, about this situation. And as the man my father raised, the man he raised to take care of my mother and sisters in times like this, it's clear that I don't know what the fuck I'm doing. I can offer suggestions and step in to help, but my help isn't always wanted.

How do you balance taking the lead and staying in the role of your parents' child?

"He had a really rough night," Mom says, her tone packed with the exhaustion she tries to hide from me. "He kept trying to find his keys so he could go to work, and then he went into the garage and got angry because he thinks someone stole his truck."

I frown. "How did you handle that?"

She sighs, gripping the countertop while the bacon crackles in the pan beside her. "I told him that I'd be upset if someone stole my car and that we'd check on it this morning. Then he was angry that I wouldn't let him go to work. But what do I do? Confuse him more by telling him that he retired years ago? It's a nightmare."

"You're handling it the best you can," I say, squeezing her shoulder as my heart splinters in my chest. The focus is always on Dad now, and what he needs and what's best for him. Mom's suffering, too. And it's moments like that where I wonder how much she suffers in silence. "It can't be easy to navigate this." *Especially since Dad never raised his voice once to you until he got sick.*

"It's not, Drake. It's not." She sags under my palm briefly before standing tall and sniffling. "But we can do hard things, and this is a hard thing we must do. Right?"

"This is a hard thing, and we will do it together. Preferably leaving Evie out of all important decisions because her answer to everything is a beach house."

Mom laughs, picking up her fork. "It is, isn't it?"

"Again, you raised her," I say, giving her shoulder another gentle squeeze.

"No. That's on your father. He's the one who spoiled her rotten."

"Sure. I wouldn't take the blame for that either," I tease. "Is Dad awake now? I heard the TV on and figured he was in there. I mean, the whole neighborhood probably can hear that TV …"

"Tell me about it. I'm ready to buy earplugs or accidentally lose the remote." She grins as she removes two strips of bacon and places them on a bed of paper towels. "We had a slow morning and just eased into the day. He seems pretty good. Tired, but his mind is pretty clear."

"I'm gonna go say hi."

She reaches for a plate. "I'll bring your sandwich to you."

Each step I take toward the living room feels like the beat of a drum. Pictures of my sisters and me hang on the walls, reminiscent of a time when the old man sitting in a brown recliner with his back to me was a six-foot-three, barrel-chested behemoth who could bench-press a small car. Flames burn a hole in my chest as I approach my dad, a shell of the man he once was.

"Hey, Pops," I say, keeping my voice light and easy.

He flinches, gripping his armrests, and it takes a split second for him to recognize me.

"Drake!" He stands, shoving himself up with shaky arms. I don't rush in to help him. He's capable, and I know how defeating it would be for him to think he was weak in my eyes. *I'll never let that happen.* "How are you, boy?"

Dad pulls me into a hug. He pats my back and runs a hand along the top of my head like he did when I was a child.

"I'm good," I say, as he releases me. I search for the remote and turn the TV down. *No wonder he didn't hear me come in. I can't hear myself think.* "How are you? You look great."

"Oh, yeah, I'm doin' just fine. Your mother takes damn good care of me." He sniffs. "Do I smell bacon?"

Laughing, I take a seat on the sofa under the window. "Yeah, I don't know how you can smell it over the sound of the TV."

Dad chuckles. "That's what your mom says all the time. Tells me to turn it down. Hell, if you can't hear it, you might as well turn the damn thing off."

"She might not be mad about that." I toss one of the million throw pillows out from under my ass. "She's making me a sandwich. You know Mom. She has to feed me as soon as I walk in the door."

"Yeah, you gotta let her do that. It makes her happy, and there's nothin' I like more in this world than to see your mother happy." He takes his seat again, exhaling in a rush as his back rests against the chair. "How was the trip out here? You came in from Chicago—no, you're in Nashville now. That's right."

"Yeah, I'm in Nashville. The drive up was easy this morning. No farm equipment hogging the roads. Great weather. Couldn't have asked for a better trip, really."

He nods. "I heard your sisters are coming today."

"Why does everyone call them my sisters? They're your daughters."

He chuckles, his cheeks growing rosy.

"Yeah, Mom said they were coming this afternoon to hang out with you for a while." I make a face that makes his chuckle turn into a full-bellied laugh. "Lucky you."

"Your mother thinks I can't be here alone." The laughter subsides and a somberness sweeps across his features. "She hid my keys from me. Hell, she hired a neighbor boy who doesn't know shit from Shinola to mow our lawn." He throws up his hands in exasperation. "Can you believe that? The kid doesn't even get the lines right, and he just about killed your mother's rose bushes." He huffs, clenching the armrests. "I don't know what we pay him but it's double too much."

"I think she just wants you to enjoy your retirement, Pops."

He scoffs again but lets it go. "How's work going? You still with the podcast?"

My chest warms. These days are infinitely easier than the days he thinks I'm still in high school. *Or the days he tries to ground me for what he construes as "talking back."*

"Yeah. Still with the podcast. It's going really well, actually. I might get a new spot in the lineup, so that's exciting."

"What about a woman? Have you got a girlfriend yet? It's up to you to carry on the Bennett name, you know." His brows tug together. "I don't know how old you are these days, but you sure as hell aren't getting any younger."

I exchange a smile with Mom as she enters the room. "I think I have a few good years ahead of me yet, Dad. I wouldn't worry about it too much." Mom hands me my sandwich. "Thank you."

"What are we gonna do with this boy, Barb?" Dad asks, grabbing for Mom's hand.

She goes to his side and laces their fingers together. "I think he's doing just fine. Although, I wouldn't mind having some grandkids."

"I hope you are having this same discussion with your daughters. Otherwise, this is quite sexist and I'm offended."

"*Oh, hell no,*" Dad says with more emotion than I've seen him have in a while. "My little girls aren't having kids for twenty more years. You watch your mouth."

I take a bite of my sandwich, the bacon perfectly crisp yet buttery, and try not to laugh. I'm not sure if this is one of those confused moments where he thinks his girls are teenagers, or if he's going into protective dad mode. It's hard to tell.

"Have you met any nice ladies lately?" Mom asks, batting her lashes. "Since Dad brought it up."

"Do you mean have I met anyone in the grocery store or biblically?" I ask, smirking at her.

Mom gives me a look that elicits a chuckle—and that just makes her stern side-eye sharper. *And funnier.*

"You're a Bennett," Dad says, puffing up his chest. "I know you're getting nookie somewhere."

Mom smacks him in the chest.

"Happy to talk this out with you, Pops, but not sure Mom needs to hear those details."

He pokes Mom in the side. "Your mom's still pretty frisky."

My teeth sink into my sandwich, but Dad's words hit just as I start to swallow. The combination isn't great. I begin to choke as Mom chastises Dad and I try not to die while erasing that sentence from my brain.

"Well, you are," Dad says, staring up at her like she's a pin-up model.

"Edward." Mom's cheeks flash bright pink. "*Enough.*"

"You wanna continue this conversation, Mom?" I ask, clearing my throat. "Or do you want to use this opportunity to segue to something else?"

"I just want grandkids," she says. "I don't care about your … exploits."

"Well, when I meet a candidate to have my children, you'll be the first to know."

Mom pats Dad's chest. "Make it sooner rather than later." She winks before heading upstairs, telling Dad she's going to change their bedsheets.

I take another bite of my sandwich as Dad settles back in his seat again.

The house settles and grows quiet. Occasionally, Mom's singing flows down the stairs and I'm reminded of her cranking up the music on Saturday mornings when I was a kid, giving no fucks that I was trying to sleep. It was infuriating then. *Now?* I don't hate the memory.

I finish my sandwich and let my mind wander to the work I have to do at home and what my schedule looks like next week. Just as my eyes get heavy and I start to yawn, Dad speaks.

"When you do find a woman, find one like your mom," Dad says out of nowhere.

My gaze whips to him, surprised that we're still on the topic. *Has he been thinking about this the whole time?*

"She's always been beautiful," he says, his voice almost

distant. "But she's smart as a whip. Funny—my lord, that woman could make me laugh." His chest rumbles as he chuckles. "I was a sucker from the moment that I saw her."

"From the moment you saw her, huh?"

He shrugs. "I was in love with her from the moment I saw her smile. I knew right then that I was going to forget about trying to play sports. I'd give it all up just to be able to take care of her."

I shift in my seat, setting my plate on the coffee table.

This isn't a conversation we've ever had before. Dad's always been open to discussing anything with me, but we've never broached his feelings for Mom. I know he's always loved her. That's never been a question. But even when I was having problems with a girlfriend or we've offhandedly talked about marriage or families, he's never told me their origin story like this.

"One day, Drake, you'll know the reason none of the other women ever made the cut. It'll be because the woman standing in front of you was out there waiting on you to find her."

"I think the woman for me has been hiding because I've had my eye out for her for a while."

He gives me a half grin. "Of course, the woman for you is hiding, kid. If she knows you, she knows you don't accept anything that you don't have to work for."

"Oh, come on, now …."

"The hell if that ain't the truth. Think about it. Have you ever been happy with anything that was just given to you?" He rolls his eyes. "No. You haven't."

Is that true? I ponder his statement, going back through my life to test his theory. In high school, I was pretty much given the point guard position because no one else could handle the ball—and I quit after my freshman year. I double majored in college because my communications degree felt too easy, and I worked my ass off to take the tight end position with the Illinois Legends from a talented veteran who thought he had the spot secured. *Hm* ....

Dad sighs, lifting the footrest of his recliner and getting positioned for a nap. "One day, you'll meet a woman who makes your heart beat different. When that happens, your heart is hers. There ain't no fighting it, son."

He exhales, closing his eyes and resting his head against the chair. His breathing evens out and soon, he's snoring.

The sun's rays beat down on me through the window, bathing me in warmth. It's cozy and peaceful, like I'm insulated from the world's troubles. I, too, close my eyes and rest my head against the sofa with Dad's words rolling through my mind.

I've always believed in a love like he was talking about. I guess from watching my parents show love and affection not just to us kids, but to each other, the idea of finding my soulmate has always been something I expected would happen one day. I imagined it would just happen—that I'd turn a corner and she'd be standing there.

The problem is that I *haven't* found her.

My career was all-consuming for a decade, and football was my life well before that. I've had more than my share of nookie, as Pops calls it, but none of those women were *the one*. That was fine because I didn't want to spend my time in that arena, anyway. Then I shifted trajectory and things changed.

A grin touches my lips.

It all changed when I started armchair quarterbacking.

I stifle a chuckle.

Gianna Bardot—you kill me.

Among other things ...

Gianna is the only woman who has made me pause. She's the only woman who I can't just slide out of my brain. It's like she holds a spot in my head and refuses to let go, overriding my defenses. I look forward to seeing her, finding things to talk about over coffee in the break room, and wondering what it would feel like to have a woman of that caliber beside me.

It's not *just* sex that crosses my mind when I imagine her—although I've imagined bending that woman over every surface known to man. *Fuck.* But I also imagine watching movies together, making dinner, and sharing a bottle of wine. Laughing. *Living.*

That's great—perfectly normal, even. But it's not realistic.

Gianna is a dream girl. She's the kind of woman who really only lives in men's dreams. The fact that she's real is wild ... but it doesn't change reality.

I've listened to her podcast enough to know that she doesn't look at love the way I do. I've also seen the men she chooses to date and there's not one commonality among them and me. Although I have theories about it all, it doesn't really matter. I simply can't get involved with a dream crusher.

Not unless I want my own heart broken.

CHAPTER
FIVE

Gianna

"I don't think I can do it," I say, reviewing the proposal in my hands. "It's just … unauthentic."

Francine slips off her tortoiseshell glasses and withholds a sigh. Instead, she licks her lips to calm herself, I think. "That's totally understandable, and I commend your integrity. But maybe we could reframe this proposal and see it in a different light."

"Frame away."

She lifts her copy of the document and rereads it.

Rain pelts the windows of my small but cozy office at Canoodle Media. A battery-operated candle flickers on the bookshelf to my right, casting a pretty glow against some of my favorite books. Biographies of my heroes and coffee-table-style art books are neatly lined up. Romances, though, far outnumber the others. A plug-in fragrance booster sends ribbons of floral through the room, scenting the air as if we're in a rose garden. It's the most creative I could get while still staying within corporate guidelines.

Francine shifts her weight, still scanning the paper. I slide back in my chair and fidget with the edge of my newly chipped fingernail.

The week has flown by. Monday was spent engaging with my audience—responding to social media comments and questions, reviewing the endless emails sent to the podcast for content creation, and analyzing platform-specific statistics. Tuesday was filled with strategy sessions and brainstorming workshops. I've spent the day recording ad spots and approving new deals. I've barely had time to think.

I blow a bright pink bubble, and it bursts just as Francine lifts her chin. She nods as if she has just come to an agreement with the proposal in her hands.

"Okay," she says. "What if we shape the narrative a bit?"

Shape that *narrative?* I lift a brow and return her smile, although mine's a touch more facetious. "If you can shape it enough so that it says, I don't know, the exact opposite thing that it does now, then fine."

"The final decision is yours," she says. "But with your download numbers over the past couple of weeks, I think we can get them to agree to a flat-rate deal. For the price range that will command, it's worth seriously considering."

She places the paper on the corner of my desk. Her amusement with me is waning—and I get it. This sponsorship would be a feather in our cap and pour more money in one swoop than we've ever managed to score so far with *Gianna Knows Things*. That makes our whole team look good.

But it would make me feel really, really shitty. I'd essentially be a sellout, and every one of my listeners would know it. Even if they didn't, I'd know it, and I'm the one who has to live with it.

"Look, I know this deal would bring in a lot of money," I say, dropping my hands to my sides. "And I'm well aware that there's a contingent of people this podcast is responsible for financially—don't think that doesn't weigh on me. But this entire pitch centers around the idea that if you send your significant other flowers, it's a magic wand. It erases any and all fuckery. And you know as well as I do that's the antithesis of the entire podcast."

She nods, the struggle of my argument and the dollar signs swimming in her head apparent.

"I step into the recording booth every week and tell people not to take shit," I say. "I'm telling them to listen to their gut. To hold people accountable for their misdeeds, and to demand more from relationships than being a doormat." I glance down at the name on the top of the sheet. "I'm not against working with Powers Flowers in theory, but they're going to have to pitch something that aligns with my brand."

"Very well." She gathers her things and slips them into her satchel. "After all, you know best."

I snort before it turns into a giggle. "Well played, Francine. Well played."

"I can be clever now and then." She winks. "I'll have the audiogram edits that we worked on today ready for your approval tomorrow, and if the Halcyon team gets back to us, we can record their spot, too."

"Sounds great."

"What else are you working on today? Or are you about out of here for the afternoon?"

I yawn, the week's tempo starting to catch up with me. "I think I'm going to go live on Social in a bit and tease Friday's show with Mercy. Nothing fancy. I'm just going to use my phone and make it a spontaneous *I'm bursting at the seams* kind of thing."

"Smart. I love that. The guesses rolling in have been hysterical—everything from Laird Faris of Faris Wheel to that super sexy racecar driver everyone is talking about."

"Cash Ryatt? A girl can dream." I laugh. "Why do they think it's a guy, anyway? That's an interesting take."

"Because you said you had a 'mega crush' on the person."

She shrugs, grinning. "It'll just make it even splashier when it's Mercy."

I whip my desktop tripod out of my desk and set it up. "You know me. I love to be splashy."

"You, my dear, are the splashiest."

She gives me a little wave and leaves while pulling her phone to her ear.

Thunder rumbles through the air, followed by a streak of bright orange lightning that illuminates the sky. I jump, knocking my scuffed calf against my chair. *Ouch.*

The thought of searching for fresh lip gloss from my godforsaken bag is off-putting. So I find a tube of lip balm in my desk from who knows when and smudge it across my pucker. I reach for the phone, but it buzzes before I can grab it.

> Lucia: Hey, sissy! I'll be close to your house tomorrow evening. Wanna do something?

Her name on my screen makes me smile.

Doing something with Lucia usually involves margaritas and dancing—two things I love almost as much as I love her. But I know her and myself well enough to know that those things on a Thursday evening aren't conducive to a productive Friday. *And Mercy is coming on Friday.*

My smile is cheesy as I pick up the phone.

> Me: I have a big interview on Friday, so I can't really go out. Takeout and gossip at my place?

> Lucia: Yes! I'm going to try to remember your housewarming present this time.

> Me: Gifts are always appreciated.

> Lucia: Brat.

I swipe off my text app, immediately noticing a new notification from Social Messaging. The appearance of the little number in the pink bubble is enough to make me toe the edge of rage because the name at the top of my inbox is the one I expected it to be. *Pearl Jenkins—extortionist.*

Pearl: Okay, you're playing hardball. I'll decrease my asking price by another $10, but that's the least I can do. Take it or leave it. I'm done messing around with you.

My thumbs fly across the screen with purpose, reminding me why my manicure is screwed up.

Me: We've been over this a million times. I'm not interested in your price point. Yet you keep coming to me with minuscule reductions that don't change a thing. Save yourself the trouble.

Pearl: It's antique mahogany. Don't you know anything about antiques?

Me: It's missing two hooks, has a gouge in the base, and the whole thing needs to be refinished. It sat in a barn for how many years?

Pearl: A lady is selling one just like this on Social for $3,000. Mine is $2,000. I'm practically giving it away. Do your homework.

Me: Then I'll pick it up at the salvation center when they mark it down to $100.

Pearl: Fine. $1,500. Last offer.

Me: $99. Final offer.

Pearl: Complete disrespect!

"What?" I screech, staring at the screen. *Is she serious?* "I ... I can't." My finger taps to exit the app, before I all-caps berate a woman with great-grandchildren. That's the kind of energy that I don't need returned to me. *No matter how cathartic it might be.*

I push the coat tree killer out of my mind and do a quick check of my hair and makeup. Then I grab my phone, position it onto the tripod, and test my lighting. It's surprisingly flattering.

Then I hit the red button.

It takes a few seconds for the connection to link and the viewer count to rise.

"Hi." I wave to the camera. Hearts and comments begin lifting across the screen faster than I can count them. "What's going on?" I laugh as the requests to join the live roll in. Even I'm not ballsy enough to go that far and allow strangers to pop up on camera with me. *Hard nope.* "I'm in my office today, wrapping up a slew of meetings for Friday's show. Have I mentioned how freaking amazing it's going to be?"

I try to find a comment to respond to, so my fans feel like I'm talking to *them*, not *at them*. I narrow my eyes, trying to focus on the messages flowing across the bottom of the screen. Finally, I spot a straightforward inquiry that I can answer.

"I got this shirt at a thrift store on Circle Grove for fifteen dollars," I say, standing. "See? It has pockets on the side." Glancing around, I grab the tripod. "Have I ever shown you guys my office?"

The word *no* in various forms spans across the bottom of the screen.

"We don't have time for a grand tour today, but I can show you the gist of it. Hang on." I gingerly lift the tripod and turn slowly in a circle. "That's my one window, but it does look out on a park where guys play basketball on hot afternoons. Not complaining about that." I twist a little farther. "And there's my fake candle because the day I tried to light a real one, I nearly got fired. No pun intended. Those are pics of my sister and me, and of my best friends. I really need to get them to come on the podcast. You guys would love them. And I—"

"Guess who left her keys on the—*oh*."

I jump, swinging toward the sound of the very sexy, very male voice.

Drake stops mid-step, my keys dangling from his finger like he's teasing me. Like he found them somewhere … personal. *And my phone?* Aimed *directly at him*. I couldn't have focused better on him if I'd tried.

He flinches in surprise, not expecting to be thrust into the spotlight.

"I'm live," I say, smiling at him. "Say hi."

He flashes me a quick, apologetic grin before turning his attention to the phone. His recovery from surprise to swoonable is impressive. And hot as freaking hell.

A dark Henley—blue or black, I'm not sure—shows off the ridges of his shoulders and the thickness of his chest. His arms fill out the sleeves until the fabric stops, bunched just above his powerful forearms. His smirk is the classiest version of porn that I've ever watched. And his tone? Thick, rich, and charming.

"How's everyone this afternoon?" he asks.

His chuckle stirs something deep in my core. I blame it on exhaustion … and on calling off my date with Matthew last weekend. A girl has needs, and mine are currently unmet.

"You guys need to settle the fuck down," he says, licking his bottom lip through a grin.

I can practically hear the women moaning through the screen. I almost want to drag the phone down his body as a treat for my fans, but I don't. Asking for his consent while in front of the camera doesn't feel fair. *Although a part of me thinks he'd love the attention.*

"Why do they need to settle down?" I ask it as if I'm oblivious to how they're melting down right now.

"Let's just say our demographics are very, very different."

The sparkle in his eyes is downright dangerous.

"This is why you knock before barging into my office," I say, setting the tripod on my desk as memories of Friday's comment section cross my mind like a ticker tape.

"The door was open, first of all." He rounds my desk and stands just off camera. "Second, I found your keys in the break room and thought I'd be a good Samaritan and return them before you spend two hours digging through that hefty bag of yours."

I sit in my chair and scoot my phone toward me. The commentary is a shitstorm, as expected.

BREAK ROOM? LIAR.
Oh, nice try. We know how you got her keys! 😉
I bet that dick is fire.
I knew you were dating! @photogirliepop18 Told you!
GO LEGENDS! #numbereightysevenforever
Your kids are gonna be so gorgeous. 😚
Marry me, Drake!

"Let's get one thing clear before rumors start," I say, laughing. "Drake and I are *not* a thing." I point at him as I talk to my audience. "We're not dating, and I don't know whether any part of him is 'fire' or not."

"This is excellent for a man's ego," Drake says, crouching beside me as the comments speed out of control. "I'm all fire, thank you," he says, chuckling. "No, her keys were in *the break room*. Not *my bedroom*. But thank you for thinking I could pull a woman like her."

I knock him with my knee. That only deepens his smirk … and raises my body temperature about three thousand percent.

"I don't even remember having them in the break room," I say, forcing a swallow and regaining control of my thoughts.

"Why does that not surprise me?" he mumbles, eyes lighting up at the phone. "I missed your name, but yes—Go Legends. I'll be back in Illinois soon for a game."

I roll my eyes. "If you want to talk sports, go to your office. We talk about fun stuff here."

"Then let's talk about fun stuff."

"Okay," I say, laughing. "I thought you said that you listened to my podcast."

"I do."

"Then you should know that our definition of *fun stuff* is relationships. Breakups. Gossip." I slide my gaze to him. "Sex."

He looks at me over his shoulder with a smirk. "Sounds fun to me."

Our gazes collide, the energy between us shifting. In one way, it's reminiscent of the way it feels when I look at Audrey or Astrid across a room. We're on the same page and have each other's backs. There's a comfort, an ease that's built into that kind of friendship. But, in another way, it's a lot like I'm looking at a man just before he rips my clothes off.

"Fine," I say, meeting the challenge in his eyes. I'm not about to broach sex, but bantering a bit certainly won't hurt my ratings. *And who am I to deny the people what they want?* "I was discussing flowers with my producer today."

"What about them?"

"Do you think if you're in a relationship and fuck all the way up, that sending a bouquet of roses helps your case? Or is it a distraction from the transgression?"

His lips press together as he thinks. "I mean, I think sending roses to your woman—or whatever flower she likes, if she likes them—is always a good idea. But do I think it helps my case if I've messed up?" He shrugs. "I guess it depends on what I did."

"What offense do you think it *would* help?" I ask.

He grabs the edge of my seat and adjusts his crouching position. His knuckles brush against my thigh. I do my very best to ignore it as a flurry of goose bumps runs along my skin beneath my clothes.

"Let's say we got into an argument over something small," he says, "and the next day I want her to know that she's on my mind and I care about her. Then, yeah, I think flowers help. Don't you?"

"Oh, this isn't about me," I say, laughing.

He shrugs. "Sure, it is."

"Trust me. We don't have time for this to be about me."

His eyes narrow. "You're telling me you wouldn't like flowers? Because I call bullshit."

My jaw falls open, and I laugh again. "Well, it's a good thing you'll never have to apologize to me after a fight because I don't like flowers. They remind me of dead people. You walk into a funeral home, and what's the first thing that hits you? *The smell of flowers.* I love massive bouquets for the people who like them, but that person isn't me."

He grins. "Funny. I thought I distinctly smelled roses when I walked in here."

He's right, of course, but damn him for noticing. *Does this man notice everything?* Still, I'm not about to concede his point. That would be too easy.

"Drake, I think I know if I like flowers or not."

"I think you'd love to get them. You don't want to have to ask for them, and you don't want them only sent when you're pissed. That's what I think."

His blue eyes peer into mine as he casts a smug grin my way. *This bastard.*

"Don't you have sportsball to talk about somewhere else?" I ask, knocking my shoulder gently against his. He's a rock and doesn't budge. "It's baseball season, you know."

He holds my gaze for a split second longer before turning to the camera. "If you agree with me, drop my name in the comments. If you agree with Gianna, drop hers. I'll personally go through and count them tonight and see what the people think."

I laugh as he stands, towering over me, and try to remain unaffected by the whiffs of his cologne as he moves. He turns to the door. Each step he takes sends another wave of comments begging him to stay.

"Thanks for the keys," I call out.

He stops in the doorway. For a moment, I think he's going to say something—probably an innuendo that won't do either of us any good—but he leaves with a smirk instead.

I clear my throat and remember that I'm live. *Shit*. I grab my phone, palms sweaty, and smile. "Now that we've been rudely interrupted, let's go back to me teasing about how amazing Friday's show is going to be. Any guesses?"

As the names roll in mixed with a slew of inappropriate comments, I try to clear my head of all things Drake.

Because he has a way of throwing everything off its axis.

Including me, apparently.

CHAPTER
SIX

Gianna

"They're still commenting?" I ask, pulling my blankets over my body with one hand. My other clutches my phone. "Holy shit."

I scroll down the comment section of my video, but it's all the same thing in various formations.

Drake
Drake
DRAKE 🤍
DRAKE I LOVE YOU
DRAKE
Drake of course 🛡️
Every girl loves flowers—especially flowers from Drake Fucking Bennett. 😍
Gianna. #girlgang
DRAKE 🌻
Drake 🌼
I'd take anything Drake is willing to give me. 🫠
Drake

DRAKE
Drake!!
Drake 🤍🤍🤍🤍🤍🤍
Drake #GoLegends
Drake
DRAKE 🪶
Drake
Check your DMs, Drake!

"Traitors," I say, switching off my screen. "All of them."

I toss my phone to the other side of my bed, switch off the bedside lamp, and close my eyes. Sleep comes quickly … and a dazzling smirk, a set of chiseled abs, and a bouquet of beautiful flowers accompany it.

Even my subconscious is a backstabber.

CHAPTER
SEVEN

GIANNA

"And I thought I've seen some wild shit," I say, flipping through Wildfire's website as their music plays from my computer's speakers. Page after page is filled with pictures from concerts and meet-and-greets spanning the globe. The energy captured in the snapshots, the smiles—*and a lot of bare skin*—is the visual definition of *having the time of our lives*.

I click on the document that I've been working on all evening.

"Women famously throw bras and panties at men on stage. What do guys throw at you?" I say as my fingers fly across the keys. "What's the weirdest thing a fan has thrown on stage?"

That should instigate an interesting story time.

I've only completed two interviews on *Gianna Knows Things* and precisely zero before that. And the two interviewees were a jewelry designer with an interesting take on relationships, and a girl who went viral on Social by getting dumped on Valentine's Day. *She was so much better off without that fuckhead.* Both were fun. I enjoyed the conversations. But neither of them was a famous drummer who wears Viking braids and has a chokehold on the music industry. The pressure not to screw this up grows a little heavier each day.

"No," I say as doubt begins to creep into my head. "I am enough for this moment."

I take a long, deep breath and blow it out slowly. All the while, I silently repeat the mantra that has gotten me over every hurdle of adulthood.

The setting sun's rays filter through the bay window overlooking the backyard, filling my living room with the prettiest glow. It's exactly as I imagined it when I first saw the house with a real estate agent a few months ago. As soon as I turned the corner from the foyer and cast my sights on this space, I knew it was special. I felt it in my bones.

And I was right.

I wake up inspired. When I come home from the Canoodle offices, a sense of peace spreads over me like a warm rain. I paint with joy, create with heart—living the life that baby Gianna dreamed for herself … in my very own house.

The only thing I ever wanted was to be a homeowner. It was an odd goal for an eight-year-old and definitely earned raised eyebrows a time or two. In second grade, my teacher instructed us to write our Christmas List for Santa Claus. I wrote boldly, in all caps instead of script, just in case Santa struggled with cursive, too, that I wanted a house of my own.

Instead, I got to have lunch with our school counselor to ensure things were okay at home with my family.

"Yup," I said, squirting the sauce packet onto the pizza crust from my Lunchables. "Our house is just boring. We can't paint the walls or hang up my art or use glitter. I want to have my own house and live there forever and make it beautiful." I sprinkled the cheese on top of my makeshift pizza. "And I'm definitely not using doilies."

A warm pressure builds in my chest at the memory, and a sense of gratitude settles over me. "I did it. All by myself."

And that is the best part of it all. I did it alone. The girl who didn't see the harm in doing things her own way or why that was so humiliating to her parents made it on her own.

"Hey, sissy!" Lucia's voice echoes through the foyer. "I'm here, and I come bearing gifts."

I smile, lifting my gaze to meet hers as she rounds the corner. Her dimples settle in as she grins at me.

"Well, *gift*," she says, laughing. "I come bearing *a gift*. But one is better than none." She proudly holds up a jar. "This is Matilda."

"That's my gift?"

"Yes," she says, rolling her eyes.

"Ah, you shouldn't have."

She steps over a canvas and mounds of buttons, then thrusts the jar into my hands. "Be nice. You'll hurt Matilda's feelings, and then she won't grow. You'll have no one to blame but yourself."

I turn the glass container in my palms and take in the ... *pancake batter?*

"It's sourdough starter," she says, sliding out of her bright red heels. "I made her. Well, I actually got her mother, Monica, from my neighbor a few months ago. But I've kept her alive. And, in return for my impeccable mothering, Monica has produced many, many loaves of amazing sourdough bread. And bagels! You can make bagels with Matilda, too."

"You gave me sourdough starter?" I ask, unable to keep the giggle out of my voice. "And to think that I was expecting a bottle of wine or the number of that hottie you work with."

"Oh, this is much better than wine—and that hottie is engaged. Sadly." She plops down beside me. "Have you ever smelled freshly baked bread? If someone could figure out how to bottle that scent, I'd wear it every damn day."

I snort. "That's one way to get eaten."

She laughs, shaking her head at me. "Anyway, I emailed you instructions on how to care for Matilda. I have high hopes that she'll be as delicious for you as Monica is for me. It's a game-changer, really. Once you get good at it, you can add in olives and onions and cheese—all kinds of stuff."

I peer into the jar at the glob of beige bubbles. There's not a chance in the world that I'm going to become a sourdough mom. But this gift, as off-the-wall as it appears, is really the most me-coded thing she could've given me. It's an acknowledgment of my homeowning dreams without making it weird. *Lucia knows I hate it when things are sappy.*

"Thank you for this," I say, setting the jar on the coffee table. "I'll do my best not to kill it."

"Her, Gianna. Do not. Kill *her*."

"Right. *Her*." *Lucia has issues.* My attention whips back to the bubbling gunk as a thought rushes to the forefront of my brain. "Wait. Is it actually *alive*?"

"Yes, it's alive."

"*Oh.*"

"Read the email. I explained it all there." She sighs and tucks her feet under her. "I'm starving. What are we doing about dinner?"

"Burgers from The Cesars? They deliver now."

"Add bacon, no onion," she says. "Can I SocialCash you some money?"

I grab my phone from under a pillow beside me and pull up the app. "No, I got it. They screwed up my order last time and gave me a gift card, so it's basically free tonight."

"Love that for us." She chews on the edge of her nail, glancing around the room. My chaotic lifestyle has always made her a little itchy. That apparently hasn't changed. "So what's with the buttons?"

"Some of those were Grandma's, and some were Mom's. I forgot that I had them until I moved."

"Why are they on the floor?"

I add fries to our order and submit it. "Because I wanted to do something with them besides filling a cookie jar."

"*So* … you tossed them on the floor?"

"No, smart-ass. I was going to affix them to the canvas with a hot glue gun and try to recreate the fruit bowl painting that hung in Grandma's kitchen. But then I thought it would be super cool to cover the canvas with fabric and sew the buttons on instead of using glue, which would take forever. So I figured I'd work on it while I watched *Dancing with Famous People*, but there's no table in here." I shrug. "And that's how they wound up on the floor."

My sister smiles lovingly at the mess. "I forgot about that painting. I always thought it was so beautiful."

"Well, I did spend more time sitting at the table in time-out growing up than you did."

Together, we cackle, because, yes, I really did spend a *lot* more time in time-out than my beautifully behaved sister.

The final beams of light drift from the room, and darkness covers the windows. Lucia's shoulders relax, and she falls deeper into the couch cushions. *I know the feeling.* It's impossible not to relax when you feel so insulated from the world.

"I love this house," she says. Her voice is soft, the words floating through the air. "I've never experienced a place so quiet."

"I love it, too."

She turns her face to mine and smiles. "It's so funny to think of you, of all people, thriving in this environment. But you really seem to be happy."

"It's my little retreat. I can go into the world and set off fireworks—wreaking havoc and anarchy wherever I go—and then I slink back here and shut the door and leave all of that out there."

We exchange a look, an understanding that requires no words. Lucia has done the same thing in her own way.

As daughters born to two highly successful and respected professionals, my sister and I were expected to follow suit. Behave like little ladies. Dress appropriately. Take piano and violin lessons and, for the love of God, don't embarrass the family.

I was never great at any of that.

"How are things in your world?" I ask. "Are you still seeing the fireman?"

Her eyes light up. "We're going out Saturday night. Our schedules are at odds most of the time, so we don't really see each other during the week. But we've gone out at least once a week for the past six weeks, so I think that's a good sign."

"That's a great sign. How's the sex? Still hot?"

"Oh, Gianna," she says, shrinking like she's melting down at the thought of her fireman. "I've never been so thoroughly fucked. I didn't even know you could fuck in so many different positions. He's had me on top, on bottom, bent over every surface in my house—twisted into a pretzel." She giggles. "He must sit around the fire station reading the Kama Sutra or something."

"Does he have any friends?"

She lifts a brow. "What about Matthew?"

I wrinkle my nose and shrug noncommittally.

"Let me guess," she says, "you're over him."

"Well, if I wasn't before you went in-depth about the fireman, I would be now." I laugh. "He's ... *fine*, I guess. I don't know. The last time we fucked, I had to get myself off, if that says anything."

"But I thought you liked him? Didn't you have good conversation? I swear that you told me that the two of you stayed up talking all night."

I roll my eyes. "What good is conversation if he can't fuck?"

"Oh, Gianna ..."

I shrug, uncertain what she wants from me. She knows me well enough to know that Matthew didn't have great odds at longevity. I can't think of a man who has made it more than two months.

Lucia and I are a lot alike, but we have a few significant differences—one of those being how we view relationships. Strangely, her take on them mirrors most of the women who call into my podcast. Our thoughts are so far apart that it's comical we share the same DNA.

My sister believes with all her heart in romance. Flowers, dates, and handwritten letters professing one's undying love— the girl thinks that falling in love is something that happens to you. I, on the other, very opposite hand, understand that romance is performative at best. At worst, it's manipulation in the most heartbreaking way. Love exists, for sure. But *falling in love* is irresponsible. It's *reckless*. It's a situation in which you're without control, relying on emotions that can mask red flags and hoping that an unreliable chemical explosion inside your body isn't misguiding you.

Yeah. That's all too much for me.

And if our parents' relationship was a model for anything— I'd rather opt out now.

"So who is the big interview tomorrow?" Lucia asks. She stands at the sound of the doorbell, grabs Matilda, and heads to the foyer. "I'm going to put the starter in the fridge so you don't forget."

"I couldn't forget because I didn't know that to begin with."

"Now you do." She disappears around the corner. "Who did you get to come on the show?"

"Francine got Mercy Malone from Wildfire," I say, a burst of excitement lifting my energy levels. "She's going to be sitting across from me, chatting with me like we're friends. How can this be real?"

The door opens, then closes. "Mercy Malone? Are you kidding me?"

"I know. Who would've thought that I would be interviewing a rock star?"

Lucia returns, Matilda-free, and inspects the contents of both bags, then hands me one. "Me. I totally would've thought you could be interviewing a rock star. And I bet Mom would've thought so, too." She smiles as she sits down again. "She always said that you couldn't stop talking if your life depended on it because you're just *so magnetic*." She rolls her eyes, but her grin is all affection.

"Would've been nice of her to acknowledge that earlier and stop grounding me for everything. I spent half my junior year of high school in my room, sneaking out for a couple of hours of freedom once you all went to bed."

I unwrap my sandwich, but before I can take a bite, my phone buzzes beside me. I reach for the device to silence it, but pause when I see the name on the screen.

A smile touches my lips.

Drake: Stopped to grab dinner. The current count is me—2,574 comments, you—143, no side/random commentary—2,032. I think it's safe to say that I win.

I tap out my response, unable to wipe the smile off my face.

Me: You did not count them. Don't lie to me.

Drake: Don't lie to you like you lied to me?

Me: What are you talking about?

Drake: I'll leave you with these …

"Cheeky bastard." I laugh.
"Who?" Lucia asks.
"A guy I work with."
She hums. "You don't mean Drake Bennett, do you?"

> Me: I don't want flowers, real or emoji.

> Drake: Good night, Gianna.

> Me: I really don't!

> Drake: Okay, dream crusher.

> Me: 😑

> Drake: 😉

"Yup," Lucia says in a tone that I don't want to indulge. "It was Drake."

I set my phone down and grab my burger. "How do you know?"

She shrugs, grinning as she takes a bite of her food. I take a giant bite of mine, too. I'm starving … but I also don't want to continue this conversation. I'm well aware that he's … *him*, and I'm sure I appeared amused at his message.

But neither of those means anything.

If they did, I'd be as silly as every other woman in the world when it comes to that man. And I'm way too smart for that.

After all, Drake Bennett is nothing more than a coworker and a friend to me. And I always enjoy excellent banter with my friends.

Even the ridiculously hot ones.

CHAPTER
EIGHT

"You can't be serious," I say, scanning the stats that my producer, Mario, loads onto the screen in front of me. "The odds that the Bobcats walk away with a championship this season are trash. I know you grew up in Indianapolis and your old man was a big fan, but that doesn't change reality."

Ron Jeffries, a sports analyst for over thirty years and sometimes a guest on *Sports Take with Drake Bennett*, groans through my headphones. The man bleeds green, the color of his beloved Bobcats, and will fight anyone who dares to speak anything but accolades about his team. Needless to say, we quarrel often.

"How can you say that?" he asks me as if *I'm* the fool between us. "Caparelli is on a streak. He's had a hit in fifty straight games. His batting average is over four hundred, and he's been intentionally walked twenty-one times. Couple that with their dominant pitching this season, and it's hard to lose a damn game. There's no way we don't end with a ring. Not a chance."

"Those stats are great, but the team batting average is under the Mendoza line, and no player is good at getting on base. And if you want to talk about pitching, their entire staff consists of two guys who can reliably get the ball across the plate with a better chance than not getting blasted out of the ballpark. You can't get away with two pitchers these days. This isn't 1920, you know."

He chuckles. "I'm going to hate coming back here in a couple of months and telling you *I told you so.*"

"Don't lose too much sleep over it because it's not going to happen."

My chuckle joins his as Mario gives me a sign from his spot in the sound booth.

"Thanks for coming by again this week, Ron," I say, grinning. "It's always good to see you. And I'd love to have you back as soon as the Bobcats fail to make the postseason."

"You're lucky I like you, Bennett."

I laugh as a short stinger, like a crowd cheering, leads me into the wrap-up.

"That's it for this week's episode," I say into the microphone. "I'd like to thank my guests for joining me this afternoon. And make sure you tune in next week to catch Branch Best, wide receiver for the Illinois Legends. He'll be here to talk about the upcoming football season and his new charity, Sunny Days, whose goal is to raise money for childhood hunger. We'll be discussing ways that you can get involved, including a competition that I'll announce live on the show, featuring one-of-a-kind Legends merch. It's gonna be great." Mario points at me. "And that's my take. See you next time."

The outro music plays as I slip off my headphones and set them on the table.

My shoulders sag as I get to my feet. I stretch my arms overhead, loosening the tension that inevitably creeps into my body when I'm broadcasting live. I used to think that I secretly harbored a fear or anxiety about it. After doing this for two years, I understand that it's less about being nervous and more about the chair I use. But once I leave this room, it's out of sight, out of mind.

The computer screen lights up as the streaming numbers and viewer metrics are shared with me. I glance at them, not paying too much attention because Lincoln Landry, Tennessee Arrows baseball team's GM, was my first guest. He never fails to deliver great stats. But as I turn to grab my notepad and pack up, I notice the metrics look suspiciously long.

"Holy shit," I whisper as I absorb the information in front of me. "What is going on?"

"Are you seeing that?" Mario asks through the speakers.

I look over my shoulder. "Are those numbers real?"

"Yup. I watched it grow while you were live. Johnny called from upstairs and said they noticed it, too. Apparently, they're calling it the Gianna Effect."

A slow smile slips across my lips. "The Gianna Effect, huh?"

"I heard you debuted on her channels yesterday, and there seems to be a crossover between her fans and yours." He smirks. "Not saying they aren't sports fans because many women enjoy sports—and a lot of them are smarter about sports than most men, but I think it probably has more to do with that … what's my wife call it? Tall, dark, and handsome?"

I laugh, shaking my head. "Followers are followers. Maybe I'll have to start streaming shirtless or something."

"Let me know when that's going to happen so I can call off work that day." He fiddles with his computer, then looks at me again. "All right. That's a wrap for today. Johnny wanted me to come see him right after the show, so I'm going to swing by his office before I take a late lunch."

"If I don't see you again today, have a good weekend, Mario."

"You, too."

He waves before disappearing from the booth.

I begin putting my things into my bag, pausing now and then

to check the updated numbers. The full video has been posted to my channels by the guys upstairs. The likes and comments are out of control. I scroll down about halfway, not sure what to expect, but am pleasantly surprised to find most of them are legit sports questions or comments. A few trolls. Limited requests to do inappropriate acts. A shit ton of private messages, none of which I'm inclined to read at the moment. But the overall consensus is *Sports Take* got a major boost in visibility … thanks to the Gianna Effect.

My teeth tug my bottom lip between them.

She has an effect, all right.

It's not a complete surprise that Gianna has this kind of power. Her fanbase is rabid in the best way. Listening to her show is a MasterClass in marketing. Her content is her signature, and she doesn't shy away from it. She's vulnerable in a way that her fans can connect with, and her followers aren't just an audience—they're a community.

The woman is brilliant. Her mind is as fascinating as her mouth, and her competence as sexy as her body. There's no woman like her. I've looked.

I grab my phone to put it in my pocket when it lights up.

Elodie: Talk me out of adopting a baby.

"Holy fuck." I flinch and reread my older sister's text. "Someone must've kidnapped her."

Me: Understood.

Elodie: Understood what?

Me: 😶

Elodie: ???

Me: Don't worry. I got you.

Elodie: I'm so confused.

Me: That makes two of us.

I grab my coffee cup from this morning and toss it in the trash.

Elodie: I asked you to help me not adopt a baby.

Me: And I acknowledged your cry for help. I'm on the phone with the police, giving them your location. Help is coming.

Elodie: 😐

Me: 🙌

As expected, my phone rings, and my sister's name is on the screen.

"Yes?" I ask, grinning.

"What the hell is wrong with you?"

"What the hell is wrong *with me*?" I ask. "You're the one talking about adopting a kid."

She whines, "I know." Her sigh is long and very, *very* dramatic. "I just met a friend for lunch, and she brought her three-month-old. Now I smell like baby lotion and spit-up, which should be gross. But it's doing weird things to my uterus."

"You know we have a mother and a sister, right? Because I have … Well, I don't want to say that I have no experience with uteruses, but it's usually the cervix when I—"

"*Oh, my gosh.* Shut the fuck up."

I laugh, leaning against the table.

"It's just that all of my friends are getting married and having babies," she says. "And I'm quickly becoming 'The Aunt,' if you know what I mean. I'm starting to think that's all I'm ever going to be. Always the aunt, never the mom."

"Have you been drinking?"

"Drake—"

"No judgment. This is a judgment-free zone. You can treat this like a safe space."

She growls, making me chuckle.

"All right," I say. "I'm done joking. Please, drag me into your crisis. I have nothing better to do today."

"I'm going to overlook your sarcasm."

I consider teasing her again, but stop short. As the oldest of the three of us at thirty-six, Elodie is typically calm and confident —even if her ideas and plans of execution equal mine when I was ten years old. But there's a slight panic to her tone today that has me backing off from giving her shit.

"Drake, do you think I'm too old to have kids? Have I missed a window?"

"No, I don't. You're thirty-six, not fifty-six. Hell, I think you can still have kids when you're fifty-six." I run a hand down my jaw. "Didn't you just say that your friends are having kids? Aren't they the same age as you?"

"Yeah, but they're settled. Most of them are married. All of them are in committed relationships. The only thing I'm committed to is paying taxes and my nail tech. And not in that order."

I laugh. "Did something go awry with the veterinarian you've been seeing?"

"I ended things primarily because he works so much. We rarely see each other now, and I don't like the idea of sitting at home waiting for him day in, day out—which is a fair point."

Sounds like she's called in to Gianna's show for advice. The thought makes me smile. "Absolutely."

She pauses, the energy through the line shifting. "But what if I made a mistake?"

"The great thing about mistakes is that you can fix them. Worst case, you learn from them."

"I don't even know whether this baby thing has anything to do with him or not. I just know that when I held the baby today, it felt so natural. For the first time in my life, I could imagine myself holding a child of my own, and I don't know what to do with that."

This might be a revelation to Elodie, but it's not to me. She's always been someone who loves people. She loves making others happy and taking care of them. There's never been a day when I didn't see a child in her future.

Is that why she's calling me? Does she need me to tell her that? Or does she just need a place to think about this out loud, and she knows I'll always have her back?

"I think you need to take a deep breath and relax a little before you go filing adoption papers, okay? I'm not saying don't adopt. But, if you're going to do it, you need to give it more than fifteen minutes of thought."

"It's been twenty, but fine." I can hear her relax through the phone. "Are you going to Mom and Dad's on Sunday?"

"I plan on it."

"Good. Just don't bring this up in front of them or Evie. I might even be over it by then. Who knows?"

"Yeah. Who knows?" *Me.* I know that she'll have forgotten all about this by then. "On another note, how did Dad do the other night? Evie sent me a few pictures and said it was going great, but Evie could be in a burning house and miss the fire."

Elodie laughs. "It went pretty well. He got confused a few times, and we had to remind him where Mom went. He also tried to cheat in every hand of euchre. But, if you think about it, both of those things are pretty normal for him. Mom said his memory gets worse as the night goes on, most of the time, so she refused to let us stay the night. I think she didn't want us to see it."

My heart aches as that bit of information pierces it.

I've tried to be respectful of my parents' privacy as they navigate this new diagnosis. I'm sure Mom feels helpless, and I know she wants to take care of Dad herself. It can't be easy on her. But, so far, she seems to have found a new routine and is managing it reasonably well. At this point, having my sisters and me come barreling in, demanding answers and removing their agency, especially Mom's, is disrespectful.

But where is the line? How do we help?

"I gotta go," Elodie says. "I have a meeting in ten minutes, and I'm still sitting in my car from lunch."

"Call me later if you want. Otherwise, see you on Sunday."

"Thanks, Drake."

"Love you."

"Love you. Bye."

"Later."

I end the call and slip my phone into my pocket. My head lifts toward the door when it creaks open. Juni from reception smiles from the doorway.

"Hey," she says. "The papers you had me get from the Tennessee Royals are on my desk. I can put them in the mail room or bring them to you in a bit."

"I'll grab them before I leave. Thanks, Juni."

She nods and backs out of the room.

I exhale, ensuring I have everything I need before I leave for the day. My head is still spinning from my conversation with

Elodie. I'm not sure what to think about that. As I hoist my bag onto my shoulder, a sound captures my attention and shoves all thoughts of my sister out of my brain.

Gianna's laughter.

My stomach tightens as I lean toward the sound, wondering what she's laughing about. I can imagine her smile and the way the corners of her eyes crinkle when she's happy. The thin gold rings that adorn her little fingers are probably catching the lights above her. I wonder if she's wearing red or pink lipstick. I also wonder why she chooses one over the other on any random day.

There's so much about her that I don't know, so much that she keeps locked up behind the set of walls that she's built around herself. I wish that I knew why she constructed those, too. She never keeps any male *friends* around for long and seems to pick the lowest fruit on the tree, yet neither of those things bothers her.

If she thinks love is a choice, why does she choose the men she does?

I guess that if I knew the answer to that, I'd be the one giving out relationship advice.

"Better stick to sports, Bennett," I whisper and walk out the door.

CHAPTER
NINE

Gianna

"Okay," I say, surveying the scene in front of me. "I think I'm ready."

The small round table that Juni helped me lug from the storage area has been placed perfectly in the center of the room. The size and shape give a friendly, conversational vibe like two old friends chatting away, and microphones just happen to sit in front of them. I kept my signature canary-yellow chairs and placed them across from each other. I fought a finance bro over those when I first started working at Canoodle. Screwball thought he could just waltz in and claim ownership of my furniture because he liked it.

He learned a lesson that day, courtesy of moi.

"Now to find some lip gloss and we'll be good to go," I mumble, reaching for my bag. But just as my hand hits the strap, my phone glows with an incoming text.

Audrey: Good luck today! I'm tuned in and cheering for you. I know you're going to do great.

Astrid: I just kicked Gray and Brooks out of the cabin so I can listen. SO excited for you, Gianna.

The way they remember little things that are important to me never ceases to amaze me.

My thumbs dance on the screen as I tap out my response.

Me: I didn't sleep at all last night, so I overcompensated in the caffeine department. Three cups of coffee and an energy drink, and now I'm jittery. I'm not sure if I have too much confidence for this interview or if I'm in way over my head. I also don't know whether wearing a Wildfire concert tee was a smart or cheesy choice, but I did it anyway. I mean, I look good, but is it too pick me?

Audrey: It's a great idea. It'll likely make Mercy feel more relaxed, and if nothing else, it'll be a great icebreaker. You can tell her that you saw her in Atlanta last year. That will form a connection.

Astrid: I agree with Miss Smarty Pants over there.

I grin as my shoulders slump in relief. Even if they're just telling me what I want to hear, because there's no time to change if this was the wrong choice, I'm grateful. The validation feels good.

> Me: Do you have any questions that you want me to ask Mercy? I might be able to slide in a couple of requests. 🫤

> Astrid: I'm guessing backstage passes for her next show isn't what you mean. 😈

> Audrey: Please ask her if she feels like she has an ethical responsibility for how her work is interpreted. Or does she feel that once she releases the music that it no longer belongs to her, so the burden of interpretation doesn't either?

Typical Audrey. Snorting, I type out my response.

> Me: I was thinking more like—What rock star is the best fuck? But I guess we can get philosophical.

> Astrid: Of course, you were. 🙄

> Audrey: Whatever you ask her will be brilliant, just like you. 🤍

"Oh, sweet Auddie," I say because even though it reads like she's full of shit, she's not. She actually believes I'm brilliant and Astrid is a genius and we're both goddesses. Audrey Van is the best of the best.

Me: I love you guys. Thanks for hyping me up.

Astrid: We're just telling you the truth. Now go crush this interview.

Audrey: And text us when it's over. Good luck!

Me: 🖤

I set my phone to Do Not Disturb and toss it in my bag. For a moment, I peer into its depths and consider rappelling to the bottom for my lip gloss. *It's not worth it.*

Francine walks past the windows overlooking the hallway and waves before entering the room. "Hey, you. How are you feeling?"

"Buzzed on caffeine, battling impostor syndrome, and simultaneously on the verge of puking and needing a hamburger. You?"

She laughs, swinging a set of headphones from her index finger. "I can have a burger waiting on you when you finish, if you'd like."

"Why are you so nice to me, Francine?"

"Not that it's tit for tat, but I do remember someone throwing me a surprise party for my birthday last month," she says. "That person also got a signed Royals jersey for me to give to my husband for our anniversary and refused to take any money for it, and she also—"

"Stop. Geez. I have a reputation to uphold around here."

"Sorry. I forgot." She winks and turns to the door. "Mercy should be here anytime. I'll give you a heads-up when I hear that she's arrived."

A flash of excitement washes through me. "That would be great. Thanks."

My stomach tightens just enough to notice as I turn on my computer and look over my notes once again. Three a.m. Gianna did me a favor and put them in meticulous order. I have a page filled with Mercy's history and backstory, another listing her professional accomplishments, and a third with miscellaneous facts that I thought were interesting or could come up during our chat. I also have a flow of questions to guide me in case I get performance anxiety.

That would be a first.

I take a deep, steadying breath and remind myself that this is fun. Sure, it's my job, but it's also an amazing opportunity. And, if all goes right, I might find myself in the Thursday slot after all.

"Gianna."

The urgency in Francine's voice has me whipping around to face her. As soon as our eyes meet, I stop dead in my tracks. The pale pink lipstick clinging to her lips is pressed into a thin line. Shoulders back and chin lifted, she's the picture of trouble.

"What's wrong?" I ask as my stomach careens to the floor.

"Don't panic."

"That instantly panics me."

She holds a palm out as if it will steady me. "I just got a call from Mercy's team. She's been in a car accident."

"*What*?" I grip the edge of my chair. "Is she okay?"

"I was told that she has some cuts and bruises, but they're going to take her to the hospital as a precaution. Apparently, a semi-truck driver lost control. They believe it to be a medical emergency—a heart attack, probably—but he smashed into Mercy's SUV."

The news ricochets through my brain, barely making sense. "Is *he* going to be okay? Was anyone in the car with Mercy?"

"I'm not sure. Most of the information is being held close to the vest, as you can imagine. Mercy's publicist made it sound like there weren't any serious injuries, but that could be a misunderstanding on my part. I'm just uncertain." Her chest rises and falls beneath her pretty cream-colored blouse. "Mercy is obviously not going to make it this afternoon to the interview."

The interview. Right. Shit.

I glance at my watch.

What do I do now?

"We aren't allowed to say anything about the accident on air," Francine says. "They'll put out a statement later."

"Oh, of course not. I wouldn't want to out her like that. It's not our business to share."

Francine nods. "We have about ten minutes to figure out how to handle this. Do you have any ideas? Any preferences? I know you're prepped for Mercy, but could we do call-ins?" She nibbles her bottom lip. "That doesn't really explain the promised fireworks, though."

I look at the ceiling, regretting all the yapping I did this week about today's show. It could've been left as a true surprise. If it had, then I wouldn't be in this situation.

"Do you have any clever ideas?" Francine asks. "You work well through chaos."

Think, Gianna. "Well, we could say that our guest had an accident, right? And just not say her name?"

"Maybe. But news will break this evening that Mercy was in an accident in Nashville. If you say that, people will put two and two together. We're better off not to touch it at all."

"Okay. Let's take a step back," I say, pacing the room. My heart pounds with each step I take, reminding me that every second that passes brings us another moment closer to the start of the podcast. "The worst-case scenario would be that something bad happened to Mercy or someone else in the accident. This just … sucks." *How can you fix this?* "I've played this up for days, and now I'm going to show up on air with a smile and an empty chair."

"Eight minutes doesn't give us much time to work with. You could just not go on today. We can say you're under the weather and run a previous segment. Oh!" She points at me, her eyes lit up like a Christmas tree. "I know. We can run the live you did with Drake. People have gone feral for that."

They have … And we could …

My attention is snagged by something over Francine's shoulder. Something tall, muscled, with bright blue eyes.

The Tilt-A-Whirl I've been riding for the past couple of minutes screeches to a halt.

Drake *isn't* Mercy Malone, but something tells me my viewers would be just as happy to see him for an hour. And it wouldn't exactly be a hardship for me, either.

A quiver rumbles through my stomach as I check the time. *Am I out of my mind? What would we talk about? What would I ask him? How do I make it as exciting as I've promised everyone?*

I have no idea. But with time ticking, I don't really have another choice.

Blood pounds through my veins, roaring over my eardrums. Sweat dots the back of my neck as adrenaline kicks in fast and hard. I'm not sure what kind of crisis my body is anticipating, but I know the one I'm about to give it.

"Francine, we have seven minutes," I say, forcing a swallow down my throat. "Please get to your booth because we're going live."

Her brows arch in surprise, but a grin smooths the reaction. "You got it."

I follow her to the doorway. As she exits, I reach out, wrapping my fingers around Drake's forearm, and pull him to a stop.

He lifts a brow, grinning. "That's one way to say hello."

"Drake, I need you."

"I knew it," he says playfully. "Glad you're finally on board."

I roll my eyes. "Are you busy right now?"

"If I were, I'd cancel all my plans for you. Why? What's up?"

Did he just flex his biceps? Damn. "This isn't the time for jokes." *Or foreplay.*

He smirks. "Who said I was joking?"

Other podcasters and support staff move past us, giving us curious looks as they go. A clock ticks in the back of my brain, reminding me that time is not on my side. Neither is privacy standing in the middle of Canoodle.

"Come here," I say, dropping his arm and stepping into my recording studio. "Shut the door behind you."

"I like where this is heading."

I take a deep breath. *Three minutes.* "Keep this between us?"

"Absolutely."

This isn't going where he thinks it's going, and that's a shame. I wipe any indication of levity from my features. "Mercy Malone was supposed to be my guest today, but she's been in an accident."

His eyes go wide, but he doesn't speak. Thankfully.

"I have three, maybe two minutes to find a replacement and—"

"What do you need?" He stares at me earnestly. "How can I help you?"

Francine taps the glass and holds up two fingers. *Fuck.*

I was so organized. The planning was done. I had a flow chart of topics, memorized Mercy's life history, and even dug her concert T-shirt out of the back of my closet … *for nothing.*

"Need me to fill in?" Drake asks, already slipping off his jacket. "I think we've already established that I'm quite the draw."

"Will you?"

He sits in the chair across from my computer and adjusts the mic. "Do you have a game plan for this, or are we winging it?"

Relief touches every piece of me as I drop into my seat. My entire body takes a breath. I start to speak, but choose that same moment to look up … and into those clear pools of blue. The genuineness in them pauses time, and the frantic pace of my brain finally eases.

I sense Francine motioning at me to be ready for the intro and see out the countdown flashing on my computer screen in my periphery. The corner of Drake's lips tilt to the sky in a mischievous smirk and I'm hit with a connection—the familiarity of him. I didn't realize how much I needed that until now.

"Let's wing it," I say, putting on my headphones. "Are you ready?"

He puts on a set of headphones that were sitting by the mic. "I'm always ready."

I grin. "Then let's make some magic."

CHAPTER
TEN

GIANNA

"Ready?" I whisper as the final notes of the opening bumper wrap the intro.

Drake smiles in a way that's truly unhelpful under the circumstances, but I shove that out of my mind and focus on the task at hand.

"Welcome to a very special episode of *Gianna Knows Things*," I say, exiting the tabs I had open with my notes for Mercy. I won't need those. "Before we get into why today is going to be so exciting, I want to take a moment to welcome my new listeners who may or may not have found me through a spontaneous live video." I roll my eyes for Drake's benefit. "I have no idea what all the commotion has been about."

I pause and twist toward Francine. She gives me a thumbs-up. Technically speaking, everything is a go.

"I've loved seeing all of your guesses this week about my special guest," I say, getting comfortable. "Some of you have been quite creative, and whoever started the petition to get Lincoln Landry on my podcast—God bless you. It'll probably never happen, but I love that energy."

Drake wrinkles his nose, moving his hand side to side as if to say that Landry is overrated. Unable to miss an opportunity to screw with him, I fan my face and blow out a breath. This earns a glare from across the table.

"Today is going to be a lot of fun," I say, giggling at Drake. "And, since many of you seem to be sports fans from what I can tell with the Landry comments, you'll be especially stoked about who is sitting across from me. We're just going to go with the flow and see how things turn out. We might take questions, and we might not. Feel free to drop them in the comments or submit them on our website, just in case. Francine, my producer extraordinaire, will be keeping up with them."

She makes a face at me through the glass.

My stomach flutters in anticipation of the announcement of Drake. He's calm, cool, and collected. But I guess I am, too, when I'm walking into a situation where I'm the main character. It's easy to be confident when you're the star. As much as I hate to admit it, he's the star of my show today, and these women are going to lose their damn minds.

He drags a fingertip across his lower lip, the corners of his mouth curling toward the ceiling. It's a friendly, yet heated gesture, the waves of which scatter beneath my skin. We've shared the same space hundreds of times, and we've even shared the same screen recently. But there's something different about this—something conspiratorial and indulgent, as if just being here is somehow crossing a line.

"Without further ado, it's my pleasure to announce that none other than Drake Bennett, host of Canoodle's own *Sports Take with Drake Bennett* is here for the next hour." I take a breath. "Drake, welcome to *Gianna Knows Things*."

He grins smugly. "Thank you, Gianna, but the pleasure is all mine."

I can hear the echoes of my listeners swooning in the distance.

"Let me start this afternoon by relaying the results of our

poll," he says. "If you missed that conversation, it's posted on Gianna's socials. Overwhelmingly, I might add, your listeners agreed with me that sending flowers, or whatever your significant other prefers, post-argument is a good thing."

"Whoa. Okay," I say, laughing. "That's not necessarily what happened."

"Really? Because I was there and I've rewatched that video more than a few times."

He did? For reasons unknown to me, that makes me happy. "Great. Then you realize that you called for a poll just after arguing with me about whether *I* like flowers. One could easily construe that the real survey was not a theoretical situation, but specifically about whether I was being honest about wanting flowers or not."

"Doesn't matter. The audience overwhelmingly agreed with me. I think my last count was two hundred thousand to two."

I laugh, shaking my head at him. "You could add together every comment on all of my socials, and it wouldn't reach two hundred thousand." I adjust my headphones, the apples of my cheeks aching from smiling so much. "But let's add to that total by bringing up the legendary Lincoln Landry."

Drake sighs, rolling his eyes at me.

"In my intro, I mentioned that many of you guessed Landry as my guest today. Since he's a baseball player, and Drake is a sportsball analyst, I thought we could get his *sports take*—see what I did there?—about the legendary centerfielder."

"You want to talk about sports?"

I smirk. "Generally, no. But I think there's a definite crossover when it comes to our personal areas of expertise on Lincoln Landry."

"Want to know what's legendary?" he asks, his eyes narrowing. He knows exactly where I'm going with this, and the fact that it seems to bother him is far too entertaining.

"Sure."

"Eight seasons and over five hundred receptions. Fifty-two

touchdowns, a red-zone nightmare, and has one of the most memorable catches in postseason history with a tip-to-self, one-handed, through-contact grab that sealed the Illinois Legends' ticket to the championship."

He sits back, his arms crossed over his chest, and smirks.

I might not know a ton about sports, but I also don't live under a rock. He's not talking about Lincoln Landry. He's talking about himself. I remember that catch vividly, watching it in the middle of The Swill on a rainy Sunday evening. Everyone who understood anything about football was highly impressed by the skills required to pull off that catch. *I* was highly impressed with his obliques on the replay.

"Funny," I say, feigning ignorance. "That doesn't sound like baseball."

"You've got to be—"

"I'm kidding." I giggle. "Everyone, if you didn't know, Drake is more than just a handsome face." *And amazing body.* "He also had a Hall of Fame-worthy career as a tight end with the Illinois Legends."

He lifts a brow. "You know that I was a tight end?"

I'm not sure if it's his question or the way he asks it that catches me off guard. But it's clear I knew that, and I'm not about to admit that I went home from The Swill and looked him up—mainly for pictures. This doesn't seem like the time or place for that.

I clear my throat. "Let's take a call from the audience. Francine, do you have one for us?" Drake pins me to my seat with his stare as I read the words on my computer screen. I ignore him, refusing to make eye contact. "We have Hannah from Chattanooga on the line. Hey, Hannah."

"Hey, Gianna! I'm so excited to talk to you. I call in here every single week and finally got through."

"Welcome to the show."

"Hi, Hannah," Drake says, oozing with charm. "Thanks for calling in."

She squeals. "Oh, my gosh. I can't believe I'm talking to Gianna *and* Drake. My boyfriend is a huge fan of yours, and he's going to die when he finds out that I talked to you today."

Drake chuckles. "I really like the excitement over here. I usually get guys wanting to fight it out over statistics."

"I'm happy to make a cameo on your show," I say, wiggling my eyebrows. "We could do my version of fantasy football."

He can't keep a straight face. "Not happening."

"Hannah, what do you need to know?" I ask, laughing at Drake.

"So my question is personal, obviously," she says. "But how do you deal with fear in a relationship? Like, my boyfriend is great, and we're in love for sure. But I know that his parents—who have always been super nice to me—expect him to marry someone in another tax bracket, let's say. If we continue to date, they're going to pressure him to leave me, and I don't think there's anything that I can do to overcome that."

Ouch. "Well, my first reaction is to say *fuck them.*"

Hannah laughs, but it's tight. Her apprehension is palpable. I want to go on one of my little rants, but I wait so Drake can hop in because once I get started, I can't stop.

"Wow," Drake says, running a hand down his chiseled face. "That's rough. I'm sorry that you're going through this. It must be hard."

"It is," she says. "I don't know what to do. Do I keep going and hope for the best, or end it now and save myself more memories to cry about later?"

Drake's gaze meets mine. The ferocity in them could scorch the earth, but the tenderness alongside it would soothe the burn. The intensity steals my breath, and a lump settles in the base of my throat.

His jaw, dusted with a day's worth of stubble, flexes, and it might just be the sexiest thing I've ever witnessed. A man annoyed by the treatment of a stranger? Watching his protective instincts kick in just inches from me?

Take me now.

"Do you want to go first?" I ask him.

He nods. "I have two sisters, Hannah. If one of them came to me with this situation, I'd suggest they talk with their guy about his intentions. Make sure they were on the same page. Because the one thing we can't do is read people's minds, and there's no way to know if he feels the same pressure or what kind of future he sees with you without asking him directly." His brows pull together. "Have you had a conversation like that with him?"

She sighs. "Kind of. He's acknowledged that I'm not too far off base with my suspicions about his parents, but he sort of dances around it. I mean, I know he loves me. We've been together a year and a half. But, even if he says he wants to marry me, can that marriage survive? Or am I just being too dramatic about all of this, which is what he usually thinks is happening?"

"If a man tells you that you're being too dramatic—*red flag,*" I say. "He's deflecting. Some call it gaslighting. The issue at hand here isn't how big your feelings are, but why you're feeling them in the first place. The fact that he doesn't want to acknowledge and work through that is a huge problem for me."

"So what do you suggest she do?" Drake asks, curiously.

Run. "My advice is that it's time to walk away, and it has nothing to do with his family."

He leans forward, focusing on me as if he has forgotten that a camera is aimed directly at us for the livestream. "You don't advocate for a conversation?"

"There's no conversation to be had. She tried. He blew her off." I shrug. "Let's pretend this goes the distance and they get married. The worst-case scenario is that she's right and the parents start playing games to break them apart. Then what? Her feelings are going to get bigger. She's going to be more panicked and in far too deep to extract herself easily. Is he still going to think she's just being dramatic? If he's not listening to her now, he's not going to be more willing to answer just because she has a ring on her finger. Conversely, he'll probably want to listen to her even less."

"He's not a bad guy," Hannah says. "Really. He's not. It's his parents who are the problem."

I hear it in her voice—the conundrum that is love. She thinks she fell into this mess when, in reality, she made this choice. She chose to love this guy, even though his family probably tolerates her at best. Yet she seems to forget that just because she made one choice doesn't mean she can't make another. It doesn't mean that she's given up the fundamental right to make as many choices as she needs to be happy—and I hate that for her.

But that's also why I'm here. *Lucky for her.*

"That might be true. They might be the root of the problem, but if your boyfriend isn't willing to stop that root from growing, it's going to invade your life—and you know it," I say, wondering why I always have to be the bad guy. "It might be time to take an axe to that proverbial tree."

Drake holds his palms to the ceiling like he doesn't understand how we got here, like I hooked a left when we were turning right. "I still think you try to have a conversation before you go all lumberjack on the guy."

"Nope," I say. "Put on a flannel shirt and get to work."

Francine holds her head in her hands. *Sorry, Francine.*

"*Wow.* I apologize that my friend here is crushing your dreams," Drake says to Hannah. "Just know it's not personal. She does this to everybody."

Drake and I exchange a smile. Warmth flickers in my chest from the twinkle in his eye and the reference to his *dream crusher* nickname for me. Despite being watched by hundreds, maybe even thousands of people, it feels like it's just us for the briefest moment. There's something great about that.

He leans back, stretching his arms overhead. His shirt rides up just above his waistband, giving me a glimpse of the obliques that don't appear to have lost any definition from his Legends days. Not that I'm looking.

"Regardless of what you choose to do, we wish you the very best," Drake says, sitting upright again. "Thanks for calling."

"Good luck, Hannah," I say.

"Thanks for having me. I love you guys," Hannah says before Francine disconnects the call.

I motion for Francine to hold all calls for the moment. If things get awkward, we can grab a question from the Social comments because the look on Drake's face—pure amusement— needs exploring.

"What?" I ask, curious.

"You're just so … ruthless."

"Ruthless?" I burst out laughing. "Why am I ruthless?"

"You're ready to end Hannah's relationship without even knowing the guy's side of the story. You don't just walk away because of something that *might* happen. How can *that* be a deal-breaker?"

I smile. "Oh, Drake. Anything can be a dealbreaker. Dating is an interview at the end of the day. You're essentially hiring a guy for a role. If they're not exactly what you're looking for or don't check all the boxes, you remove them from contention and carry on with the search."

He starts to speak but stops. Instead, he licks his lips and analyzes me. He doesn't try to hide that he's doing it, and I don't hide that I'm aware of it.

Finally, he sighs. "You really don't try to fight for rela-tionships?"

"Not with guys. I'll fight to the death for my girls. But when it comes to a guy and the ship starts to go down, I'm not putting on a life vest and hoping for the best. I'm jumping overboard and looking for a nice big … yacht."

"That's so fucked up," he says, chuckling.

"At least we both know it when I do it, as opposed to most of the men who use another *dinghy* and don't tell me about it." I blow out a breath. "Look, most women give men way too many passes. The guy ghosts them before their date? They accept his bullshit answer. He 'forgets' his wallet at home? They pay for dinner. They catch him on a dating site and believe him when he says that he hasn't logged on in months." I snort, embarrassed that I've been guilty of the same crimes. "Life is too short to mess around with unworthy men."

"Who the hell are you dating?" he asks, laughing. "Do you intentionally search for assholes or what?"

"I have a type, okay?"

He snorts. "What? The feral, unemployed type?"

"Hey, I'm not judging you based on your women of choice," I say, laughing, too, even though I have no idea what kind of women he sees.

"I would be more than happy to be judged based on how I treat women, thank you very fucking much."

My lips twist to try to hide my grin.

"Let me ask you a question," he says, resting his forearms on the table. "When you start dating a guy, do you expect it to last? Do you think you're choosing qualified applicants for the job?"

My eyes stay on his for a beat longer than necessary as one corner of my mouth lifts. "What are you getting at?"

"How long was your longest relationship?"

What? I peer across the table at him, wondering where he's going with this. The look he gives me is innocent enough, but it feathers a flame in my stomach, nonetheless. Maybe it's the curiosity in his eyes. Perhaps it's the sexy grin that accompanies it. Either way, my instincts tell me to tread carefully. Despite the warning, I'm intrigued.

"Seven months," I say. "His name was Calvin. He was an Aries."

"What caused you to bail on him?"

"He was a prick, for one. For two, *he was an Aries*. And three, he didn't check off enough boxes to warrant a life jacket, so to speak."

Drake grins mischievously. "When you met him, you thought he was capable of passing the interview?"

"When I met him, I was three martinis in, and he was a six-foot-two security guard with curly blond hair and a *very* wicked tongue."

"I'll take that as a no," he deadpans.

"You can take it however you want." *I certainly did.*

Drake sits back slowly with his gaze trained on me. *Like he's getting comfortable.* His blues twinkle, and I don't know what to make of it. He's plotting something, and whatever that is amuses him.

My heart races at the unknown. I finger the edge of my shirt under the table, fighting the urge to cut to an ad. I've lost control of this conversation, and it's my damn podcast. *Worst of all?* I don't know how to take it back—and that's a position I've never found myself in before.

"I think the advice that you give comes from a history of dating the wrong kind of guy, and if you dated better men, you might have a different perspective." He pauses, fighting a grin. "Maybe you *need* that kind of experience to round out your worldview. It might save some hearts."

On the surface, it sounds casual—but the challenge is unmistakable.

"What are you getting at?" I ask. I may not fully understand the challenge, but I'm not backing down from it. "I like the guys that I like. I can't help it."

"You like being treated like shit?"

"I think you're overgeneralizing."

"Try me." He smirks. "Let me prove you wrong."

"Excuse me?" I ask, my brows pulling together.

He takes a breath. "Date me for six weeks."

What the fuck? I lean away from him, processing his words. There's no way that I heard him right.

"Date me for six weeks," he repeats. "We can document it here for your fans. It'll help your ratings if nothing else." He shrugs like he knows he's got this in the bag. "You can think of it like an experiment to make you a better podcaster."

If a pin dropped in the room, it would sound like a bomb.

It takes a full five seconds for me to partially process what he's saying. *He wants to date me?* I have so many questions and no idea where to start. So I jump right into the middle of it.

"You want to fake date me to get our ratings up?" I ask.

"No." He grins. "I want to date you for real to prove that your *one-size-fits-all* approach to relationships doesn't work."

I'm vaguely aware of Francine reacting in the sound booth, and my phone lighting up like a Christmas tree. But I'm anchored in place, heart racing, and staring into the eyes of … my new boyfriend?

I've done much, much crazier things in the past with much, much lesser men than Drake.

Which is kind of his point, but I won't admit that.

"Okay," I say, wrapping my head around his proposition. "You want to date me. For real. For six weeks. All to prove that I need to expand my dating horizons so I can be a better podcaster?"

"Yeah. I mean, it won't hurt that you'll get to spend time with a nice guy for once. Hell, you might even like it."

I laugh, and the sound is much more maniacal than I intend or expect. For some reason, this makes him smirk.

"You don't think I'll fall for you or anything, right?" I ask, smirking right back. "Because I won't. You're not my type."

He snorts. "From what I've heard, I'm happy about that. I'd hate to be lumped in with that group."

"Very funny."

"I'm basically a public servant, trying to stop the destruction of dreams and futures. I'm just doing this as a public service. I'm not trying to make you fall in love with me."

"Good. Because no man can make that happen."

"You can't make love happen, Gianna. It just does."

Yeah, right.

The heat between us builds, clouding my head and making it hard to think clearly. I don't know what this will entail or why he's doing this, but it will help my podcast. I bet my viewership is setting new records today. *And dating in this year of our lord comes with sex, doesn't it?*

As if he can read my mind, he winks at me.

Fuck it. What do I have to lose?

"Deal," I say, smugly. "You have six weeks to broaden my horizons. We'll update my followers each week on how it's going. Cool?"

"Cool. And, if at the end of the six weeks, you realize that I'm right …"

"I won't."

Francine's celebration from the sound booth reminds me that we're live. *Shit.* I glance at the clock. *We're nearly done with this episode anyway.*

"We're going to wrap up today's show a little early, friends. After all, I don't know how much more excitement I can pack into one episode. So I will see you next week with hot takes and cold truths about …. my new boyfriend." *That sounds so weird.* "See you guys later."

"Goodbye," Drake says as he gets to his feet.

The outro music begins to play, and I slide off my headphones. Drake follows suit. I have no idea what we do now, or if he was joking, or if this is some skit he wants to keep up for views. There are so many unanswered questions on the tip of my tongue.

"I'll text you tonight," he says, grabbing his jacket off the back of the chair.

"Okay …"

He gives me one final lingering smile. "This is going to be fun."

"I …"

He's out the door before my voice catches up with him.

I fall back into my seat and take a long breath, trying desperately to get my wits together.

What the hell just happened here?

CHAPTER
ELEVEN

Gianna

"Let's look at the bright side," Audrey says, stepping over the button mess still scattered on my living room floor. "The messier things get, the better you operate."

"Or we can look at the other bright side." Astrid laughs from Audrey's phone, which is propped against a box that Lucia had delivered to me this afternoon. "Drake Bennett is going to be one hell of a fuck."

"Well, there's that, too," Audrey says with flushed cheeks.

I dip my brush into a blob of crimson paint and splatter it against the canvas. Each droplet drips and runs down the white background in vivid streaks. It reminds me of the energy buzzing through my body and the heat blooming in my chest. Not to mention the ache between my thighs. It's intense and exciting … and a bit worrisome from a practical standpoint.

But when have I ever been practical?

"You know, that setup looks like the makings of a serial killer documentary," Astrid says, her voice momentarily cutting out. Phone service is bad on the ranch, we've learned. "Clear plastic sheets covering a corner of your living room. A drop cloth with red droplets. Your art could pass as blood play. It's very … Dexter of you."

I lean back and take in the impromptu studio. It was unintentional, but it does look a little … violent.

"So what does this mean? I heard the show, but … are you really dating him?" Audrey asks, flopping on the couch. She curls her feet beneath her and sinks into the plush cushions.

"I saw the way Drake was looking at her," Astrid says. "There's nothing fake about it to him. I guarantee that."

I bite back a smile, happy that my back is to my friends so they can't see that Astrid's commentary is kind of what I want to hear. I'll never date Drake—not really. He's too traditional and jaded about what it means to be in love. But the more I think about fake dating him for real, whatever that means, the more I like it.

There's just one question that remains, and I can't answer it. Or maybe I'm afraid to. *What's in this for him?*

The question plagued me all afternoon and followed me into the evening. When most guys want to date me, I know exactly what they're after, and I'm more than happy to deliver. Honestly, I'm usually in it for the same reasons. But with Drake, I'm not sure what he wants to get out of this aside from the obvious: ratings.

"He's clever," I say, pushing the brush a little too hard against the canvas. "He said on air that he wants to prove that my approach to relationships is wrong because I only date losers, essentially. But that's to *my* benefit. My show will reap those rewards. The only benefit that I can see him getting out of this is numbers. His stats this week will be incredible. He's tapping into a new demographic because my podcast is basically a free hunting ground for him. And when we're neck and neck for the Thursday slot, I have to assume that's his takeaway."

"Wow. I didn't think of it like that," Astrid says.

"Me either," Audrey says, sighing.

I add some yellow paint to my used egg carton and dab my brush into it.

Today has been a roller coaster of emotions, and I haven't had time to sort it all out. Every high was chased by a low, only to be followed by another high. It's exhausting, even for me as someone who admittedly loves drama. I had to turn off my phone before I left the office. Incessant calls, constant text alerts, ceaseless chirps notifying me of Social comments and messages. It was all too much—especially since I don't know what to say for once.

"Playing devil's advocate here. What would you say if he isn't doing it *just* for ratings?" Audrey asks. "How would you feel about that?"

I switch back to the red paint. "It would depend on what his objective is, I guess. Is he just wanting to have fun? Great. There are a million ways in which I can imagine fun with that man. Is he looking at it like a science experiment? That's … not as fun." I study the art in front of me. "Either way, I don't think he's being exploitative. He's not that kind of guy."

"Are you going to go on dates?" Astrid asks. "Have you talked to him?"

"He said he'd text me before he left, but that was the last that I've heard from him. I guess we'll go on dates. How serious is he about that? Are we monogamous for the next month and a half? Is that even necessary?" I shrug because I simply don't know.

Audrey glances at my phone on the coffee table. "Your phone is off. Do you know that?"

"Yup."

"Well, you can't hear from him if you literally can't hear from him." She giggles.

I just need a little time to get my thoughts together before I deal with Drake.

Astrid groans. "I wish I were in Nashville. I should be there with you guys."

"When are you guys coming back to town?" I ask, creating an arch with the brush over a yellow blob.

"We'll be back in January for the rugby season," Astrid says. "But we do have a few meetings up there soon, so we'll make a long weekend out of it so I can spend some time with you guys."

"You can stay with me," I say, etching a few trees into the paint with the back of my brush. "I have three extra bedrooms. Tell Gray to bring his cowboy brother. He can share my room with me."

"You'd kill Hartley, Gianna," Astrid says, laughing.

I laugh, too. "I'd be sure that he went out with a smile."

"You'd better clear that with your new boyfriend." Audrey picks up her phone.

"Hey, where are you taking me?" Astrid asks.

I look over my shoulder as Audrey props Astrid against a pillow on the couch. Then she reaches for the box Lucia sent. I told Audrey to open it earlier, but Astrid called, and we got distracted.

"Why do you have a proofing basket?" Audrey asks, pulling things from the container. There's a basket, a couple of oddly shaped tools, and what looks like bonnets. "Are you into baking all of a sudden?"

"What the hell is that stuff?"

"This is a proofing basket for sourdough," she says. "These are liners and covers for it. You have a scoring lame, a dough whisk, and a bowl scraper."

I wrinkle my nose and set the egg tray on a bench I carried in from the garage. "I thought bread making was supposed to be easy."

"I've been baking bread for Gray." Astrid beams. "I did a cherry chocolate chip loaf the other day. And I did a pistachio brown sugar loaf for Hartley. He said it was the best bread that he's ever eaten."

A smile pulls at the corners of my lips. "If he wants to eat, I can help him out with that."

"*Gianna*," Audrey says.

"I meant sourdough, Auddie." I unfasten my overalls and let them fall to the floor. "I swear."

"Oh, that's cute," Astrid says. "What are you wearing?"

"This outfit is brought to you by my friend insomnia." I dance in a little circle, showing off my chocolate-brown shorts and tank to my friends. "It's so comfortable, and I think it was like fifteen dollars because I did get it on sale."

Audrey frowns. "I wish my insomnia purchases were that cheap."

As soon as she says it, regret sweeps across her features. Astrid and I exchange a look. If Audrey is making impulse purchases, something's amiss. That especially worries me, considering how down she's been lately.

I move Astrid back to the coffee table, and then I sit next to Audrey.

"Are you okay?" Astrid asks her.

Audrey plays with the end of the ribbon in her hair, looking anywhere but at us. Her big blue eyes are foggy, as if she's holding back tears. I reach for her hand and squeeze it.

"What's going on?" I ask softly.

"I almost bought a ticket to Boston the other night," she says. "And then I remembered that it's different now, so I bought a new pair of running shoes that I don't need."

"New shoes are never a bad decision," I say, trying to bring some levity into the conversation.

Audrey *almost* smiles.

Andrew, Audrey's brother, lives in Boston and is best friends with the guy who broke her heart. She's avoided visiting Andrew for weeks, and it's killing her not to see him. But she says she doesn't know how to act around him and his friends, including Dipshit, and that she needs time to come to terms with reality. Which—*fair*. But the cloudiness in her eyes just about breaks my heart.

"I feel so ... boring," Audrey says as a single tear streaks down her face. "I'm a dud."

"That is so not true," Astrid says.

"If you're a dud, what's that make me?" I ask, pulling her into a quick hug. "You're beautiful. You're sweet. You have a literal doctorate. There's never a moment when you don't know the right thing to say, you know what fork to use in fancy restaurants, and there's not a person on earth who could say a bad thing about you."

She pulls away, running her fingers beneath her eyes. "You have to say that. You're my best friend."

"True," I say. "But that doesn't make it a lie."

"I don't know anything, really," she says. "Sure, I know what fork to use. Good for me. I don't know how to talk to men. I can't flirt. I've had sex with one guy, and I have no idea how to give a blow job—and there's no way to fix any of it."

"I'll set you up with some porn, and that'll fix the blow job issue." I grin as her jaw drops to her lap. "I'm teasing you. Don't look so horrified."

"See? I've never watched porn. The thought of watching two people have sex makes me so nervous. It feels ... illegal."

"Well, it's not. In this state, at least. And it can be so hot to watch people get it on. It's a fetish for some. I was at this party once and—"

"Before you start watching porn with Gianna, really think about this, Auddie," Astrid says, side-eyeing me. "You don't want to change who you are to try to attract a guy."

I point at Astrid. "You just missed out on a great story."

"I have no doubt," she says, grinning.

"But she's right," I say, turning to our friend. "If you want to try new things because you're interested, then I've got you. But there's nothing wrong with you the way you are, and there's nothing wrong with embracing that. If a guy doesn't want you like this, fuck him—literally or figuratively. It's up to you."

Audrey gives me a sheepish smile. "Anyway, is there any news about the hall tree?"

I hate leaving this conversation the way it stands. Audrey losing her self-confidence because of some asshole from Boston is asinine, and I want to be sure she understands that. But this is the most she's opened up to Astrid and me about this, and I don't want to push.

Well, I want to push, but I won't. We'll go at her pace, even if it's slow as molasses.

I groan. "Coat Tree Woman has issues. She messages me four or five times a day. I finally quit opening them, but I think that makes her even madder because the messages came in faster after that."

Astrid's head whips to the side, her cheeks pinking immediately. "Don't you dare come in front of this phone. I'm talking to Auddie and Gianna."

"Hi, Gray," Audrey calls out.

"Hey."

"Bring our friend back, asshole," I say.

"She's mine now," Gray says. "Deal with it."

I laugh. "Keep talking shit. I still have my Taser, you know."

"You and that fucking Taser." He chuckles.

"I gotta go," Astrid says, giggling. "Keep me posted on the Drake situation, Gianna. Love you, Audrey. Call me anytime."

We say our goodbyes before she disappears from Audrey's phone screen.

The house grows quiet. Audrey leans her head back against the couch and closes her eyes. I want to be pissed at Dipshit—I *am* pissed at Dipshit—but I doubt he knows that he broke Audrey's heart. I hope not, anyway. Because I can't imagine anyone hurting this girl, destroying her self-esteem, and being okay with it.

And I *really* don't want to go to prison.

I consider turning on my phone but decide against it. Even

though I'm dying to know if Drake has texted me, I want to wrap my head around this situation before I respond.

"Date me for six weeks. We can document it here for your fans. It'll help your ratings if nothing else. You can think of it as an experiment to make you a better podcaster."

"You want to fake date me to get our ratings up?"

"No. I want to date you for real to prove that your one-size-fits-all approach to relationships doesn't work."

A coy smile spreads across my face. If he's being honest and really wants to do this, I can have some fun with it. With him.

Heat spreads through my belly and into my core as I think of what this experiment might entail. I've always told myself that Drake was best kept in my dreams, but that was to protect the sanctity of the workplace. If it's to benefit the workplace …

It's not like I'm actually going to fall in love with him.

So, what could possibly go wrong?

CHAPTER
TWELVE

DRAKE

"Heads up!"

I spin around just in time to catch a basketball aimed straight for my head.

"Sorry about that." A guy on the other end of the court holds his hands out for me to pass the ball back to him. We've exchanged pleasantries in passing a few times. He's always seemed like a decent guy, but the ball to the head makes me reconsider that assessment. "I completely missed that pass."

I fire a bounce pass his way and then turn back to Jory.

Jory Plath, a winger with the Tennessee Royals rugby team, wipes his forehead with the back of his hand. We met two years ago when I moved into this building and quickly bonded over sports and a shared love of pizza. When he called me on my way home from the office and asked if I wanted to shoot around for a while in our building's gymnasium, I was all too happy to take him up on his offer.

After the day that I've had, I need an outlet to release some of this energy that's still buzzing beneath my skin, or I'm going to go crazy. It's also nice to think about something else for a minute. Distance sometimes provides clarity.

"I just don't know if I want to do it anymore, man," Jory says, banking a shot off the backboard. "A part of me thinks I'd miss rugby like crazy if I retire. But then I think about not hurting every fucking day, settling down in one place, maybe getting a dog, and suddenly, it doesn't seem like such a bad idea."

"A dog?" I chuckle. "That feels so random."

"You know what I mean, asshole." He tosses me the ball. "How'd you know when it was time to retire?"

I step to the three-point line and launch a perfectly arched shot over the rim. The net swishes as the ball slides through.

This question comes up surprisingly often, especially in conversations with other athletes. It's hard for us to walk away from a game that we've been playing since we were children. It's the only reality we know. It's often the only thing we're good at. But my retirement story is complicated and includes discovering Dad's rapid mental decline. That played a huge factor in my decision, but that's not a topic I want to discuss.

"How'd I know?" I ask. "Well, I took a look at my bank account and then took a call from my mom." *Which isn't a total lie.*

He laughs, nodding as he rebounds my shot. "Been there, done that—in that order."

"We won three championships in five years, and I didn't feel like I had anything left to prove." *Which isn't a lie either.* "I had to commit to another three to five years with the team, with at least two of them being rebuilding seasons, or go home. And honestly, I played for eight years without major injuries. It felt like tempting fate if I stayed."

"It was that simple, huh?"

"Hell no. There wasn't anything simple about it. But I knew in my gut it was the right thing to do, and I always follow my gut."

He snorts, setting the ball down and swiping his water bottle off the bench. He takes a quick drink. "Well, I wish mine would tell me more than to stop drinking cow's milk. The last time I tried to figure out what my gut was saying, I woke up with a wife." He curls his lips. "That's why I stopped listening to that sonofabitch."

"I didn't know you were married."

"I'm not." He gives me a toothy grin. "Anymore. *Thank God.*"

"Are you serious?" I ask, unable to read the goofy fucker.

He shrugs before trotting to the basket and shooting a free throw.

I take a ball from the rack by the window overlooking the courtyard and dribble it from one hand to the other. Football was my bread and butter, but I've always loved basketball. The smell of a gymnasium—sweat mixed with stale popcorn—reminds me of high school. The acoustics are nostalgic. I've spent many hours bouncing a ball as I work out a problem or regulate my nervous system when I'm stressed.

Like now.

"Date me for six weeks. Let me prove you wrong."

"Deal. You have six weeks to broaden my horizons."

The thought of *broadening her horizons* makes my dick so hard I wince.

I have no idea what got into me today, or why I decided to shoot the shot I'll never really get to take. There's a damn good reason I friend-zoned Gianna on the first day that I met her. She's impossibly perfect in every way but the one that matters.

Regardless of whether this was a wise decision on my part, the choice has been made—and she co-signed it.

I'd better enjoy the next six weeks because I won't get them again. I'd better figure out how not to get crushed by the vixen, too.

"Are you about ready to call it for the night?" Jory asks. "I got up early as shit, and I need a shower. I smell like a locker room."

"Yeah. Might as well."

We walk side by side to the benches lining the court and gather our things. I sneak a peek at my phone—still no response from Gianna. I'm not sure if this is one of those "no news is good news" type of things or not.

"Want to grab some dinner on Sunday?" he asks as we head for the exit. "They opened a new surf 'n' turf place near the stadium. Some of the guys on the team said it was good."

I sling my bag over my shoulder. "I'm going to my parents' house for dinner on Sunday. My dad is … going through some stuff, so I try to get back and help my mom as much as I can."

"You're a good dude, Bennett." He starts down the long hallway to his bank of elevators. "See ya when I see ya."

"Later."

I forgo the elevator and take the steps instead—all nine stories of them. It's a long haul, and by the time I get to my floor, my thighs are screaming. It hurts like a motherfucker, but it gives me something to think about besides Gianna.

Mr. Hernandez waves at me from the end of the hall as I slide my key into my door. I return his gesture before stepping inside my apartment, then I drop my shit and head straight for the shower.

I peel off my shirt to hop in the shower when my phone buzzes from my pocket. I dig it out and try to hide my disappointment that it's not Gianna.

"Hey, Evie."

"We have some things to talk about," she says. "And I'm just a little pissed that I had to hear your news through the grapevine and not from you personally. Do you know how much clout I lost today from being the only person in my office who didn't know you're now dating Gianna Bardot?"

I blow out a breath that feels like it originated in my toes. A grin dances on my lips. Even though we're not *really* dating, even though we are, I like the sound of it.

"My apologies for not calling you with such important news," I joke.

"It's Gianna Bardot, Drake," she says, like I'm a child. "This is quite possibly a bigger deal than you signing with the Legends."

I laugh at my sister. Only she would think that.

"So tell me what happened. Give me every little detail," she says. "I need something juicy to share with the office on Monday to save face."

"Did you listen to the podcast?"

"No, I didn't listen to the podcast. Some of us have to work in the middle of the day—although I do plan on listening to it when I get home … and out of this traffic." A horn blasts in the background. "This is the fast lane, asswipe!"

"Settle down." I chuckle. "Damn. You sound like Dad."

"There is one tractor in the slow lane, and this grandpa decides to match his speed in the fast lane. I'm the third car back, and I can't see the end behind me." She honks again. "Back to Gianna."

"It's complicated."

"Well, talk to me about it. Let me help you *un*complicate it."

I laugh. "You've never uncomplicated anything in your life. As a matter of fact, I can't think of a situation where you didn't complicate things unnecessarily."

"Rude."

I slip off my shorts and toss them into the laundry bin. I don't know what to tell Evie. But I guess I'd better get used to talking about it because it's going to be a thing for the next month and a half.

"It just kind of happened," I say, reaching in and turning on the shower. "We were talking to this woman on the podcast about whether she should stick it out in a relationship or bail. I said she needs to have a conversation; Gianna said to jump ship. One thing led to another, and I'm daring her to date me for six weeks to prove that not all guys are assholes. To balance the equation a bit, if you will."

"So are you really dating or not? Because I'm going to be devastated if this is a prank."

I laugh, checking the water temperature. *Perfect.* "I told you. It's complicated."

"What are you getting out of this?"

"Honestly?"

"No, lie to me," she says, snorting. "Yes, honestly."

I pace the room and ponder the question, which isn't as straightforward as it seems. Sure, I think it's a good thing for Gianna to experience a nice guy. God knows that she deserves more than being ghosted and having to pick up the check at dinner. But there's a selfish part of it, too—and that part of it feels a little … pathetic. But if there's anyone I can confess that to, it's Evie.

"Okay," I say, taking a towel out of the linen closet. "Here's what I'm getting out of it. Gianna is a woman who I'd consider spending a lot of time with. But she's also the woman who I'll never get to spend a lot of time with because she and I aren't really compatible."

"Why the hell not?"

I smile. "Because she doesn't even believe in love, I don't think. She bails on relationships. She's a fucking maneater, Evie." The thought makes me chuckle. "So I guess this is my way to have a few weeks with her without *actually* dating her." I stop myself. "Don't get me wrong. I'm going to date the hell out of that woman. But I'm going to do it knowing it's for six weeks and then it's over." *Hopefully, that'll keep me from getting crushed.*

"That's an interesting take on things, but I hope it works out for you. I also hope we can double date so I can hang out with her."

I shake my head. This conversation has gone on long enough. Evie got the information she wanted. Now she'll use it to her advantage. *Baby of the family shit.*

"Hey, I have a shower running, so I need to go," I say. "Are you good? You don't need anything?"

"I will corner you on Sunday with prepared questions."

"Thanks for the warning."

She giggles. "Love you, Drakey."

"Love you, Evie."

She hangs up before I do.

The bathroom is steamy. The scent of eucalyptus from the branches my housekeeper hung in the shower a couple of weeks ago wafts through the air. I take a long breath, filling my airways with the cool, minty, almost medicinal scent. My lungs expand, tingling before I exhale.

I stare into the foggy glass, seeing a muddled reflection of myself. My stomach is a ball of nervous energy thanks to my sister's questions. But they were helpful, too. Strangely, I feel better about this situation now than I did before my sister called.

I'm just going to have fun with it. I'll make sure that if it's only six weeks, it's the best damn six weeks that Gianna ever has. She won't be able to look back on this time without smiling and wishing she had more of it.

I turn toward the shower. Before I take a step, my phone lights up.

She finally responded.

> Gianna: Yes, I'm free tomorrow at seven. Care to tell me where you're taking me on our first date?

Guess that means she's not backing out. I hold my breath as I type out my response, trying not to sound too eager. *Play it cool, Bennett.*

Me: It's a surprise. I have everything handled.

Gianna: But what if I want details?

Me: You don't always get everything you want.

Gianna: Yeah, I usually do. 😌

"I bet you fucking do," I say, reaching into the shower and switching it from hot water to cold. If this conversation keeps going this direction, I'll definitely need a cold shower when it's over.

Me: Not this time.

Gianna: This doesn't bode well for our relationship, boyfriend.

Our relationship. I blow out a hasty breath.

Me: How can I make an impression if I treat you like every other guy does?

Gianna: I can think of ways. 😈

"Yup." I groan as my cock grows rock hard. "Cold shower it is."

Gianna: So this is a real dating experiment? Meaning, it's for science, but it'll be real for all intents and purposes, right?

Me: You better tell Matthew to fuck off. Does that help?

Gianna: Oooh. Are you a possessive boyfriend, Drake?

Me: Are you a jealous girlfriend, Gianna?

Gianna: No. I'm confident that I can keep your attention for six weeks.

"There is no doubt about that."

Gianna: If this is a real relationship, then I should treat you like I would any other guy who I'm dating, right? And not like my coworker? Or should it be my coworker who dared me to date him as a science experiment?"

Me: This will only work if you treat it like a real relationship.

I'm playing with fire. I'm playing with so much fucking fire that there's no doubt that I'm going to get burned. *Why does that sound so tempting?*

Gianna: So I should totally send you nudes …

Me: PLEASE.

Gianna: 😒 No nudes before the first date.

Me: I knew I should've made our first date tonight.

Gianna: You missed an opportunity.

Me: Guess I'll have to do what I do every other night then.

Gianna: What's that?

I grab my cock and give it a nice, tight stroke.

Me: I'll talk to you tomorrow.

Gianna: Don't be late.

Me: I wouldn't dream of it. Good night.

Gianna: Night. 💋

Memories of her lips assault me. And now, visions of her body naked … *Just how far does Gianna plan to go?*

This is going to be the longest, *hardest* six weeks of my life.

CHAPTER
THIRTEEN

GIANNA

"If all else fails, I look hot."

I give myself a final once-over in my floor-length mirror, turning side to side to get a full view of my outfit. The black leather pants I bought on sale a few months ago came in clutch. I was starting to think I'd never find a place to wear them. They paired perfectly with a champagne camisole that I stole from Lucia, a pair of black heels, and a few thin gold rings, necklaces, and a bracelet. It gives exactly what I wanted it to give—namely, fuckable.

My phone rings on the bed, and I reach over and grab it. Astrid's name is on the screen.

"Hey," I say, putting her on speakerphone and dropping her back on the bed. "What's up?"

"Are you ready for your date? And why am I looking at the ceiling?"

I groan. "You're so needy." I pick her up and prop her on my dresser. "Better?"

"Much. You, my friend, look amazing. Seriously. Drake isn't going to be able to help himself."

"That's the plan."

As surprising as it is, I've been more excited for this date than I have been for one in a long damn time. There's something fun about it. There are no expectations. He could take me to a drive-thru, and I won't be upset about it because it doesn't matter. If we go sit by the river and have terrible conversation, that's fine. If he wants to take me back to his place to fuck as most men prefer, I'm *seriously* not going to be upset about that. *Why? Because this isn't for real. It's fake for real. Who cares?*

"Do you like my hair like this?" I ask, twisting my head so she can get a glimpse of the back. "I left it kinda messy on top but pulled it back at the nape of my neck. It's too late to fix it if you hate it, so lie to me if you must."

"It looks great. I love it like that. And your makeup is perfect. Did Lucia do it or you?"

"I did it, thank you very much." I pucker my lips and add a dollop of gloss to the center of my lips. It makes my Cupid's bow pop. All the attention I can bring to my mouth tonight, the better. "I got a little wild with the eyeliner, but I think I smoked it out enough that it looks all right."

"What time is he supposed to be there?"

"He said he'd pick me up at seven. It's currently …" I glance at the clock. "Six fifty."

Astrid yawns. "Do you know where he's taking you?"

"Nope." I sweep her off my dresser and carry her to my closet to grab a cardigan and my purse. "I don't have a clue where we're going, which made it hard to decide what to wear. He just said he had it handled, which, may I add, is so super hot. A guy takes control, and all I have to do is show up and enjoy myself? Yes, please."

I hold up my accessories and make sure they look good with my outfit. I like what I see.

"Men taking care of things is so sexy," Astrid agrees. "I remember the day when Gray set up an appointment with an attorney for me. I didn't ask him for help. He just saw a need and knew he could fill it, so he did." She sighs happily. "I think that cemented what I wanted in a man. Someone who can get things done, who wants to take care of me, and can problem-solve."

"You just described me. I get things done, take care of myself, and solve problems." I gasp. "Are you calling me sexy?"

"I think that goes without saying."

We laugh as my heels click against the floor. I make my way through the house, admiring the little touches that make this house so special. The exposed brick wall in the hallway. The fireplace separating the dining room from a perfectly odd, circular space that I use as a library is lovely. The molding, which probably isn't original but is old and intricate none-theless, makes my heart skip a beat. It's so charming. So special. So mine.

"Are you taking your Taser tonight?" Gray asks from some-where in the distance.

Astrid laughs, shaking her head.

"Nope," I say. "He's not the kind of guy who warrants a Taser, unlike some men I know."

"Someone should call your date and warn him to bring one," Gray jokes.

"Ah, do you miss me, Gray?"

He snorts. "I miss you about as much as I miss chewing glass."

I smile to myself, placing my purse and cardigan on the table beside the door. "It's six fifty-five. He's cutting it close."

"I'm sure he'll be there," Astrid says as I walk to the kitchen. "Are you nervous?"

"No. Hey, how long do you have until your sourdough starter dies? Or whatever it does?"

"It's very forgiving. As long as you feed it and you—"

"I have to feed it?" I swing the refrigerator door open and look in on Matilda. "Why would Lucia give me something that I have to keep alive?"

The jar is as bubbly and, quite frankly, gross as it was when my sister delivered it to me. I shrug and close the door.

"Call me tomorrow afternoon if you want to bake a loaf," Astrid says. "I'm going to make some bread to take to the retirement center in town anyway, so I can walk you through the process."

"Sounds riveting."

She laughs. The sound of her laughter blends with the doorbell's tone echoing through the house. *He's here.*

"Okay, focus," I say, leaning her against a fruit bowl and stepping far enough away so she can see most of me. "Fit check. What do you think? Same rules apply as earlier—lie to me if you must."

"You're beautiful, Gianna. Those pants make your ass look amazing, and the top shows off your boobs. Shiny hair, glowy skin—you couldn't possibly look any better. He's not going to be able to keep his hands off you."

That's the plan.

I blow her a kiss. "That's why you're my best friend. Now, I gotta go. I'll call you after with all the details."

"Love you."

"Love you most. Bye."

I end the call and make my way to the front door once again. I drop my phone into my purse so it's not in my hand when I see him. *How tacky.* Then I take a deep breath, will my heart to stop thundering like a storm cloud, and open the door.

"Hey," I say as it swings far enough for me to see him. "You're here, and you're three minutes early."

"If you're not early, you're late." He drags his gaze down my body unapologetically. "Wow, Gianna. You're absurdly beautiful."

Absurdly beautiful? No man has ever called me *that* before. "Thank you. I have to say that Date Drake is much hotter than Office Drake, and I didn't think that was possible."

He lifts a brow and the corner of his mouth. "Oh, really?"

"You should know by now that I don't lie."

We face each other, neither of us speaking for a long moment. The space between us is relaxed, and I could reach out and touch him without feeling at all awkward. This isn't how first dates usually go, but then again, I'm not usually fake real dating guys I'm already friends with.

I grab my purse and cardigan and then step onto the front porch. He moves to the side while I lock up and then waits for me to descend the stairs first. *Like a true gentleman.*

"I would've brought you flowers, but I know that's triggering for you," he jokes, pulling open the passenger door of his Mercedes.

"Smelling a funeral before our date would've been a bit of a downer."

He offers me a hand as I climb into the seat. "I tried to think of something to replace it with, like candy or a puppy."

"A puppy?" I laugh. "Dear lord, don't bring me a puppy. I can barely keep myself alive."

He grins as he shuts the door and makes his way around the front of the vehicle. He moves effortlessly. A thin black sweater hugs his broad shoulders, making him appear bigger and more solid than usual. His thighs fill out the caramel-colored pants, highlighting his trim waist. The man, *my new boyfriend*, is a walking advertisement for physical fitness, and I am not mad about it.

Oh, the things I do for science.

Drake climbs in beside me, and we get buckled in. I take a moment to survey the interior. The floorboards are spotless. You can see out of every window without nary a streak. There are no straw wrappers or errant french fries like there are in my car, and the air is lightly fragranced with a scent reminiscent of his cologne.

It's like being wrapped up in one of his jackets. Or his arms. Or his sheets.

"So where are we going?" I ask as he pulls away from the curb.

"I thought we'd grab a bite to eat tonight. You haven't eaten, have you?"

"No. But even if I had, I'll always eat again."

He cracks a smile. "My kind of girl. We're going to a little place not far from here. A friend of mine and his wife opened it last summer, and it's been doing very well. It was just named one of Nashville's best new restaurants, which I find very cool."

"That's exciting. Are they chefs or businesspeople who like food?"

"She is a chef. Her name is Melissa. I believe she went to culinary school in Europe, then worked in a ton of kitchens around the world. My friend met her while eating street food in Singapore. Their story is pretty wild."

"Oh, I love that. How did they get here?"

Drake looks at me out of the corner of his eye. "Nox, my buddy, is from Nashville. Melissa fell in love with Tennessee, and they moved here about ten years ago. He quit his job last year to help her open this restaurant."

"A man supporting his woman. How groundbreaking."

He laughs. "Right? We live in this world now where we've taken the hustle culture of business and applied it to our personal lives. We've lost the idea of working together and supporting one another."

I sit back in my seat and absorb that. It wasn't what I expected to hear.

He's not wrong. I know that because I've seen it with my own eyes. With my own parents. They couldn't set aside their individual goals and power trips to create a safe, warm space for Lucia and me—or themselves.

"Have you been married?" I ask, the thought suddenly occurring to me. I don't know a lot about Drake, really, and maybe his insight comes from experience.

"Uh, no. Why?"

"I don't know anything about your love life post Jessica. Maybe there's an ex-wife that I need to be aware of."

He grins at me. "No ex-wives. You're in the clear."

"So have you had a lot of relationships? Where does this foundation you're spouting come from?"

"I've had a few relationships, but nothing close to marriage." He flips on the turn signal and makes a left at the light. "I guess my foundation, as you call it, comes from watching my parents. They've been married for almost forty years."

"Whoa. That's a long damn time."

He chuckles. "It really is. They dated in high school and got married as soon as Mom found out she was pregnant with my sister Elodie. Mom likes to say that no one thought they'd make it and that sometimes her desire to spite them outweighed her desire to choke Dad."

"She sounds funny," I say, smiling.

"She's pretty great." He regrips the steering wheel. "What about your parents? What are they like? They must've been pretty exceptional to have you as a daughter."

I half laugh at his words—appreciative of the compliment—but also aware of the irony.

I turn my attention to the scenery out the window. Not looking at Drake gives me a moment to gather my thoughts and figure out what to say about my mom and dad. I don't want to paint them unfairly, but I want to be honest, too. *How do I be respectful but accurate—and fair all the same?*

It's a fine line.

"They were good people," I say, choosing my words carefully. "Dad worked for the government, and Mom was a college professor. They were very successful, *very busy,* and so damn smart. In retrospect, I think that's why they fought all the time and demanded perfection of me and my sister, Lucia. It was exactly as you said—a dog-eat-dog household."

He frowns, reaching across the console and giving my hand a gentle squeeze before pulling it back to the steering wheel. No words were exchanged, no sentiments shared. But that little touch, a quiet acknowledgment of my truth, makes my breath halt in my throat.

"Here we are," he says, pulling slowly into a parking spot at an adorable tapas place. The parking lot is busy. The group currently exiting the building is laughing and smiling. *All good signs.* "They have so many options on the menu that I'm fairly certain they'll have something you like. If not, I have a backup plan."

"Which is …"

He kills the ignition. "Cook you something myself."

"At your place?"

Our eyes meet, and the heat that passes between them could burn down the entire city. The air is charged, so thick with energy that it's nearly alive. Drake's gaze drops to my mouth, to the exact spot I highlighted with gloss, and then he licks his lips painfully slow.

A half smile paints his lips as his sight returns to mine.

"*And that,*" he says, grabbing the door handle, "is why we aren't going with the backup plan."

"But …" I protest, but he's already out the door.

Dammit.

CHAPTER
FOURTEEN

GIANNA

"This is *adorable*," I say, gasping as I step inside Hess.

"Do you like it?" Drake asks, grinning because he already knows the answer. *How could he not?* This place is fabulous.

The space is bright despite the hour, with beautiful peach walls and fantastic maize-colored chairs. The drinkware reminds me of my favorite Depression-era glass in all the delicate, pretty colors. The music is soft but upbeat, and the art on the walls—sketches, sculptures, and tons of whimsical, mixed-media pieces—is nothing short of iconic. *But the copper accents with a slight patina?* I'm in heaven.

Off to the right is a piece of art composed of pages of books. Figures are painted onto the pages with each person or animal interacting with the words. A rope swing looped around a *G* with a tiny mouse sitting on the seat. A woman has a leash tied around the word *walk* as if she's taking it on a leisurely stroll and a chef stands at the word *cook*, using the two *O*s as skillets. It's whimsical and so much fun.

"Are you ready?" Drake whispers from behind me, his breath hot against the shell of my ear.

I hum as my core clenches and goose bumps race along my skin. My body sinks toward him, desperate for contact. "If you really want to cook me dinner, keep it up."

His chuckle rumbles through me, and I feel it *everywhere*.

Drake nestles his hand in the small of my back as he guides me through the restaurant. His touch is gentle, his fingertips barely pressing the silky fabric of my cami into my skin. It's a taunt. A tease. Hopefully, it's a taste of things to come.

"Here you go," a young man says, placing two drink menus on a table. "Jackie will be right with you. Enjoy."

Drake thanks him and pulls out my chair. Once I'm seated, he sits across from me.

"This place is amazing," I say. "How did I not know it was here? It's so close to my house, too."

"You would've heard about it sooner or later. It's getting a lot of press."

I pick up a menu and scan the offerings. There are so many choices that sound delicious. I can imagine being here with my friends, ordering drinks and laughing about our day. *Astrid should have Gray bring her here. She'd love it.*

"Do you know what would be fun?" I ask, spotting a mocktail section that would be perfect for Audrey.

"Yup."

His tone—rich and rough—captures my attention. I lift my gaze from the menu in time to catch a roguish grin on his face.

"The backup plan didn't have to involve cooking," I say, casually. "You don't need a kitchen to eat, if you catch my drift."

"This is our first date."

"So?"

"So first dates are for getting to know each other."

I start to suggest how I'd like to *get to know him* but stop myself. I think the fucker is being genuine. *Does he really want to get to know me?*

This was not what I was expecting, although I'm not certain

what my expectations were, exactly. I suppose I assumed this science experiment would be face deep—that is, until he was face deep between my legs. We'd have fun, create stories to yap about on the podcast, and exploit the workplace relationship loophole that we seemed to have found. I'm not sure what purpose getting to know each other serves in this six-week escapade.

Jackie chooses this moment to appear at the side of our table with a wide smile and bouncy red curls. "Welcome to Hess. I'm Jackie, and I'll be your server this evening." She fills two soft blue glasses with iced water. "Is this your first time with us?"

"I've been here a number of times," Drake says smoothly. "But this is my girlfriend's first visit."

His declaration startles me, as does the swift wave of warmth that rolls through my insides. When men have called me *their girlfriend* or *their woman* in the past, it's been icky—like they were trying to control me. It was a proverbial boot on my throat every time, and I instinctively resisted. This time, though, it's less *boot on my throat* and more *air rushing into my lungs*. He doesn't spit it out like ownership; he speaks it with pride.

Less like he's chosen me and more like he's lucky that *I* chose to spend time with *him*.

Huh.

"Oh, nice," Jackie says, placing two new menus on the table. "If you need any recommendations, please let me know. I'm kind of an expert around here."

"Okay. What are your favorite drinks?" Drake asks.

She smiles as if this question just made her day. "Well, we have a great prosecco. All our white wines are good, but I love our tempranillo. As far as cocktails, our lychee mule is very popular. You can never go wrong with the mojito or the sangria. But if you go with the sangria, just get the pitcher. Trust me on that."

"Jackie, I love your passion about the drink menu." I giggle.

She shrugs happily. "It's a perk of the job to be able to

genuinely recommend things to customers. You can't go wrong, no matter what you choose. I say that with my whole heart."

"So what do you think?" I ask Drake. "What sounds good to you?"

"I always get a Mexican lager they carry from a local brewery. Although, I did have the lychee mule once and I'd order that again if I wanted something different."

I wrinkle my nose. "I'm not a beer girl, but I love sangria."

"Got it," Jackie says. "Glass or pitcher?"

"He's driving," I say, laughing.

Jackie laughs, too. "Great. I'll work on that while you peruse our menu. Again, let me know if you need recommendations."

"Thank you," I say. Once she's gone, I look at Drake. "She's so nice."

"I've never had bad service here. You know, the level of service is highly underrated. It's one of the things that immediately comes to mind when you consider going back to a restaurant."

"So true. My friends and I have two places in our rotation and a big part of that is because of the staff. For example, one of our favorite servers, Kim, just got a new puppy. How do I know that? Because when we walk through those doors, we feel like family. It's great."

"Tell me about your friends. What do they do?"

"Audrey is my doctor friend."

Drake chuckles. "The philosophy doctor with a specialty in tetanus?"

"That would be the one." I grin. "Astrid works for Renn Brewer. He owns the Tennessee Royals."

"No shit."

My brows pull together, not understanding why that bit of information received that response. "No shit."

"My buddy, Jory, plays for the Royals."

"Oh. What a small world. Astrid's fiancé is Gray Adler."

Drake nods his head, surprised, I think, but impressed, nonetheless. "Adler is a fucking beast."

"I've heard he's a fan of a certain sportscaster."

"You should hook us up."

I laugh. "Are you breaking up with me already? I'm not opposed to a threesome, you know. But I can't do it with my best friend's fiancé."

"Not a problem. I don't share."

My smile is coquettish. "It's hard to share something you've never had."

His eyes darken, but Jackie arrives with our drinks before he can reply. I would love to hear what he came back at me with, but there's something fun about leaving the conversation just like that.

It won't hurt the man to let that marinate for a while.

"Here you go," Jackie says, setting Drake's drink in front of him. She pours a glass of sangria for me and leaves the pitcher on the edge of the table. "Have you thought about what you'd like to eat?"

"Everything looks amazing," I say, wondering how to narrow it down. "How do people decide?"

"My advice is to order a few plates each and see what you like," Jackie says. "We can kind of go from there."

Drake looks at me over his menu. "I'm thinking the stuffed dates, potatoes bravas, chicken skewers, stuffed peppers, and definitely the chorizo clams."

He rattles off his dishes, and then the pressure's on me. There are so many I want to try, but my eye is drawn to the Hess Sampler—four of the owner's favorite dishes named after their children: the Max, Mav, Cove, and Casio.

Once Jackie has taken our menus and departed, Drake and I settle in. He picks up his beer, leaning back in his chair with a cool confidence that puts me at ease.

"You were saying something earlier about something being

fun," he says. "We got interrupted before you could tell me what it was."

I take a sip of my sangria and nearly die. It's the best damn sangria I've ever had.

"I was thinking about how fun it would be if we, as a part of our dating experiment, ran a giveaway of some sort and sent a couple here on a date. Maybe a blind date where we match the couple or something. People could nominate themselves, and we could play matchmaker. Doesn't that sound like a good time? And it would give your friend some bonus exposure."

Drake snickers. "Look at you. One date with me and you're wanting to bring people together instead of tearing them apart."

"Ha. Ha. Ha." I take another drink. "Speaking of the podcast, how much of this are we sharing with the public?"

"Have you checked your socials today?"

I shake my head.

He takes a deep breath and blows it out slowly. "It's wild, Gianna. These people are more invested in our lives than we are. It's hilarious." He takes a swig of his beer. "I think we're going to have to give them something, or they'll riot."

"Maybe we can record something—a two-to-four-minute thing—that we can post on Social every Monday or something. We can catch them up on whatever happens, so they feel included. And if we don't have a date or nothing to report, we'll just make something up."

"I get six weeks to date you. You better believe I'm going to want all the time you'll give me."

I study him as I sip my sangria, feeling the alcohol and the sweetness of the fruit play on my tongue. This date has been so easy—surprisingly easier than most dates I go on. It's been so easy, in fact, that I forgot it was a date for a while. It just felt like catching up with a super-hot friend.

"In the back of my mind, I was worried this would be awkward," I admit.

"Why?"

"Because this just kind of happened. It's not like you asked me out after we met in a bar. You dared me to date you in a spur-of-the-moment segment on my podcast with thousands of people listening. It's not like you could back out."

"I can do anything that I want to," he says. "But I want to be here, with you. How often does a guy like me get to date a girl like you?"

Who is he kidding? Guys like him—beautiful, delicious athletes with charm and money—date whoever they want. They're usually supermodels and Social influencers with perfect bodies and curated homes, though. Not ordinary girls with cellulite, buttons strewn across her living room floor, and a Matilda that she doesn't know what to do with.

"Men like you date women like me all the time," I say, grinning.

"Impossible." He leans forward, his eyes twinkling beneath the lights. "Because there aren't too many girls out there like you."

"Now you're just telling me what you think I want to hear."

He laughs. "Hardly. I think you want to hear something that you can use as a springboard to jump ship. Isn't that your modus operandi?"

"It's not like I set out to do that. I just refuse to stay in situations that waste my time. That's smart. That's resource management."

He rolls his eyes. "Maybe, but the resource you're managing isn't your time. It's your emotions. You pick guys who treat you like shit or have some other fatal flaw so that you have an out."

"Not true. I just have a type that's unfortunate for me. At least I'm smart enough to acknowledge that and not marry one of them and be miserable for the rest of my life."

Jackie carries a tray to our table and places tiny plates between us. The presentation is as incredible as the restaurant itself. Each dish looks as though a chef crafted it especially for us. Once we're set with silverware, she tops off my sangria and sets Drake up with another beer, then Jackie leaves us to it.

My stomach rumbles from the delicious aroma of the food.

"This looks and smells divine," I say, trying to decide which plate to tuck into first. "Look at the beets. That color is magical."

"Try one of these." He lifts a bacon-wrapped stuffed date with a little toothpick. "This is my favorite thing on the menu."

I start to reach for it but quickly assess that there's no way for me to take it from him with my fingers. A grin twitches against my lips as I lean forward. "This isn't what I thought you'd be putting in my mouth tonight."

His eyes blaze—the usual oceanic blues shifting into a raging storm as he inserts the date between my lips.

"*Oh*," I moan, my lashes fluttering closed. The savoriness of the bacon mixed with the bite of blue cheese harmonized with the buttery mouthfeel of the date. "I could eat these for the rest of my life."

"They're good, huh?"

I sigh, licking my lips and opening my eyes. "You should never use *good* to describe what I just tasted. It's incredible."

We make our way through our dishes, sharing with each other and trading notes. Drake prefers things with a richness, while I gravitate to the spicier options. It's fun noting where our tastes crossover. When Jackie returns, we're quick to order another round of things to try.

The restaurant quiets, nearly half of it empty, and the sky through the windows is dark. A slow, sweet buzz hums through me with every sip of my sangria, and Drake's easy, just-right smile from across the table heats my core.

So far, tonight has been fabulous. Drake has surprised me in so many ways. He's an interesting person and much deeper and more thoughtful than I expected. Surprisingly humble for being such a "thing" in the sports world. As I look back on the past few hours, it stands out to me how he asks questions and seems to not just know the answer but to know *the why* behind them.

No one ever does that. And on the rare occasion someone does, it isn't sincere.

But Drake? His intentions truly feel genuine.

I can't think of a dinner date that I've enjoyed more. Not one comes to mind—not even close. That thought makes me smile.

"I've had a great time tonight," I say, wrapping my hands around my glass. "Thank you for bringing me here."

"I'm glad you are enjoying it as much as I hoped that you would."

"What made you think I'd like it?" I ask, curious what linked me with Hess in his mind.

He sighs, seeming to choose his words carefully. "I don't know. You're both beautiful, for one. That's the most obvious thing."

"You know," I say, grinning, "you're pretty quick to shower me with compliments for a guy who I've worked with for months."

"I've thought about saying them for months. Now I can."

"Oh, really?"

He shrugs. "Yeah. That can't be a huge surprise, and it's part of the fun of this whole thing. I have a window to say everything I want before I have to go back to being your coworker. I mean, you and I would never be together under normal circumstances. I want to fall in love and have a family." He pulls his brows together. "I'm not sure what you want."

I understand what he's saying, and he's not wrong. If it weren't for this dating dare, we wouldn't be together. I've said it a hundred times. Still, hearing him say it so matter-of-factly has a little sting to it that I have a hard time shaking off.

"What *do* you want, Gianna?"

I roll my head in a slow circle, trying to work out some of the tension that has just settled in my shoulders. It's a fair question, especially for a getting-to-know-you first date. It's just a question that I don't like to think about.

"Do you mean after we leave here or …" I joke, hoping he takes the bait. But, of course, he doesn't.

"I was thinking more broadly."

"I'm not sure," I admit. "It's not something I sit around and ponder."

His brows pull together. "You don't?"

"Should I? Are there pondering sessions that I didn't know about? Do we bring our own drinks and sit around a campfire and plot the next ten years?"

He takes a long slug of his beer, watching me over the bottle.

I've clearly piqued his curiosity, and my follow-up question didn't help. People think about their future all the time. It was Astrid's favorite hobby until she met Gray, and I'd bet that Audrey thinks about it at least ten times a day—maybe more. But when I think about the future and wonder what it will look like for me, I get an overwhelming urge to paint something.

Still, it *is* a fair question. I'm not obligated to answer it, but I should. I should at least try.

"No one has really asked me this before." I sigh. "I mean, my friends do. But they're both at places in their lives where they need to focus on themselves. They're not too worried about me in the foreseeable future. They know I'll be fine."

"But is fine good enough?"

I shrug. "What do you mean?"

"Are you content with being *fine*? Don't you want to be happy? Comfortable? Fulfilled?"

"Who said I'm not happy?" I ask.

Frustration dusts his forehead.

"Listen," I say. "I'm happy right where I am. My goal in life was to buy my own home, and I recently did. I'm fulfilled. I'm comfortable. I have the best job ever, a new boyfriend, and Matilda."

"Matilda?"

"It's a long story," I say as Jackie places another round of plates between us. "What I'm trying to say is that I understand why people want a five-year plan, and for people like you and Astrid, it works. For people like me, all I see are things written in permanent marker, and that feels so … permanent."

He chuckles, but I can tell he doesn't quite understand. "Thanks, Jackie."

"Of course," she says. "I'll be back in a bit. Enjoy."

"What are you trying first?" I ask, surveying the spread. "The stuffed piquillo peppers are so pretty."

"The empanada is calling my name."

I smirk. "Do you like things that call your name? I'm taking notes."

"And I'm trying to show you a new way of dating." He watches my lips wrap around the pepper. "You're making it hard—literally and figuratively."

I lick a bit of tomato sauce from my lips. He shakes his head as he looks away.

"Why do you care so much, anyway?" I ask.

He sets his empanada down and studies me as if maybe he's not sure either. Finally, he sighs, seemingly content with his deduction.

"Maybe I just want you to see that not all men are … unsafe. Self-serving, maybe," he says. "Or it's possible that I dislike you carrying an eject button in your back pocket like a lifeline, and I want you to see how it feels to be safe in a relationship. Just in case you put together a five-year plan at some point and change your mind about things."

We exchange a look, then a smile, and then something else transmits between us—an energy that I can't quite name.

Even if I could, I'm not sure that I want to. Because some things are better left unread.

CHAPTER
FIFTEEN

"Don't even think of opening that door yourself," I say as I turn off my SUV.

Gianna withdraws her hand from the handle and places it in her lap. "My apologies."

I slip out of my seat and step into the brisk autumnal air, pausing to stretch my arms overhead. Mid-stretch, I feel her attention on me. I glance at her out of the corner of my eye and catch her watching me with a slight tilt to her lip. I let the stretch last a moment longer than necessary, smirking as her gaze travels down the length of my torso.

So, that's why she agreed to stay put.

I stifle a chuckle and reorientate myself. I should've known she let me have my way because Gianna Bardot doesn't do anything that she doesn't want to do.

She agreed to date me …

The evening went far too quickly … and far too perfectly. My mind keeps searching for something to focus on—a moment of poor conversation, a bored look on her face, or if she seemed not to be into me. Only one thing comes to mind, but I'll think about that later.

Our gazes meet through the passenger's window as I round the side of my vehicle.

A sheet of steel separates us, but her stare crashes into mine so hard that it nearly knocks me off balance. My heartbeat quickens. I'm aware of every pulse in my temples. A war commences inside me, logic versus lust—instinct versus reason, and the push and pull of it is an exquisite torture.

Honestly, I'm not sure how I've resisted her innuendo. It's like having the gift you've always wanted right in front of you, and you manage not to peek. *Fuck, how I want to unwrap her and play with her all damn night.*

But if this is how she operates with other men, it's easy to see why she refuses to wear a life preserver and risk going down with the ship. The ship isn't worth it. Hell, it would be a waste of resources.

Men are going to generally put forth the least amount of effort that they can get away with to reap the maximum reward. *Gianna?* She's the ultimate prize. Why would she, or should she, be willing to fight for something, or someone, if they weren't willing to do the most for her?

I get it now. That part makes sense. Eject the hell out of there.

But I fail to comprehend why she's complacent with this setup. *Why doesn't she demand more? Is she scared of falling in love, so she pretends she can control it? Is she just so jaded about relationships that she feels like this is the best it's going to get?*

I don't want to think that I know what's best for her because she's an intelligent, grown woman who can make those decisions for herself. But I have an inkling that she does want to be pursued. Just like flowers, I think she's afraid to ask for more—or even to expect it. That maybe it's not worth the hassle or disappointment.

"Let me help you," I say, offering her my hand.

Her fingertips lay in my palm as she steps out of my vehicle.

"Ooh," she says, shivering. "It got cool fast."

I retrieve her cardigan from the seat and close the door behind her. "Turn around."

I brush her hair off her shoulders, sweeping my knuckles against her bare skin. She shivers again, and I wonder if it's from the chill or my touch. I drape her cardigan over her narrow shoulders, letting the tops of my hands run the length of her arms as I draw them away from her body. The contact does nothing to help my internal battle. My blood grows hotter, and my cock grows harder.

Walking away from her tonight is going to take every bit of restraint that I can find. *But I must do it.*

"So this is the Goal House?" I ask as we walk up the sidewalk toward the brick home with black shutters. The shrubs could use a trim, and my dad would have a fit over the leaves in her yard. But it's a nice home with a big front yard tucked into the end of a cul-de-sac. Not what I expected from her, but it still somehow fits.

"Yup. This is Goal House." She glances at me over her shoulder. "I love that name for it."

"I've always liked it when people name their houses. It's so elite."

She giggles. "Does your house have a name?"

We take the steps to her porch, and she fishes her keys out of her purse. My breath tastes hot as anticipation kicks in. *How will this go? Do I kiss her? Do I go in?*

Internally, I groan. I can't go in. If I go in, I'll fuck her.

"No," I say, my balls beginning to ache. "I live in an apartment. When I moved back to Tennessee after I retired from football, I didn't really know how long the podcast would last or where I wanted to end up. So I just rented until I get a long-term plan in place."

"And you were on my case about not having a plan," she teases.

"I have one now."

She hums, twisting the knob and letting the door swing open. "Does it include coming inside for a drink?"

Fuck. Me.

Her tongue drags along her bottom lip, leaving a wet trail behind it. My eyes are glued to that sexy little mouth, and all I can think about is having those lips wrapped around my cock. Life is so unfair.

"I can't," I say, clearing my throat.

She arches a brow. "What do you mean that you can't?"

"I don't fuck on the first date."

"That's fine," she says, tracing my jawline with the tip of her finger. "I do."

My chuckle is strangled with need and regret. This is the start to a scene that I've fantasized about a thousand times while coming in my hand. It starts here and moves just over the threshold, where she falls to her knees, looking up at me through those fucking lashes while sucking my cock down her throat.

"See," I say, nipping at her finger. Her giggle is nearly my undoing. "That's why we can't. This is supposed to be a new experience for you."

She groans, rolling her eyes. "Fine. We'll do anal on the first date. That's never happened before."

I grip the doorframe to keep myself from grabbing *her*.

"You're the one who said this was real," she says breathily, standing so close to me that if I breathe too deeply, we'll touch. "What's wrong with fucking your boyfriend?"

It's now or never. I either walk off this porch and drive away in the next five seconds, or she's going to be bent over the first surface in her house. And as much as I want, maybe even need to do that, I can't. Because if I do that, I'm just like every other fucker in her life.

Tonight has been better than I hoped. Gianna has surprised me at every turn. I knew she was interesting and that we had things in common, but I didn't expect her to be such easy company. The conversation flowed like water from one topic to the next. And she was so great to the restaurant staff, even straightening the table as much as she could so it would be simpler for them to clear after we left.

And watching her try each plate, tasting each dish as if it were a work of art? *Yeah, I can't be thinking about her lips wrapped around anything right now.*

"Good night," I say, pushing away from her and walking down the sidewalk.

"Are you serious?"

"Get inside and lock the door."

"I don't even get a kiss good night?"

Once I'm on the other side of my SUV, I pause. She's on the porch, hands on her hips, clearly upset with me ... and it's the cutest, sexiest thing I've ever seen in my life.

"One of these days, I'll make it up to you." I smirk.

"Fine." She drops her hands and smirks back at me. "I'll make you regret this."

"I have no doubt."

Gianna sighs as if she's done with my games. "Stop messing around. You're not really going to leave."

Before I can banter with her anymore and find myself climbing those steps once again, I hop in my vehicle, wait until she's in the house, and then speed away while I still can.

CHAPTER
SIXTEEN

GIANNA

He left. That fucker really left.

CHAPTER
SEVENTEEN

Drake

I left. I really fucking left.

CHAPTER
EIGHTEEN

"There's my boy," Mom says, wiping her hands on a kitchen towel. Her smile is a little brighter, a little less forced than it's been recently. "How was your drive?"

"Excuse me," Evie says from the sink. "Why do you sound so happy when he shows up? When I show up, it's like, '*Oh. Yay. Evie's here.*'"

Mom rolls her eyes. "That's not true."

"It is true," I say, tugging Evie's ear as I walk by her. She smacks my hand away. "She loves me more."

"Be nice," Mom says as she pulls me into a big hug.

The house is warm and filled with the unmistakable fragrance of pot roast and apple pie, evoking nostalgic childhood memories. It's the scent of late nights after football practice, of Sunday afternoon dinners and chilly fall evenings. It's comfort in its simplest form.

Dad and Elodie's voices trickle in from the family room over the sound of one of Dad's Westerns. Evie complains as she returns to doing the dishes—a chore everyone knows, because she never fails to remind us, is her absolute least favorite. Mom stirs something on the stove, content that her family is home, and for the moment, life is as it should be.

"Where's the boyfriend, Eves?" I ask, peering over Mom's shoulder into a pot of noodles.

"Like I'm going to bring him here. We just started dating."

"What's that supposed to mean?" Mom asks. "Why wouldn't you bring him here?"

"Oh, let's see. How far back should we go?" Evie sighs with the drama only the youngest child can provide. "Tony Rosedale. Brock Lon. Kyle Stannus. Then there was Xander Willoughby." She looks at me over her shoulder, her lips pressed into a thin line. "Remember what you did to him?"

I lift a brow. "Remember what *he* did to *you*?"

"I remember he never talked to me again. That's what I remember."

"Who are we talking about?" Elodie asks, giving me a quick hug.

"Your siblings are discussing why Evie won't bring her new boyfriend home," Mom says.

Elodie fights a grin. She understands. Unbeknownst to Mom or Evie, Elodie was the one who told me that Tony fucking Rosedale grabbed my sister by the neck and shoved her against a wall. She didn't rat out Brock or Kyle, and I can't remember how I discovered Xander's misdeeds. But word gets around in a small town, and my older sister made sure certain things got back to me.

"So how far along are we in the list?" Elodie asks. "Have we hit David Darrow yet?"

"*Thank you*," Evie says, grateful to have support. "I'm glad that someone understands what a cockblocker Drake is."

"Evie Mae!" Mom gasps. "What did you just say?"

"Don't you have to have a cock to block?" I ask, teasing my sister. "Or are you using your boyfriend's cock as the proverbial cock in this equation?"

Mom groans, looking at me and pointing toward the living room.

"Sorry, Mom," I say cheekily. "I'm just trying to understand what's happening."

"Get out of here and go say hi to your father," she says.

Evie sticks her tongue out at me as I walk away.

I make my way toward the sound of a gunfight over a card game, taking my phone from my pocket. I glance at the screen, wondering if Mario texted me back. A grin splits my cheeks when I spot Gianna's name on the top of my alerts.

Sorry, Mario. You're going to have to wait for a reply.

Gianna: Have you checked your socials? O M G

I lean my shoulder against the wall and type out my response.

Me: No. Why?

Gianna: Francine called me this morning and told me to look. I've gotten fifteen THOUSAND new followers since Thursday, and I'm pretty sure I can never use the direct message feature again. Do you know how many dick pics I've received over the past few days? Do girls send you pics of their boobs?

Laughing, I shake my head. *Only Gianna would ask that.*

Me: On occasion. They're never solicited. 😉

Gianna: Well, you tell those hoes that you have a girlfriend now and the only boobs you're going to be seeing for the next six weeks are mine. I mean, theoretically. You don't seem like you want to see them.

Me: You don't appreciate that I wanted to focus on your mind first?

Gianna: I did have a great time at dinner. The drop-off afterward? Not so much. 😔 But you did pick out the perfect first date spot. I keep thinking about those chicken skewers. 🤤

Me: Any requests for our second date?

Gianna: Is sex off the table? If so, boo. 🍆 But I also love your taste in restaurants, and feeding me is never the wrong answer. But inside. Eating and fighting bugs on picnics is not my idea of a good time.

An idea crosses my mind, and I can't type fast enough.

Me: Do you have plans for Friday night?

Gianna: Is this your way of asking me out on a second date?

Me: I'll pick you up at six. Wear closed-toe shoes, jeans, and a cotton top.

Gianna: That does not sound sexy at all. I'm guessing sex is out of the question.

Me: You could wear a trash bag and be sexy.

Gianna: Charmer.

She's going to want more details, and I'm not going to give them to her. Anticipation is half the battle. So I slide the phone back in my pocket and round the corner into the living room. The gunfight has stopped, and the cowboys appear to have swapped the saloon for a brothel. Dad is stretched out in his recliner, the remote in his hand—dead-ass asleep. His breaths sound like he's blowing raspberries.

"Is he asleep?" Elodie whispers from behind me.

"Yeah."

"Mom is on the phone with Aunt Vivi. Wanna take a walk?"

I nod. "Sure."

We step out the back door into the yard where we rode bikes, built forts, and chased lightning bugs as kids. The big oak tree used to hold a tire swing that Evie fell off and broke her front tooth. Our playset is long gone, as is the sandbox, but it still feels so much like home.

The older I get, the more this shit matters. I have championship rings, my highlights are played on sports channels to this day, and I've been more places and done more things than people usually do in a lifetime. But as that slows down and I take a moment to take stock of what I have, the more I realize that the most I ever had was here. In this house.

"Still having baby fever?" I ask as we mosey toward the lake at the back of the property.

She tugs her hoodie closer to her neck to fend off the cool breeze. "I think I just need a new hobby. I mean, would I like to have a baby?" She considers this. "Yeah, I think I probably would. But I want to have it with a guy I love and have a whole family, a dog, and a white picket fence. I don't want to do it alone."

"Makes sense."

"What about you?" she asks. "Evie called me the other day to tell me about your new girlfriend. By the way, we decided not to talk about it in front of Mom unless you brought it up. We're afraid it'll set her up for a big letdown when she finds out that it's only for, what, six months?"

"Six *weeks*."

"How's it going? I listened to Gianna's podcast on the way over here, and it was hysterical. I've never listened to her before. You two couldn't be more opposite if you tried."

"Yeah, well ..."

She's not wrong—at least from an outside perspective. But I'm not sure that she's right.

The only moment last night when things felt a little bumpy was when I asked her what she wanted in life. It was the first time she paused. It was the only time she stiffened. She rolled her head around her shoulders like she was trying to ease the stress that the question caused.

But why?

I lay in bed last night long after we got off the phone— because she called to thank me for dinner—and thought about these things. Nothing makes sense, yet so much makes sense at the same time.

She can list all the reasons she *should* be happy, but falls short of saying she *is* happy. Her goal in life was to buy a home, yet permanence makes her uncomfortable. She faults men for being hedonistic douchebags, but then faults me for not treating her like a piece of meat.

Gianna may say things that make us seem miles apart, but when we're together, it doesn't feel that way at all.

"She's complicated," I tell my sister.

"In what way?"

I kick a rock down the path and think about how to explain it. "Gianna's very independent and knows what she wants ... except she doesn't. I asked her last night what she wanted for herself in a few years, and she said it's not something she thinks about often. For someone as smart and successful as she is, I find that surprising."

"People can be ambitious and still shy away from being

strategic. You can be strategic and not ambitious. Think about it. They're not mutually exclusive."

"I guess." I lift my face toward the sky, letting the sun warm it. "What bothers me most, I think, is that she has this extroverted personality and says everything that's on her mind without thinking twice about it. But as I get to know her, I wonder if she's hiding behind that. Is the outlandish shit she says—the innuendos and sarcasm—there to shield her from something?"

Elodie considers this, her brows pulled together. "Could be."

"She said no one had asked her what she wanted out of life and that her friends knew she'd be fine. And I asked her if *fine* was okay. Didn't she want to be happy? I mean, doesn't everyone want a life where they're happy?"

"What did she say?"

I sigh. "She said she was … comfortable, I think. Fulfilled. But she stopped short of saying she was happy."

"Maybe she doesn't know what would make her happy. That happens to people. Hell, it's happening to me right now." She grins at me. "I wanted a baby a few days ago. I was convinced it would make me happy. Now, the happiest scenario that I can fathom is going home to a quiet house, a glass of wine, and a true crime show. Those things are mutually exclusive."

"But what if she knows what she wants, what *would* make her happy, and is afraid to want it? It would explain her approach to relationships. She always has an eject button, always has an out."

"It's possible." Elodie shrugs. "It's a theory that makes sense. But remember that you can't make someone else happy. They have to choose that for themselves."

We walk in silence the rest of the way to the lake. I pick up a few stones and skip them across the still water. Elodie sits on a boulder on the shore and watches me search for the smoothest rock that I can find.

I'm treading on thin ice when it comes to Gianna, and I feel the proverbial cracks under my feet. This was supposed to be just fun—a way to get a dose of a woman I knew I could never truly have. After all, who is goofy enough to fall for someone when you know it's going to be over in a few weeks?

Unfortunately, I might be that goofy son of a bitch. And that scares the piss out of me.

"If I tell you something, you can't say a word to Mom or Evie," Elodie says.

"You know that I won't."

She takes a breath. "I got a job offer in Raleigh."

I face her with a stone in my hand, water droplets sliding through my fingers. "North Carolina?"

"Yeah. It's … far. About a nine-hour drive, I think. I didn't apply for it. A girl I used to work with moved there and is doing the same things she did with us, but she's getting almost twice as much money. She called me a couple of days ago and asked if I wanted to come work with her."

"What did you say?"

"I said I didn't know."

I chuck the rock as far as I can across the lake. The plunking sound it makes as it falls into the water is the same way my spirits nosedive at my sister's news.

She hops off the boulder and dusts off her hands.

"Do you want to take it?" I ask.

"I don't know, Drake. I mean, the money is amazing, and there are bigger opportunities for advancement. And she said their benefits package is out of this world." She takes a shaky breath that I know all too well. "But how do I leave here now? Mom said that Dad has had a couple of good days, but how long will that last? What happens when he gets worse? Mom can't do this alone forever. I know we agreed to give them their space for a while, but we're going to have to be more involved at some point—and I'm the oldest daughter."

My palm grips the back of my neck as my sister verbalizes the things I've been mulling over for a while. They're questions that I can't answer. I'm not qualified to answer them. But I also know this isn't on my sister, oldest daughter or not, to feel the weight all alone.

I look into her eyes and see what I need to see.

"You gotta take it," I say through the tightness in my chest.

Her eyes, the color so similar to mine that it's disturbing, grow wide. "What?"

"You should take it. Ask yourself what you would do if Dad weren't sick. That's your answer."

"But I can't leave you and Evie here to handle it."

"Why?" I chuckle. "Evie might be worthless, but I'm very capable."

She laughs, brushing tears away from the apples of her cheeks. I pull her into a hug, and the way she clings to me tells me she needs it.

"Dad would want you to go," I say softly. "I followed my dreams, and you and Evie picked up the slack while I was gone. It's your turn."

Elodie pulls away, drying her eyes with her shirtsleeves. "Why does being an adult have to be so hard?"

"Because you're a good person."

She leans her head on my shoulder as we stand facing the lake. Fish jump, breaking the surface and sending sparkling ripples across the water. It's peaceful—and I think both of us need a blast of peace.

Finally, she stands and stretches her arms over her head and turns toward the house. "I haven't mentioned this to Evie, so please keep it between us."

"Of course."

I follow her up the path, both of us quiet as we try to make sense of our thoughts. Elodie has a tough decision to make. I fear I might have one of those on the horizon, too.

My phone buzzes again, vibrating against my leg. I stop walking and pull it out. "Go on, Elodie. I'll be right there."

"Okay."

I swipe open the screen.

Gianna: Just got off the phone with Francine. She's suggesting a moderator for our dating chats. She thinks it might be helpful to have someone ask us questions so we can answer as a couple rather than as podcasters. Peak entertainment value, I think she said.

Me: Fine with me.

Gianna: I suggested Juni. She mentioned wanting to do more technical things, and it might be fun for her.

It might be fun for us, too.

If I have five weeks left with Gianna, I'm going to make damn sure they're fun.

Me: Sounds good to me.

Gianna: Ok. Enjoy your family.

I smirk.

Me: I'd rather be enjoying you.

Gianna: DONT YOU DARE DO THIS TO ME NOW.

Me: 😏

Gianna: You wanna play? Game on, buddy. I play to win.

A smile ghosts my lips. Little does she know that if she wins, so do I. And I like the odds of playing for keeps.

CHAPTER
NINETEEN

GIANNA

"How was your weekend?" Francine leans against my office door with a smug grin on her face.

"If you're asking how my date was with my new boyfriend, it was great," I say, laughing. "Every time I call him my boyfriend, I feel like I'm in middle school again. But it's so fun."

"Between you and me, if I were younger and single and Drake Bennett wanted me to call him my boyfriend, I wouldn't blink twice." She laughs, too, and enters my office. "I take it things went well?"

"He took me to the cutest place to eat called Hess."

"I've heard of it," she says, nodding along. "A friend of ours went there for their anniversary last weekend and raved about it. I heard more about their brussels sprouts than I've ever heard about brussels sprouts in my life."

"Whatever they said, multiply it by a thousand. It was seriously the best food, the best ambiance, the best everything."

"The best company?" She smiles knowingly. "I have to say, I didn't see this coming between the two of you, but it's great. It makes sense. And God knows it's good for our show. I asked

Tommy to get our reports from last week early, if possible. I have a meeting with the executives this afternoon, and I want solid data on hand. This dating bet has just propelled you into outer space, and I want to make damn sure they know it."

It makes sense? What the heck is she talking about?

My mind wanders, wondering if other people think Drake and I *make sense*. The idea of the office chattering about us amuses me more than it should. Are they whispering at the water cooler about how they saw this coming? Because there's no way. I don't believe that for a second. We aren't two people you pull out of a lineup and think, *Oh, those two go together like bread and butter.*

Right?

I shake the thought out of my head and focus on work. "When do you think they'll have a decision about who they're moving to the Thursday slot?"

She shrugs. "I was hoping we'd know something by now. I'll poke around about it today and see if anything shakes out."

"Keep me posted."

"Will do. Now, Juni will get in touch with you shortly. She was thrilled when I asked her to be the moderator for you and Drake. You should've seen the look on that girl's face." She laughs. "I didn't know whether you wanted to do it in here or in the studio, since it was more of an informal thing. But if you need me in the booth, just text. I'll be around until one thirty, then I head into meetings for the rest of the day."

"Great. We'll probably record it in here as long as Drake doesn't object—and I can't see why he would."

"Sounds wonderful." She heads to the door. "I'll let you get back to it."

"Thanks, Francine."

I exhale, sitting back in my chair and letting my mind replay our conversation. I never dreamed that I'd be in contention for the prime slot until Francine mentioned it, but now that the excitement has simmered down, I don't want to get my hopes up. The odds still aren't in my favor, and even if they were, I don't want to be disappointed … although I'm already imagining the office conversion I have planned for one of the bedrooms in Goal House.

"I have to say, I didn't see this coming between the two of you, but it's great. It makes sense."

This line bounces around my brain like a Ping-Pong ball. I must admit that I had more fun with him on Saturday than I've had in a long time. And it really felt like a date, which was nice. There was intention and forethought, and it really felt like he curated the night for me. *Who knew those things could be so sexy?*

"You gotta stop thinking about him," I groan, grabbing my phone. I haven't spoken with Audrey since Saturday, when I updated her and Astrid about my date.

Me: Auddddiiiieeeeeeee.

Audrey: Hiiiiiiiiii.

I smile. That's a good sign.

Me: Whatcha doing?

Audrey: I just got out of a yoga class. I thought it would help me get out of this funk.

Me: Did it work?

Audrey: Meh. I don't know what's wrong with me.

Me: I'm making sourdough tonight. It should be entertaining at the least if you want to come over and watch me try to be domestic. I'll even buy you dinner.

Audrey: Thank you. That's very sweet. My mom asked me to meet her for sushi tonight. They're leaving for Vegas on Thursday.

Me: Is Andrew fighting?

Audrey: No. They're just going for the fun of it.

Me: Well, if you change your mind, come hang out with me. Or come over after dinner, and we can have some fresh-baked bread for dessert. Bring your jammies, and we can have a midweek slumber party like irresponsible adults. I know you've never tried that before, but maybe that'll bring you out of your funk.

Audrey: We'll see.

Me: Don't "we'll see" me. It sounds like my mother, and it makes me want to sneak out and go on the hunt for a delinquent.

Audrey:

Me: Call me if you need me. Love you, Auddie.

Audrey: Love you, Gianna.

She didn't cartwheel emoji me once. That's concerning.

I read through our conversation, analyzing each of Audrey's responses. She's going out and doing things to try to feel better. That's progress. And she knows it's just a funk. That's good, too. Hopefully, Mrs. Van will be able to lift her spirits at dinner.

If not, I'll just bring her to my house and force her to paint. It always helps me.

I start to close my phone and move on with my day when my gaze lands on my second-to-last response.

Don't "we'll see" me. It sounds like my mother, and it makes me want to sneak out and go on the hunt for a delinquent.

I haven't thought of this in years. So many nights I'd sneak through my bedroom window and dart into the night, telling myself that I needed freedom. In retrospect, I probably needed the opposite. I probably needed attention. But doing something over the top was the only way to get more than a half-assed conversation at dinner, and I'd stopped trying to impress my parents years before. They made it clear that I would never live up to their expectations, and I chose to believe that.

Eventually, pissing off my parents became a badge of courage —a war patch. Dating men on motorcycles covered in tattoos, much too old to be with a sixteen-year-old girl, was where my power was harnessed. The more my parents tried to strip me bare of who I was as a person—no art, no rap music, no colored streaks in my hair—the more I pushed back with all my might. I craved some form of control over my existence. I wanted someone to love me for who I was and not what they wanted me to be, even if it was a liar named Dale waiting for me on a bike at the end of the darkened street.

This isn't an epiphany. I've known this since my parents sent me to a therapist in high school to try to root out my *behavioral issues.* But seeing the words typed out by my own fingers hits different.

I scroll to my sister's name on my phone.

Me: Was I a bratty kid?

Lucia: Obviously.

Me: I'm serious.

Lucia: Anchor me into this conversation. What are we doing? Where are we coming from?

I get to my feet and pace around my office. My brain is spinning too quickly to sit still any longer.

Me: I don't have a five-year plan.

Lucia: Are we supposed to have one? Who is checking?

Me: Audrey just told me "we'll see" and I could hear it in Mom's voice. And I just had a moment when my past and my present kind of collided.

Lucia: What does that have to do with a five-year plan?

"I don't know," I say, groaning. *But they feel linked.*

Me: Forget it.

Lucia: No, you weren't a brat. Mom and Dad were hard. I remember all six hugs they gave me, and I'm not sure Dad ever told me he loved me. But no one is without issues, Gianna. I'm sure we both have shit that a few good night kisses could've fixed, but we are who we are. And I'm proud of us both. We're doing the best we can.

I hold my phone to my chest and stare out the window. *We're doing the best we can.*

Are we? Lucia has curated an intentional life that she loves. She's doing the best she can—the best anyone can. *But am I?*

Me: I'm proud of you, too.

Lucia: 🤍

Am I doing the best I can?

I noticed Drake's pause when I told him about my house and fulfilled life. He didn't look convinced, but being the gentleman that he is, he didn't call me out on it. But the momentary pause was noted.

As I stare out the window, I note the sun is out, but the rays don't quite touch the ground. The park is empty. Everything below is still. It's like it's all waiting for something. *More sun? Rain? Snow? A thunderstorm?* The world is clinging to the bleakness until something comes to bring it back to life.

Hmm …

My life has been shaken up recently, and it's felt a little sunnier.

A smile touches my lips as his name comes to mind. He's felt like warm sunshine and powerful thunderstorms all in one.

Never did I imagine that I'd be going on dates with a guy like him and *talking*. Staying up late at night texting about everything and nothing. Plotting outfits to drive him out of his mind because he thinks it's cute to frustrate me sexually.

I open the coat closet and check out my reflection in the full-length mirror on the back of one of the doors.

A black skirt with a texture that makes you want to touch it in a length almost too short for the office. A white tank that hugs every inch of my torso and the wicked curve fading into my hip. My hair looks intentionally messy—like I just rolled out of bed like this. A pair of heels makes my legs look impossibly long. But the *pièce de résistance?*

A red lip that will undoubtedly draw Drake's attention right where I want it. *To my mouth.*

I told you that I play to win.

Movement catches my attention, and I glance over to see Drake walking through the doorway. He stops mid-stride as his attention lands on me and his eyeballs nearly pop out of his head.

"Holy fuck," he says, his Adam's apple bobbing.

"Hey, babe."

"Gianna." He chuckled. "*Fuck me.*"

"I've tried. You won't." I wink at him as I strut by on my way to my desk. My skin sizzles from the heat of his gaze. "Francine talked to Juni, and she's going to call me in a bit to see when we want to sit down with her. I thought we could do the segment in here, so it feels a little less staged and more fun."

He runs a hand down his face as if trying to regain his composure.

"Mario asked if I'd record an ad for your show," I say, clicking around on my computer mostly so I don't stare at him. My outfit worked. I have his attention. But to play this correctly, he can't have mine. "It's for an energy drink, I think. I said it was fine with me, but he needed to run that through you and Francine first."

Drake moves swiftly to the door. It closes with a *pop*, and the lock snaps shut.

And I nearly combust.

The room shrinks an inch a second. The temperature rises a degree with every step Drake takes toward me, like a predator hunting prey. He's a picture of perfection in dark denim, a black long-sleeved shirt, and bright white sneakers. If he added a backward black cap, I'd be dead.

He stands in front of me so close that a piece of paper wouldn't slide between us. His cologne taunts me with its understated yet sensual notes. My libido has been out of control for days no matter what toy or touch I use to try to quell it, so I might not be strong enough to be this close to him.

I may have flown too close to the sun on this one.

"What are you doing?" he asks, amusement lacing his voice.

"I'm working. What are you doing?"

He smirks. "Don't play coy with me."

I got him right where I want him. "Are you bothered by something?"

His lips twist. He's entertained but also irritated.

"It's Monday," I say, as if I'm oblivious to the heat in his eyes. "And—"

"And you're dressed like *that*." His gaze blazes a trail down my neck, between my breasts, down my torso. It stops between my thighs, lingering long enough to make me pant. "Are you trying to get my attention?" He splits what little room there is between us. "Congratulations. You have it. *You always have it.* All you're doing today is making me want to break every workplace code of conduct and fuck you right on your desk."

Yes. Yes, fucking please. "I won't tell."

His head dips ever so slightly toward mine. "You're trouble."

I hum, my blood scorching through my veins.

"Do you need confirmation that I want you?"

"Wouldn't hurt."

"Every fantasy I have has you in it," he says, lowering his

head even farther. "But this ..." His hands grip my waist, his fingertips cinching into my skin. I yelp out of surprise, then moan as my knees turn to Jell-O. "This is beyond my wildest dreams. To have you in my hands ..." His face drops lower. "To have you this close where I could taste you ..."

"I'm not wearing any panties," I whisper, my voice filled with need. "You could taste me in lots of places right now."

Adrenaline shoves through my veins, and blood rushes over my eardrums.

His fingers dig into my hips. The peppermint on his breath is a delicious contrast to the heat of his body. My heart pounds, anticipation heightening, and I find myself leaning toward him.

Wanting him. Needing him.

Desperately needing him to touch me.

"Just one ... more ... thing," he says, the words dusting across my lips.

I moan, clenching my core as if that alone will keep me from falling apart.

His eyes sparkle. His mouth hovers above mine. My breaths are audible as I lug them in the small space between us. It's as if he sees right through me.

"*Game on, buddy*," he whispers, cracking a deep, mischievous smirk. "I play to win."

His hands fall away from me, and I gasp for breath.

"You fucker," I say, reeling at his use of my own words against me.

A knock raps against the door, and Drake smiles victoriously. "I better get that."

"I hate you," I say, dragging air into my lungs. "I think I'm breaking up with you over this."

He laughs, earning a glare from me as he opens the door.

"Hey ..." Juni's eyes widen as she looks at me and then back at Drake. "Am I interrupting something?"

"Yes," I say as Drake says the opposite.

I sigh. *She was supposed to call first.* "Come in, Juni."

She doesn't look sure but takes a deep breath and resets herself with a bright smile. "Okay. Are you ready to get started, or should I come back?"

"No. We're ready," Drake says. "We were just getting a plan together."

"That's right," I say, staring at Drake. "We were."

His grin wobbles ever so slightly—enough for me to know he's worried about how I might respond.

And he should worry. Because I have a plan.

CHAPTER
TWENTY

GIANNA

"My ears work fine, Pearl," I say, putting her on speaker-phone and setting her on the table next to my scissors and a purple permanent marker.

"Sweetheart, I don't think that they do. You keep saying the same thing over and over. If your ears work, then you're not listening."

I shouldn't have answered her call. It's not like I didn't know it was going to be her. I saved her number in my phone the first time we talked—back when I was optimistic about buying her coat tree. *Before I knew she was an extortionist.*

A variety of aluminum soda cans are spread out on a towel in front of me to finish drying. I sifted through a box of my finds in the garage before pulling out five of my favorites. There's a bright blue, green, red, orange, and a brown one that used to hold root beer. The brown one is the one I was after when I got sliced by glass in the dumpster.

Guess I didn't get tetanus after all.

"My ears work, and I'm listening," I say, trying to determine which can to start with. "You just keep saying the same thing over and over again. But you're at one thousand dollars, and I'm at fifty bucks. We're not going to come to an agreement."

"Maybe you need to see it in person."

I roll my eyes and choose the blue one. "I'm a busy woman, Pearl. I don't have time to spend on frivolous things." I reach for the scissors and grimace. I *am* spending my evening cutting butterflies from Coke cans, but what Pearl doesn't know won't hurt her. "Besides, I trust your photography skills. You should believe in yourself more."

"Should I take new pictures for you? Because although I, too, don't have time to spend on frivolous things, I will make an exception for you."

"Oh, Pearl. You're so sweet."

"So do you want them?"

"No."

She groans as if she's exasperated with me, but we both know that's not true. If that was possible, she would've hit the limit last week. But here we are.

I put on my winter gloves to protect my hands during this procedure. They're not exactly the leather bad boys the people on the how-to videos used, but it's all I have. Sometimes, you have to make what you have work.

Besides, I'm never buying those ugly things.

I pierce the metal with the tip of a knife, then use the scissors to remove the top and bottom of the can. Then I cut a line straight down the side, and it springs open but holds its shape.

"Fine," Pearl says, sighing. "Do you want to know the truth?"

"The truth? Have you been lying to me? I thought we were friends, Pearl," I joke.

"I want to sell this damn thing because I don't want my kids to have it when I die. Okay? That's the truth."

Well, this took a turn. I wrangle the can flat and then place a cast-iron skillet on top of it.

The sun hovers over the tree line, filling the kitchen with the last rays of warmth for the day. The week has flown by. There have been so many meetings to discuss how to handle the increase in popularity of *Gianna Knows Things*. I've received dozens of requests to visit other podcasts, I was asked to speak at a conference for women in business, and I heard something today about being asked to do a reality show where they treat you like military recruits. Juni showed me a clip over lunch today. I'm pretty sure that I can handle it—I have iced water in my veins—but the screaming in my face would do me in.

I'd punch a motherfucker for that.

"I want the tree to go to someone who will love it," she says, sniffling. "That dumb old thing means a lot to me, and I figure if someone paid good money for it, they'd take care of it."

"Can I ask why you don't want your kids to have it?" It's none of my business, but she roped me into this mess. Sharing the tea is the least she can do to make up for the time she's cost me with her haggling. "Shouldn't the things you love most become an heirloom or at least a family keepsake?"

"One would think. But my kids don't want my old junk, even if my old junk mattered to me. They'll just throw it away when they clean out my house once I'm dead and gone, and it just hurts my heart to know that. I'd rather it be loved."

The thing has been kept in a barn for years. It's covered in mildew. Pieces are broken off it. *If it's so loved, why is it in such sad shape?*

I start to work on the orange can. "Won't you just be helping them clear out your shit and turn it into cash for them?"

"No." She cackles and it's clear that once upon a time, Pearl was a smoker. "Me and Jeretta, she's an old hag that I met playing Bunco a few years back, we're taking one of those SKI holidays."

She's going skiing? "Pearl, I didn't have you pegged to be such an outdoorswoman." *Especially at your age. Don't you risk breaking a hip?*

"Not skiing. A SKI holiday. Spending kids' inheritance holiday."

"Oh," I say, laughing so hard I snort.

"They're ungrateful—and mean. These kids are downright hateful. They steal from me. They tried to sell my house out from under me. Got me to sign some papers while I was in the hospital and didn't know what I was doing."

I frown. "I'm sorry they're nasty."

"Me, too. But I'll get the last laugh because there'll be nothing left, which is why Jeretta and I want to go on a cruise. We want to do one of those adults-only trips so we don't have to listen to crying babies. And who knows? Maybe we'll get lucky and find some nice old fellers with working peckers, if you know what I mean."

"Oh, my gosh," I say, laughing. "But, yeah, I know what you mean. Sometimes a girl needs a good working pecker."

Boy, do I know all about that.

I slip the orange can beneath the skillet and then begin on the green one.

Drake and I had lunch together every day this week. A couple of the days, we ran to Stupey's because it's so close, and the others we had food delivered to the office and ate in the break room. We learned from Scott in IT that there's an office pool going around about how long we'll stay together. The closest person to the right date wins two hundred bucks.

Our experiment has brought a new levity to the office, and it's been fun joking around with everyone, but it's been even more fun hanging out with Drake. I feel like I've gained a new friend, and my life is better for it.

When I date a guy, it's usually good for a while. It always feels performative, though, like I'm playing a role until the show stops. The funny thing about that is, with Drake, I am playing a role. I'm pretending to be his girlfriend. Yet this is the only role I've ever played that feels ... natural. And I'm thoroughly enjoying myself. How ironic.

"You know what, Pearl?" I ask, squashing the split green can with a dutch oven. Then I grab the red one.

"What?"

I grin, removing the top of the can. "I can't help but love a lot about this conversation. First, the pettiness of not wanting your kids to have your stuff is something I can get behind. Second, the fact that you love a coat tree this much is commendable. And third, I fully support Operation Working Pecker. I'm on a similar hunt myself."

"What are you talking about? You sound young. Pretty. Sharp as a tack. A little sarcastic at times, but you're good for a laugh. You can't tell me you can't find a man out there. I just don't believe it."

"Funny story, Pearl. I have a man. Kind of." I furrow my brow as I cut down the side of the can. "And I'm not bragging or anything, but I'm not a troll to look at. Some would consider me a catch."

"Damn right that you're a catch, and don't you let a man tell you any different."

It's obvious she doesn't know me. I laugh. "Trust me. That's not a problem."

"Good for you. So what *is* the problem?"

"The problem is that this guy I'm dating refuses to have sex with me. I know he wants me. He admits it. I'd know he's lying if he didn't. But he won't do it."

"Huh." She pauses. "Is he religious?"

"I actually don't know."

She scoffs. "Well, even if he was, most of them still get down with it these days. What's his problem?"

I can't believe I'm talking about my sex life with the coat tree extortionist. Then it hits me, and I gasp.

I'm getting Gianna'd by Pearl.

What has happened to me?

My process has gotten faster, and I make quick work of the last can. Then I remove my gloves and carefully check on the first two. They could be flatter, but this is just a test round to see if my idea works. So I grab the marker and begin drawing a large butterfly on each one.

"We've only been dating for a week," I say, leaning all the way into this conversation. I'm in too deep to back out now. "But we were friends before. There's always been some flirtation between us, so I never dreamed he'd hold out on me."

"You know, back in the day before I was married, men were different from the way they are now. You wouldn't dream of offering to pay for a soda or a tank of gas. That would be a slap in their face. They held doors open, and there was none of this honking at the curb for you to come out. *Oh, hell no.* If a man wanted to see a girl, he'd better walk his ass to the front door. And back then, sure, some of them would get nasty in the back seat in the drive-in movie or whatnot—those were my kinda guys if I'm being honest. But it wasn't uncommon to have a guy wait a few dates before he tried to enjoy female favors, if you know what I mean."

Hmm … "What are you saying, Pearl?"

"I'm saying that maybe he's like my Alfred, may he rest in peace. When he met me, he knew he had to stick out from the crowd, you know? He had to get my attention—rise above the back seat fun boys. *Earn it.* Deserve it. And maybe that's what that man of yours is doing."

Is it? I press my palms against the table and lean against them, wondering if Pearl could be right.

"If he's not rushing into things with you, that's him wanting to connect with you—make ya feel safe. He's showing you that he's not competing with anyone because he knows he's the star of your roster. Isn't that what you kids say now? Your roster?"

I giggle. "Something like that."

"He's breaking your patterns, sweetheart. That man is giving you a chance to see him for who he is … so you can choose him."

Whoa.

I push away from the table, my gaze fixed on the phone. What she's saying makes sense. Drake is going slow—far too slow despite the short time this has been brewing, but slow, nonetheless. He's giving me space. He's giving me time. And we're connecting in ways that I've never connected with a man before.

We talk. He makes me laugh. We trade stories about our childhood, our friends, and our favorite television shows. I showed him a video about an artist I just discovered at lunch yesterday, and he tried to explain the defensive formation in a football meme this afternoon. I didn't get it, but that's not the point.

The point is, maybe Pearl's right. Maybe he is trying to earn my attention. *Wow.*

"You just broke my brain," I say, picking up the phone.

She laughs, the sound ending in a cough.

"Do you take SocialPay?" I ask.

"Yes, ma'am, I do."

"I'm going to send you fifteen hundred dollars for the coat tree, and I'll be there as soon as I can to get it."

Her gasp is immediate. "Are you serious?"

"Well, we both know it's not worth three grand."

"Hell, it ain't worth fifteen hundred, either. It's probably not worth one hundred and fifty dollars, if we're taking the blanket off the baby."

"So you were extorting me!" I laugh.

"Yeah, when I didn't know you. But now that I do, I can't cheat ya. Dammit, anyway."

I roll my eyes. "I'm sending you the money. I hope it gets you on a boat and a working dick."

"Oh, Gianna. Thank you. You have no idea how much …" She sniffles, crying softly. "Just thank you."

My eyes fill with tears as I listen to her disbelief. She's right—the coat tree isn't worth a third of that price. But sometimes it's not about the money. It's about what good the money can do.

And if it can give my girl Pearl a trip to remember with her old hag Jeretta, then I'd be an asshole to stand in their way.

I open my Social app, find her name, and send her the money. A green check mark loads on my screen.

"There you go," I say. "The coat tree is mine."

"Bless your little heart, Gianna."

"I'll message you about when I'm coming for it, okay?"

"Okay. Thank you again. Thank you so much."

I smile from ear to ear. "You're welcome. I'll take good care of it."

"I know you will," she says before the line goes dead. "Goodbye."

"Goodbye, Pearl."

The grin still on my lips, I pull up my text app and find Audrey's name.

> Me: So what about a cruise?

> Audrey: For what?

> Me: I just got off the phone with a friend, and she's going on a cruise to spend her money so her kids don't get it and to find a man—probably a sugar daddy by her extortionist abilities. Although she sounds eighty. I'm not sure if it qualifies as a sugar daddy at that age. What would it be? Powdered sugar?

> Audrey: Oh, Gianna.

"A laughing emoji is better than no emoji," I say, typing again.

Me: So cruise?

Audrey: I'm good. But thank you.

Me: I have a boyfriend now so no sex parties. Want to take a girls' trip somewhere? Me and you? Astrid if she can come? What about Kismet Beach in Florida? I think Banks Carmichael is married now, but we can still have a good time.

Audrey: Maybe.

Me: Yay! I'll take that.

Audrey: Did you make your sourdough?

Me: No. Do you have any idea how many steps there are? It's like feed it, stretch it, feed it, let it nap. I don't do that for myself. I'm not about to do it for a blob of … whatever it is.

Audrey: I can't judge you for that. At least, you're honest. But I need to go. I have an appointment with a student from one of my classes in five minutes, and I need to find his essay so we can go over it.

Me: Love you. Be nice to the student! He probably has a hangover, so dim the lights and talk slow.

Audrey: Love you.

I've never been so happy to see a ridiculous emoji in my life.

CHAPTER
TWENTY-ONE

Drake

"You told me to dress like this, and you're taking me *here*?" Gianna plants both feet on the asphalt and gazes up at Table in the same way I did when I saw it for the first time. "I can't go in there."

I blow out a breath, amused by her reaction. "No one in there cares how you're dressed."

"But I do."

"And I respect that. So if you got to do it all over again, what would you have chosen to wear?"

She huffs and faces me. "I don't know. I would've researched it and figured out what was appropriate. But whatever the answer, it wouldn't have been jeans, sneakers, and a plain white T-shirt. I thought we were going on a picnic or something."

"I thought you said you didn't like picnics because of bugs."

A grin tickles her lips. "I did say that."

"Okay, then trust me." I stop in front of her, brushing a lock of dark hair off her shoulder. "When we walk in there, everyone will be looking at you. Be ready."

"That's my point. Why did you do this to me?"

"I didn't do it. I assume your mom did."

She lifts a brow, as if she's not sure whether to fight me, laugh, or blush.

"You, Gianna Bardot, are going to have every head in the place turning because you're so damn beautiful. Not because you're in jeans."

She sighs, fighting a grin. "It's such a shame that a guy who looks like you and talks like you has such a low libido."

"There's nothing wrong with my libido."

"You know what they say."

"What's that?"

"Everyone's an expert from the sidelines."

I roll my eyes, unable to hide my entertainment with this infuriating woman. "Come on."

"But—"

"*Come on*," I say, reaching for her hand without thinking. Her palm slips into mine, and we take a step in the most fluid, most *we-do-this-all-the-time* way. As soon as she notices it, she starts to pull back. But this is the moment that I've been waiting for—dying for.

The natural progression of things.

Instead of letting her break the contact, I lace our fingers together. I don't look back at her as we take the limestone steps to the restaurant slowly but intently. My grip is loose enough that she can pull away if she wants to, but tight enough that she understands my intent: I want to touch her. I want to hold her hand. I need her to know that I'm proud as fuck to walk into this establishment with her at my side, and for everyone inside said building to know she's mine.

A surge of pride and protectiveness sweeps through me so hard that it nearly knocks me off my feet. *My dream girl is on my arm. And I haven't even kissed her yet.*

Every cell in my body is acutely aware of this inconvenient fact. At first, my hands-off approach was to stand out. She's a woman who gets what she wants. *What if she didn't?* But now, it's because I want to establish a connection to her that isn't based on sex—a relationship that she can't easily toss away. I want to create a tie that's deeper than the curve of her hips and more powerful than the orgasms I'm dying to deliver.

I'm afraid to contemplate what that might mean … for us. Because I know what it means for me. I'm about to get crushed by this beautiful woman and I don't have enough self-respect to care.

"Oh, wow," she breathes, stepping inside Table. "What is this place?"

"It's pretty great, huh?"

"You think?" She takes in the lodge-style architecture with large, rustic beams overhead and a wall of windows delivering the perfect view of the golden hour. Oversized chandeliers hang from the tall ceiling in an unexpected contradiction to the log construction. It's a play on casual and sophistication that I thought she'd find interesting. "This is beautiful."

"I was hoping that it would appeal to your artistic nature in a different way than Hess," I say.

She beams up at me, and I might as well have hit the damn lottery.

I give my name to the hostess, and she asks us to follow her.

We stroll through the dining area and pass the bar where golf stories are swapped, and multi-million-dollar business deals are made. I say hello to a few people I know as we walk by. Gianna sticks to my side, and I can feel her excitement and awe. But her gasp as we enter the outside patio with breathtaking views of the Cumberland River snaking below is everything.

"Your server will be right with you," the hostess says, as I pull out Gianna's chair.

"Was that Kelvin McCoy back there at the bar?" Gianna whispers as I get seated across from her. "The country music star?"

"Yeah."

"And you know him?"

I shrug. "He probably doesn't remember my name, but we

hung out one night after a concert. A guy I used to play ball with went to high school with him."

"And I'm in jeans."

"*And* he probably checked out your ass as we walked by. You have nothing to be ashamed of. Obviously."

Her cheeks heat, but her playful smirk overrides it. "I'm glad someone checks out my ass. My boyfriend doesn't seem to want anything to do with it."

I sit back and shake my head. *If she only knew.*

"Actually, do you know what? That's not fair of me," she says.

I narrow my eyes, curiosity piqued.

"You've been such a gentleman. I was talking to my friend Pearl about this and how we haven't even kissed, and she helped me change my perception. I mean, I'm still sexually frustrated, but I appreciate your restraint. It's very sweet of you, and I will endeavor to meet your energy."

"You will, will you?"

"I'll make this easier on you. I apologize."

Why does that sound like a challenge?

"Apology accepted," I say, playing along. I don't know where this is going, but it'll undoubtedly be entertaining.

Our server, Raffi, arrives and takes our drink order. Gianna then excuses herself to go to the ladies' room.

I sit back and breathe in the cool evening air. Discreetly placed heaters blow warmth across the space. Each table has a fireplace at the center, and many diners have chosen to light theirs. The flames create a cozy, romantic ambiance that I hope my girl loves.

It's been a long time since I truly dated a woman. I've seen a few here and there, and I've asked out a handful of women since my retirement, but none of the dates felt like this. Those felt like a plau—a curated set of moves that are, at the end of the day, the means to a satisfying end. This experience with Gianna feels more real, more meaningful than all the others. And that irony is not lost on me.

My gaze pulls across the patio to the doorway just as Gianna comes through it. The sight of her makes my breath stutter in my chest. Her body is fire with soft, sensual curves in all the right places. She carries herself with the confidence that men are praised for. It's unapologetic. Poised. Fierce.

But it's the smirk for me—the wickedness extending from the curl of her lips to the glint in her eye—that has my attention.

I stand, grabbing the back of her chair and pulling it out for her. Curiosity prickles my skin as her hair dusts against my arm. *What is she up to?* I step to the side to take my seat when she grabs my wrist.

My gaze falls to hers, and I'm unable to look away. She holds it tight as she pries my fingers open one by one. Then a piece of fabric is pressed into my palm.

"What's this?" I ask, narrowing my eyes.

Slowly, with a grin hot enough to scald the sun, she reverses order, closing my fist into a ball around the fabric.

"I wanted to give you a token of appreciation." She licks her lips. "Since you can't take these off me, I did it for you."

You little fucking minx.

I bite back a growl rumbling at the base of my throat, and fight the urge to bring her panties to my nose and breathe them in. My cock throbs so hard that I'm not sure I can sit. But I play it off as best as I can, shoving the damp lace into my pocket and lowering myself into my chair.

In no way did I suggest that I wanted a sexless relationship, and she knows it. This isn't a token of appreciation. It's defiance wrapped in consent. But if that's how she wants to play this, so be it.

Raffi reappears with our iced teas. "Here you are. Have you had a moment to look at the menu?"

Gianna smiles up at Raffi. "I don't need to look. What do you suggest?"

"Oh, I love it when customers ask me this," she says, laughing. "Well, we have steaks, roast chicken, and sustainably caught fish. But my favorite is the burger. The Fernie, to be specific. Thick patty with lettuce, tomato, onion, and a little mayo. It's a little basic, I know, but sometimes you can't beat a classic."

"I'll have that," Gianna says. "Does it come with fries?"

"Yes, ma'am."

"Great."

"What about you, sir?" Raffi asks.

I slide the menus to the edge of the table. "Let's keep it easy and make it two."

"Awesome. I'll get that in. In the meantime, you're welcome to start your fireplace if you'd like. Just flip this button," she says, pointing at a red switch. "Open the valve right there *gently* and then press the igniter."

"Thanks, Raffi," I say.

She nods. "It's my pleasure."

"Have I ever told you that I love fire?" Gianna asks, turning on the fireplace. "In high school, I collected lighters. My mother found them eventually and told my dad who was convinced I was doing heroine or something, and all hell broke loose." She opens the valve … a little too wide. "It was a bad couple of weeks for me after that."

"Hey, that valve is a little—*shit*!" A whoosh roars from the center of the table as soon as Gianna pushes the igniter. Flames shoot to the sky in all their blue and orange glory, sending waves of heat in all directions. "Turn the valve down."

Her giggle is all I can make out on the other side of the blaze.

I lean to the side, the heat frying my face, and lower the intensity. "Is this your way of telling me you're a pyromaniac?"

"I swear," she says, still in a fit of giggles. "I did not mean to do that. You should've warned me."

"Raffi said *gently*. You just flung that thing open like you knew what you were doing. I was letting you have it." I can't help but laugh, too. That giggle is infectious. "I'll always take your side, but I can kind of see your dad's point with the lighters."

She taps a napkin beneath her eyes. "He probably was right in retrospect. I was a little wild as a child, and having lighters was probably—definitely—a bad idea."

"You're like my sister Evie. She could burn a place down with an ice cube. The last thing she needs is a match."

"How many sisters do you have?" she asks.

"Two. Elodie and Evie. Evie, by the way, is a big Gianna fan."

"Oh, I love her. She's my favorite sister of yours."

I laugh. "What about you?"

"Just Lucia." Her brows tug together. "I wouldn't say she's my best friend because that's Astrid and Audrey. But Lucia and I are close in a different way."

"Yeah, you're family. I get it."

She makes a sound as if that's not quite right. "Maybe. We grew closer when our parents died, and we had to deal with all of that together. And now it's just her and me, you know? We don't have an extended family because our parents were never home long enough to facilitate one." She takes a quick sip of her tea. "So maybe you're right. Maybe it is because we're family."

I clear my throat as a heaviness sinks into my chest. "That will happen with my sisters and me, too. Probably sooner than I want to think about it."

"Why?"

"My dad has dementia."

The words drop between us like a lead balloon. It's the first time I've said those words out loud to someone without the last name Bennett. Saying them aloud to Gianna feels like I've let something out of a box that I can never put back, and I'm not sure how I feel about that.

She reaches across the table and places her hand on mine. "I'm sorry, Drake."

I roll my palm over and lace our fingers together once again, giving them a gentle squeeze. Then I pull my hand away.

"Thanks," I say. "He's in the early stages, and we're all still trying to adjust. It's hardest on my mom, of course. But she's handling it like the champ she is."

"That would be awful. My grandmother had dementia, and it's tough. My parents moved her into a nursing home close to us, and she lived there for years." She takes an uneven breath. "When Mom and Dad died, they were just gone. But it was like we lost Grandma over and over. It's heartbreaking."

"Guess I have that to look forward to."

She winces. "I shouldn't have said that."

"No. I'm glad you did. Now I won't feel bad calling you when I'm sad." I smile. "Can I ask what happened to your parents?"

"Yeah. They were on vacation and driving in the mountains. A deer jumped the guardrail and ran right in front of them. They were in heavy traffic, going about eighty, the police think. And Dad had nowhere to go." She frowns. "I was nineteen."

"I'm sorry that happened to you."

She sits back as Raffi returns with our burgers. Our drinks are refilled, extra napkins placed on the table, and then we're alone again.

We eat quietly for a while, tucking into our meal and our thoughts. I hate that the levity of our conversation was ruined, but I'm glad we shared our experiences. It's nice to know she understands what I'm going through, and I'm happy to know more about where she's coming from. It helps.

"So tell me about your art," I say, hoping I've given her enough time to sort herself. Even if she hasn't, art seems like a safe topic to bring us out of the gloom.

She looks up at me with a soft smile. "Really?"

"Yeah, really. Done any dumpster diving lately?"

"Well … okay." She sets her burger on her plate and sits taller. "I'm working on the project with the cans that I was telling you about. My kitchen is covered in cut-up aluminum. I'm also in the middle of a project that I never should've started." She makes a face. "I'm trying to recreate a picture from buttons. It's a pain in the ass."

I take a drink. "I saw this guy on TV the other day who was remodeling a house. He used pennies to create a border around the edges of his office floor. I wonder if you could do something like that with buttons?"

Her eyes light up.

"They're not flat like pennies, so that would be a challenge," I say, wondering how in the hell I'm coming up with this. It's not like I've ever thought about using buttons for anything other than a jacket before this conversation. "Maybe if you built the floor up and left a little channel around the room, it could work."

"Stop talking dirty to me."

I laugh, shaking my head at her.

She fans her face. "I'm all hot and bothered now."

"There's nothing I can do about that since you gave me your token of appreciation," I say, slipping my hand into my pocket.

"Good thing we've already had a walkthrough of you just dropping me off after a date and not coming in," she says, deadpan. "Should make things easier tonight."

I clear my throat, twisting my lips so I don't give anything away. "Well, I had a proposition for you …"

She narrows her eyes as if she's not sure if I'm being serious or fucking with her. It doesn't take long for curiosity to win. *As expected.*

"I'll bite," she says, smirking. "What's your proposition, Mr. Bennett?"

The lace slides against my skin, slipping between my fingers. Imagining this on her body, touching all the places I want to lick, makes my heart race. My balls are tight. My head, both of them, are ready to explode.

"I can absolutely take you home just like I did last weekend. Or, since you compromised and agreed to no sex," I say, barely able to keep a straight face. We both know we're going to fuck. It comes down to who's willing to give in first, and teasing her is half the fun. "I thought I'd compromise, too."

She pulls back, her eyes widening. "Oh, really?"

"I mean, no sex," I say, grinning. "But if there are other things you'd like to do, I'm game."

She sinks into her chair as she yanks her napkin off her lap. "I really love everything oral."

Perfect. "Done. We leave here, and you can blow something."

"*Finally.*"

CHAPTER
TWENTY-TWO

Gianna

"This is why this thing between us works," I say, studying the side of Drake's face. "You know how to compromise. That's such an elite ability that most people can't manage, and it's such a turn-on."

The corner of his lips flickers with a grin.

With one hand on the steering wheel and the other in his lap, he navigates us through the streets of Nashville. Drake steps on the gas, pulling smoothly into the left lane. The engine roars as the vehicle lurches forward quickly. *Powerfully.* We overtake the van in the right lane easily before he deftly moves us in front of it.

That's so hot.

"Do you live far from here?" I ask, imagining his jaw clenched together while he's coming.

"Not too far."

"Good." I sigh in relief that the pent-up sexual frustration that I've been carrying for the last week will finally meet its end. "There's only so much a girl can do with a vibrator, you know?

And, if I'm being honest, I've gotten off to the idea of your face between my legs just about every night this week."

Just the thought of it now is enough to make my insides clench.

He looks at me out of the corner of his eye. "You started doing that? I mean, if we're being honest, I jack myself off to you in the shower *every motherfucking day*."

Oh fuck. My lips part, each breath shaking and coming quick. The vision he just planted in my brain—body wet, muscles flexed, his Adam's apple bobbing while his hand grips his cock and he moans my name, wrecks my libido.

"What do you think about when you're coming?" I ask. "My ass? My tits? Shooting it down my throat? Because that's going to happen as soon as this vehicle stops."

Drake cups his cock, groaning as he tries to rearrange it. "I've fucked you every way you can imagine over the last … how long have we worked together?" He takes his eyes off the road long enough to let them sear into mine. "I met you on a Tuesday. You had on a black skirt and a white top with a giant ketchup stain on the front of it." He chuckles. "I came so hard that night." He glances at me again, this time with a smirk. "My cock was buried inside you when I got off."

"Stop it," I groan, shifting in my seat. "I'm so wet right now that there's probably a spot on your seat."

He flips on his turn signal and slows. I look around, but we aren't anywhere near a residential area. It's full of storefronts and gas stations. *Maybe he's taking me to a hotel. Or a parking lot.*

That's never comfortable, but God knows that I've done worse.

"Good call," I say, my heart starting to pound. He makes a left into a strip mall. "I need your cock in my mouth right fucking …" I gasp a breath. *"You motherfucker."*

Hanging proudly, lit up in blue, are the words Blow Me with a variety of blown glass objects around it.

I shove his shoulder, making him laugh. "I hate you."

"No, you don't." He parks the car and cuts the engine. "This is going to be fun. I think you get to hold a rod, blow into a shaft —should be everything you asked for."

Sighing, I sink back in my seat and sulk—but just for a moment. Because when I think about it, it *is* pretty clever, and he executed it perfectly. *When's the last time a man planned something fun like this for me?*

Never.

He leans over the console, his eyes sparkling under the street-lamps. "You aren't really mad, are you?"

"No," I say, breathily so the heat of my mouth touches his, but our lips don't quite touch. Then I grin and lean back. "Are we really blowing glass?"

"I thought it would be fun. Have you done it before?"

"No, but I've always wanted to give it a try. I mean, what's not to love about putting glass in fire?"

He cringes. "I didn't know about your pyromaniac tendencies when I booked this."

I laugh, brushing a lock of hair off his forehead before I realize what I'm doing. He looks up at me through his thick, ridiculous lashes, and all I want is for him to kiss me. Right now, in this moment with no one around and my anticipation so high that I think I might crack, I want his touch. Just a single brush of his lips against mine. *Anything.* But the stubborn bastard isn't going to give in.

I climb out of the car, ignoring his objections and warnings about opening my own door, and meet him at the hood.

He takes my hand, lacing our fingers tightly together, and guides me toward the building. "I open your doors. We can joke around all you want, but I open the doors."

"*Okay.*"

I can't tell if he's upset with me about it or whether he's just irritated because he's on the verge of coming in his pants, too. It is a little satisfying to know that I'm not the only one spiraling.

Chimes ring, announcing our arrival. An old man with a bald

spot on the top of his head greets us with a smile. "You must be Drake and Gianna."

Holy fuck, it's hot in here. Fans buzz in the periphery, but they do nothing to cool the air. My hair clings to my neck, and I can feel sweat gathering under my boobs.

"That's us," Drake says, stroking my hand with his thumb. The smooth, rhythmic motion has a direct line to my nervous system. My shoulders drop, and the buzz from the car settles almost instantly. *How wild.*

"I'm Paul, and it's nice to meet you. Have either of you done this before?"

"No. This is our first time," Drake says.

"It could've been," I mutter.

Drake's chest shakes as he suppresses a chuckle.

"It's good to see you both wore the right clothes," Paul says, motioning for us to follow him deeper into the building. He points at a wall with aprons hanging on colorful pegs. "You're not required to wear a smock, but we have them over there if you'd like one. Today's class will be fun and easy. I don't foresee any accidents happening, but that's why they're called accidents, right?"

"Right," I say, nodding along. I remove my hand from Drake's and grab an elastic from my pocket. It takes two seconds to get my hair pulled up and on top of my head. "It's so hot in here. How do you stand this?"

Paul chuckles. "Well, it takes a lot of heat to melt glass, and this is my passion, so I guess that makes it easier. Are you ready to get started?"

Drake moves to stand behind me as we peer over buckets of colored glass bits. As Paul explains that we'll need to choose the colors we'd like to make our flowers, and fades into a story about the first thing he ever made—a paperweight—Drake slides his hands under the edge of my shirt stealthily. I hiccup a breath, trying to focus on what Paul is saying since he's clearly talking to me, and not where Drake's fingertips are biting into the skin of my hips.

"This is the furnace," Paul says, opening a door to a raging inferno. "It's about 2000 degrees in there. There's a pot of melted glass inside—but I'll be the one handling that." He closes it and opens another smaller door. It's a smaller portal to hell. "We call this the glory hole."

I try not to moan as Drake presses his rock-hard cock into my back. There's a joke to be made, but I can't make it. I can barely formulate a thought.

Sweat, cocks, and glory holes—and I'm abstinent. *What has my life become?*

"What color would you like, Drake?" Paul asks.

"Blue."

"What about you, Gianna?" Paul asks, quirking a brow at the quickness of Drake's choice.

I snort-laugh. "I'd like pink, please, Paul."

He takes a rod and explains his process of retrieving a ball of molten glass from a bin in the furnace. Apparently, he's the only person allowed anywhere near the fire dungeon, and he's all too happy to go into a detailed account of how he earned his credentials.

Once his back is to us, Drake rocks his cock against me again. "Are you wet?"

"Soaked."

"Good." He growls against my ear. "This is for the panty stunt."

I grin. "You should quit while you're ahead."

"Or what?"

"Or I'll play dirty."

Paul looks at us over his shoulder. "Gianna, you're up first. You said pink?"

"Yup."

He fishes a ball of molten glass from the furnace with a long rod. The blob on the end is the brightest orange I've ever seen, and he carries it carefully to the buckets of crushed glass bits. He explains his process of rolling the glass in the bits, then taking it back to the hole to get it all soft and gooey. He repeats this twice, giving me time to get my wits together and relax.

Serenity sweeps over me as I lean the back of my head into Drake's chest. My heart races as my brain yells at me, setting off all the red warning bells and trying to trigger panic. But when he slowly wraps his arms around my waist, the beat of his heart overshadows my body's alarm system. *And I sigh.*

This is new—to me as an individual and to us as a … *couple.* That word tosses around in my mind, all wobbly and awkward. But like the molten glass on the rod, somehow it molds into something so sturdy that I wonder if it could become a part of who I am. Because Drake is my fake real boyfriend, who's starting not to feel so fake anymore.

And that doesn't terrify the shit out of me like it should.

"Gianna, head to that bench over there," Paul says. "You're going to take that flat metal piece and, when I bring this over, you're going to press it against the bottom. We just want to make a little disc. Okay?"

"Sure thing, Paul." I take my seat on the bench and grab the instrument. Paul approaches with a giant ball of molten glass. "Press that gently against the bottom. It goes without saying that this is very, very hot. We don't want to touch, bump, or otherwise contact the rod or the glass. Got it?"

"Got it. Don't contact the rod. It's kind of the theme of the night," I mutter. I touch the metal plate to the glass until it forms the desired small disc. The process is fascinating and oh, so satisfying. The transformation is so fun. "Ooh, that's so cool. It's like slime or Play-Doh. It's not at all what I expected."

"Neat, huh?" Paul asks.

"Very neat." *Who knew people still used that word?* "I can't fathom how this is going to become a flower, though."

I look up and catch Drake watching me intently with a soft smile.

"We only have about a minute to work this glass, and then it goes in the glory hole to soften back up," Paul reminds me, motioning for me to stop. "That's good. Drop that tool into the bucket of water behind you, or the glass will stick to it. Then grab the pliers."

"How hot is the glory hole, Paul?" I ask.

Drake comes up beside me. "You just wanted to say glory hole."

"So?"

"It's about fourteen hundred degrees," Paul says, oblivious to our whisperings behind him. "Be ready with the pliers. We must work quickly, remember?"

I hold up the giant metal tongs. "I'm waiting on you, Paully."

"You sound like my wife," he says, chuckling as he lays the rod across the bench. "Have you ever made a pie?"

I stare at him. *Do I look like I've made a pie?*

"Fair enough. Crimp the edges with the pliers," he says, grabbing another pair. "See how I pull gently. Do what I'm doing."

I mimic his method, and the flower begins to take shape. "I see it. I see where we're going with this." I laugh. "I'm going to need a glory hole at my house so I can do this all the time."

Paul shakes his head and looks at Drake. "What are you going to do with her?"

Drake looks at me, his eyes soft. I can't understand what he's feeling or guess what he's thinking. But something tells me it's not about the glory hole.

Finally, he grins. "Paul, I have yet to figure that out."

That makes two of us.

CHAPTER
TWENTY-THREE

"Well, you were right," I say, facing Drake. "I can admit when I'm wrong."

He makes a face as if he's not following me. "Right about what?"

"It turns out that I do like getting flowers when I don't have to ask for them."

We exchange a gentle, simple smile.

It occurred to me as Paul was putting our flowers into a contraption to cool them, because it's a process or they'll break, just how intentional Drake was about the glassblowing date. Not only was it cheeky and appealing to my artistic side, but it was also a way for him to give me flowers. So many birds, one sweet little stone.

The more that I see of this man, the more I like him. Everything that I thought I knew about him was barely touching the surface. The depths of his kindness, playfulness, and sexiness know no bounds. Being the object of his attention becomes more intoxicating every day.

What on earth would it feel like to be the object of his affection?

He nibbles his bottom lip, a hand in his pocket, and … waits.

"Are you heading home now?" I ask sweetly, testing his resolve.

His eyes twinkle. "Yup."

"Oh. Okay. Well, thank you for a lovely evening. I had a great time."

"Yeah. Me, too," he says curiously. He narrows his eyes, hiding a grin as he searches me for clues about what I'm up to—because he knows I'm up to something. And he's not wrong.

I told him that if he didn't quit messing with me in the glass studio, I'd would play dirty.

"Good night, Drake."

I open my front door, step inside, and shut it behind me.

My heart races as I listen to his shoes against the concrete while walking back to his Mercedes. I drop my purse on the table by the door and kick off my heels. Then I rush to the living room without turning on a light so he can't see me. I stand in the shadows and wait for him to pull away from the curb.

"Shit," I say, fumbling around for the light switch. I trip over a step stool I brought in earlier to reach the top of my canvas, fall on the coffee table, knocking half of its contents onto the floor, before landing on the sofa. "You've got to be kidding me."

I find my way to my feet, manage to turn on the lights, and locate my laptop in the kitchen. *Why is it there?* I open it with one hand and peel my shirt off with the other. Thankfully, Social is pulled up from a deep dive I did last night on Audrey's crush's fiancée's ex-boyfriend.

The guy has a cute puppy.

I carry the laptop to my room, trying to type with one hand.

Me: Astrid!

It says delivered. "Ugh." Time is ticking, so I switch to Audrey.

> Me: Auddie. Are you there?

Astrid's message shows read. "Perfect." I don't give her time to respond. I sit the computer on the edge of my bed and type quickly.

> Me: I need a favor.

Astrid: What's up?

> Me: I need you to call my phone.

Astrid: Where is it?

I giggle mischievously.

> Me: It's in Drake's car. Call it. Please. Now.

I yank off my jeans and toss them in the dirty clothes basket. My bra joins it.

Audrey: Hi, friend!

Me: Never mind.

Audrey: That's not nice.

Me: Love you. Will explain later.

Audrey: I don't even want to know.

I roll my eyes, removing my hair from the elastic. It's clumpy from the sweat so I run a brush through it and hope my curls from this morning held.

Astrid: I called. Now what?

Me: Call it again.

Astrid: Why?

"Now's not the time, Astrid," I grumble.

Me: We're having a power struggle. I left my phone in his car, so he'll have to bring it back to me. I'll happen to look super hot when he gets here, and he won't be able to help himself. Then I win, and we can stop this ridiculousness, and I can get some cock.

Astrid: GIANNA.

Me: I'd do this for you!

Astrid: I'm calling for the third time. I'm just ... how do you come up with this stuff?

I run into the bathroom, grab a wet washcloth, and hit the hot spots. Brush my teeth. Mouthwash. Add a bit of red lipstick for the drama of it later, hopefully, and apply a bit of powder, thanks to all the sweat in the glass place. Then I race back to my bedroom.

Astrid: How many times do I call?

Astrid: I'm on number five.

Astrid: Are we hoping he answers?

Astrid: What if your battery goes dead?

Astrid: What if he's listening to music and can't hear it?

My computer beeps with each message, but I don't have time to answer her. I sort through my closet, searching for the red silk robe that I've had in mind for this since I devised this plan while Drake formed his flower. Finally, I find it mixed in with my winter coats. *Because why wouldn't it be there?*

The material is so soft against my skin, hitting just low enough to barely cover my ass. I cinch the tie around my waist but loosen the top so my cleavage is totally exposed, and my nipples will be, too, if I move the wrong way.

Ding dong!

"I love it when a plan comes together," I say, applying a few spritzes of my sexiest perfume. Then I shut my computer and toss it into the laundry bin. *I'm never going to find that tomorrow.*

Ding dong!

"Coming," I call in my most innocent voice as I hurry to the door. "Just a moment, please."

My heart races so fast that I'm dizzy. I've never had to put this much work into getting a man to want to sleep with me. It's annoying and frustrating, and if this doesn't work, I might suffocate him before he can leave. But as much as I hate to admit it, this has been fun.

And it's about to get spicy.

I take a breath, open the robe just a bit more, then open the door.

"You ..." He swallows. *Hard.* "Left your phone in my car."

I lean against the door and bat my lashes. "Did I? How silly of me."

His eyes scrape along my skin as they drop down my neck, over my collarbone, and between my breasts.

"I was just getting ready for bed," I say innocently. "If you want to hand it over, I'll—"

"*Fuck it.*"

———

Drake

She's in my arms, my mouth on hers, capturing her gasp of surprise and then the sweet, delicious moan of relief, before either of us can process what's happening.

We move backward, a wild tangle of hands, lips, and tongues moving, touching, *feeling*.

"*Oh*," she moans as her back smashes into the wall behind us. A painting just above her head slips from the force, swinging perilously from one screw. She giggles through the kisses, leaning her neck to the side to allow me access. "It took you long enough."

She reaches between us, slipping her hands under the hem of my shirt. Her palms skate over my skin—her nails sinking into me just enough to make me hiss. The scratches tomorrow are absolutely worth having her hands on me.

"Now's not the time to talk shit," I say, licking a trail across her collarbone.

I shove the silk off her delicate shoulders, the fabric pooling around her waist. Her tits hang in perfect teardrops—heavy and smooth with dark nipples begging to be sucked. I cup them both in my hands and draw one between my lips.

"That's the theme of our relationship at this point—*ooh!*" She moans as her eyes roll to the back of her head. "Oh, my fucking hell, that feels good."

I fumble with the tie at her hip, finally freeing it with one hand. It falls open, exposing the front of her body. The sight of her, perfection personified, makes my cock so hard it's difficult to breathe.

Rounded stomach. A deeply curved hip. Thighs that I want around my head as soon as possible.

"Holy fuck." I lick my lips. For the first time in my life, I'm not sure where to start. She's like a fucking amusement park, and all the rides are mine for the taking. *How'd I get so lucky?* "Woman, you're a fucking *dream*."

She drags the hem of my shirt up over my head and tosses it somewhere in the depths of the house. "I need to come," she says, unfastening my pants. "I've waited far too long. How do you plan on accomplishing that?"

"Wait a minute," I say, chuckling. "You're not in control here."

"The hell I'm not."

My pants fall to the floor. I kick off my shoes, then pull off my pants and socks. My cock is stretched to the ceiling with a bead of precum on the tip, aching to be sucked.

"I thought you liked giving oral," I say, stroking myself. "Get on your knees for me."

Her grin is absolutely *wicked* as she kneels at my feet. She licks her lips, a pool of red silk around her—and I nearly come undone.

"I'm only doing what you asked because I want to," she says, wrapping her hand around the base of my cock. "Just to be clear."

I plant my hands on the wall behind her. "You are welcome to justify it however you want. Just put my cock in your mouth."

She lifts her eyes to mine, rubbing the head over her lips. "Is this what you imagine in the shower?" Her tongue slips around the tip in a slow, leisurely circle like she has all night. "Did you imagine fucking my mouth?"

"Dammit, Gianna," I growl.

She giggles before sucking me between her lips. I groan as the sensations—*hot, tight, wet*—hit me at once. Her tongue swirls over the head, collecting the precum like it's her last fucking meal. She's needy, loving this as much as I am … and that's *so fucking hot*.

"I can't wait," she begins, planting kisses down my cock, "to feel you spilling down my throat." She licks her way back to the top, flicking her tongue against the head. "That makes me so horny."

"You're killing me here," I say, the ache so intense in my balls that I wince. "I—*fuck!*"

She sucks me into her mouth as far as she can, her free hand gripping my ass. I tremble, my body shaking as she pulls me in and out of her mouth with the perfect amount of pressure. The sounds she makes—*sucking, slurping, moaning*—have my breath coming out in shudders.

"Take me deeper." I hold each side of her head and guide it up and down. "Just like that."

Her spit rolls down me, over her fist, and drips onto my legs. Together, we find a rhythm that might be the most divine feeling I've ever experienced. My teeth clench as I move my hips, unable to stay still.

Faster. Harder. Deeper. My head gets light as an orgasm builds, and I know what I have to do—but fuck if I want to do it.

"Stop," I say, pulling away from her.

She rocks back, her eyes watery, as she wipes her mouth with the back of her hand. Her lips are swollen, and her cheeks are pink.

She's breathtaking.

I help her stand but instantly crave connection with her again. It's never going to be enough. I've opened Pandora's box.

My hands on her ass, I scoop her up and pin her to the wall. Her legs wrap around my waist as she captures my lips with hers. I reach between us and start to enter her but then remember that I need a condom.

"Fuck," I say, nipping her bottom lip.

Her eyes go wide as she searches mine. "What? What the fuck is the matter now?"

"I need a condom."

"Do you, though?" She grinds her soaked pussy against me. "I'm on birth control. Got a checkup last month and I'm a healthy girl."

"I got mine three weeks ago. I'm good, too."

Her back arches, shoving against the wall, as she begs for contact. "Fuck me then. Raw. I want to feel you inside me."

The mouth of a fucking goddess. "You're going to be the death of me."

She giggles, but the sound turns into the loudest moan I've ever heard as I part her flesh with my cock. She's so wet, the fluids coating her thighs in a slippery, sticky mess. The heat of her body covers mine as I press the tip against her opening.

I take a breath and shove all the way inside her.

"Fuck!" she yells, the sound of her voice echoing through the house. "Drake!"

CHAPTER
TWENTY-FOUR

His thrust is hard. Unapologetic. Intense.

Absolute fucking perfection.

I'm pinned between the wall and Drake Bennett, and I don't know which is harder.

My shoulders dig into the drywall as he slams into me again, as if he's needed this as badly as I have. Each stroke is an intentional movement. Deliberate. Like he's trying to commit this to memory through the fog like I am.

"Now this is cooperation," I say, the sound coming out in small bursts around his thrusts. I leverage myself with my hands against his thick shoulders and tilt my hips to allow him to go as deep as he can possibly get. "Just like that."

"You feel so good," he says through clenched teeth.

"Give it to me harder."

His chuckle is strained. "If I give it to you any harder, we're both going through the wall."

"I can afford renovations."

Like the good man he is, he gives me what I ask for.

He drives into my pussy so deliriously deep that I cry out.

My voice pierces the air as I squeeze my eyes shut, vaguely aware of the sound of my body colliding with the drywall. It's borderline pain and pleasure, like I might be splicing into two, and the ferocity of the sensation makes me feel alive.

A painting crashes to the floor from overhead, sending thousands of tiny beads scattering across the hardwood.

"Don't stop," I say. "I didn't like that piece anyway."

He leans forward, capturing my lips with his, and kisses me like his whole life depends on it. Our mouths move together in slow, sensual movements like we've had a lifetime of practice. There is no learning curve; we're in sync from the start.

"Bedroom?" He presses the words against my lips. "Which way?"

I motion vaguely to the right, moaning in displeasure as he slides out of me.

"I'm mad at you," I say, locking my ankles around his waist and fingers working through his soft hair.

He smirks and carries me toward the bedroom. "If this is what being pissed looks like with you, I'll endeavor to keep you madder than hell."

"We could've been doing this for the past week, but you had to try to prove a point," I say.

"Sometimes you have to sacrifice to—*whoa.*"

He stumbles over the cookie tin filled with buttons, kicking it across the room. Buttons fly everywhere like circular confetti. But as he regains his footing, he trips on a step stool—*why did I not move it after I tripped over it?*—and we go lurching forward. Drake holds me up with one arm and catches us against the couch with the other.

Impressive.

"Sorry," I say, wincing. "The life of an artist."

"I hope you have good insurance."

I tug on the roots of his hair and grind my pussy against him. "If you were an athlete, do you think you'd have better balance?"

"Excuse me?" He laughs, starting down the hallway. "I am an athlete."

"No, but if you were a real athlete. Take the last door on your left." My hips roll. The head of his cock is right there, and if I move just right … "Could you pretend you're an athlete again and run? You did run in football, right?"

He squeezes my ass until it stings. "Wait. Just wait."

"I have been. If you make me wait again, it will not end well for you."

His eyes blaze as we enter the bedroom. The light is on in the en suite, illuminating the room just enough to see. Drake marches to the bed and tosses me onto the mattress. He's hovering over me before I'm settled.

"What?" I ask, staring up at him.

A slow smile ghosts his lips. "Just making sure you're real."

I reach for him, pulling his face down to mine. His words do something goofy to my heart, and maybe if he kisses me, it'll stop. His tongue swipes past my lips, deepening the kiss. Plunging into my mouth. Exploring it. *Owning it.*

He drops kisses down my throat, sternum, and across my stomach as he scoots down the bed. The kisses are less frantic but no less passionate than before. More reverent, maybe.

I writhe beneath him, aware of my loss of control. My heartbeat quickens as he rolls off the bed. He slides me to the edge by my ankles, his eyes on me always.

I take a breath. "Why don't you—"

"Why don't you lie back and relax?" It's a statement and not a question. A carefully spoken request that's really a command, softened by his recognition of my comfort zone. "All you have to do tonight is enjoy it."

"But …"

"Hey." One brow raises toward the ceiling. "Do you trust me? Because, if you don't, I have no business being here."

I search his eyes while his words claw at my defenses. Trust isn't something I give easily. But, then again, it's not something anyone has ever asked for. I suddenly find myself straddling a line, instead of straddling him.

I want to say no. That's my instinct, my automatic response. But when I open my mouth to relay the message, my heart won't let the words come out. Naked in front of him, exposed in so many ways, giving up control doesn't feel reckless. It's a choice —a surrender instead of submission. Something he's asking me to do, not trying to take from me.

"Okay," I say. "I trust you."

"That might be the sexiest part of this whole night."

My cheeks flush as he grabs my calves and pushes my legs toward me and my knees to the sides. The air touches my freshly waxed bits, making me shiver. But the look in his eyes, devilishly hot and downright sinful, has me trembling.

"That's it," he says, as he lets go of my knees, but I keep them wide. "Keep your pussy open for me."

I lift my hips for him. "Better?"

He smirks, sliding a finger through my slit. My moan fills the air as he rocks a thumb over my swollen clit. I wiggle in a desperate plea for more.

"You're going to come on my tongue, my fingers, and my cock tonight." He pushes a finger, then two, inside me. "Where do you want to start?"

I grin at him, holding his gaze. "Tongue."

His chuckle rolls through the air, hitting my core like gasoline on an already raging fire. He dips out of view, but his hands are all over me. Hips. Ass. Stomach. He squeezes my sticky thighs as he buries his face between my legs without warning.

"Fuck!" I gasp for breath as I begin to tremble. "*Fuckkkk.*"

He inserts his fingers again, twisting them before sliding them back out. Every lick, flick, and stroke echoes through the room, mixing with my moans to create our own soundtrack. His tongue presses against my clit before he sucks it gently, sending shock waves rippling from my head to my curled toes.

This is all about *me*—and it's better than I possibly imagined.

"That's so good, Drake." He hums against my sensitive flesh. "Just like that."

I rock against his hand and face, raising my head off the bed to see his face framed by my thighs. It's picture-perfect—dream-worthy, and the sight of him like this, with my pussy in his face, is enough to send me toppling over the edge of bliss.

"Fuck!" I yell as the orgasm smashes into me, sending bolts of fire through my veins. "*Fuck*! That's it. Oh my … Ugh. I'm coming *so hard*." I clench my jaw, and my teeth grind together from the force of it all. "I can't take it."

"Yes, you can. Take everything I fucking give you," he growls, and the vibrations are a level of indulgence I never knew existed.

He clamps down on my thighs, holding me in place, forcing me to ride out the waves of pleasure. I feel his gaze glued to me. He's not missing a thing.

Finally, the intensity eases, and I sigh, sinking into the comforter. My legs are gelatin. My pussy trembles. But my mind? It's a beautiful, peaceful, but muddled mess.

I'm aware he removes his fingers because another shudder wracks through me.

"You, Mr. Bennett, are invited to do that anytime you'd like," I say, laughing.

He wipes my juices from his face, grinning. "I'll remember that."

"There are towels in the bathroom," I say, motioning toward the lit doorway.

"Hell, no. I love the taste of you."

My stomach blooms as I get to my knees, taking his body in for the first time. The man is a work of art. His physique is no accident—and every piece of it is hard.

Chiseled abs. Those lines down his obliques that make me drool. The seam of muscle running from his thigh to his knee … and that jawline. *My God.*

"You are seriously perfect," I say, biting my lip. "I take back what I said about you being an athlete. It's obvious."

"Come here."

I scoot to him. As soon as I'm within arm's reach, he wraps an arm around me and hauls me into his chest. I giggle, draping my arms over his broad shoulders and sighing happily.

Our mouths find each other's as if they're now magnetic. He parts my lips with his tongue, and I can faintly taste myself on it. There's something about being in his arms that I don't hate. I kind of love it, actually.

"You are heaven," he whispers, skimming his palms down and around me until he's cupping my ass. "I mean it, Gianna. There's nothing better than this."

I tilt my head to the side as his kisses trail down my shoulder. "You're playing a dangerous game."

"Why?

"Because if you keep feeding my ego, I'll crave the attention."

He pauses, smiling against my shoulder. "And maybe that's the point."

This man. I sag into him, floating in the clouds at the sweetness of his words. I'm not someone who enjoys being fed lines or love-bombed, and I struggle to play along with it for the plot. But that's the thing—this doesn't feel like a plot. I don't sense an undercurrent of bullshit.

If I wanted to, I might believe him.

He kisses me again. One arm holds me tight against him. His other hand comes down against my ass. The crack breaks the silence, loud and jolting. It's more bark than bite, so to speak, but the combination of the sound and the sting is so deliciously good that I can't stop the moan from spilling out of my mouth.

"Oh," he says, pulling back to see my face. He massages the spot where he spanked me. "Did you like that?"

"If your objective was to make me want you to fuck me hard from behind, then, yes. I enjoyed—*ah!*" I yelp as he smacks me again. "That makes me so wet."

"When I fuck you in just a second, I want to hear every little noise you make. Let me hear you. Got it?"

"It'll be my pleasure."

"Literally," he says, turning me around. "Bend over."

I get on all fours and look at him over my shoulder. His cock is in his hand as he caresses my ass cheek.

"Wanna fuck that?" I ask, swaying it back and forth.

"Now, *you're* playing a dangerous game."

I grin. "Why?"

"Because if you keep being so fucking perfect, I'll never be able to leave you alone."

"And maybe that's the point."

I barely get the words out before he plunges into me. I bite back a hiss as he grips my hips and holds me in place.

"I wanna hear you," he says, thrusting into me. "Do you like this? Tell me what you like."

All of it with you.

"Gianna …"

My name is a warning, a thinly veiled threat that there will be repercussions if I fail to comply. Instead of pissing me off, it turns me on. Because I know he's not going to hurt me in any way that I don't want him to.

"Deeper," I say, hissing loudly. "I love it when you go deep like that."

"I feel your pussy pulsing around my cock."

"It's about to go off again if you keep this up."

My tits hang heavily, aching from the orgasm building in my core. I arch my back, rocking into him thrust for thrust, the world around us nothing but a distant fog. I never come from this position, but it seems that's about to change.

A moan slips from my parted lips, and I whimper as his fingers nearly touch my hip bones. Deep pressure builds between my legs as they begin to shake.

"I'm going to come," I say, unable to stave it off. "I can't stop it."

"Don't. I want to feel you come on my cock."

I pant, shivering as the intensity builds. Drake tenses behind me, and I sense he's trying to wait on me to come before he lets go. The thought of him coming inside me does it.

"*Fuck!*" I scream, this one far more powerful than the first.

He drives into me, his grip flexing against my skin. I look over my shoulder to see his head tipped back and his Adam's apple bobbing in his throat. Every muscle is tense as he growls into the air.

I did this to him.

His motions grow slower, and I gently tumble back to reality. His body has one final tremble before he sags in satiated relief. A smile touches his lips that I haven't seen before, and it's my new favorite.

"A-plus work," I say, wincing as he pulls out of me. A drop of cum falls onto my leg. "That's fun."

He chuckles. "Want me to run you a bath?" He pauses. "Do you have a bath?"

I laugh, too. He's going to make me come like that and not flee immediately so that he can run me a bath? *Wow.* I decide to push it—to see how far he'll really go.

"I would like that on one condition," I say.

"Name it."

"If you take it with me."

He shrugs casually. "Done."

I fall backward into the comforter and watch him walk into my bathroom like he owns the place. With confidence and maturity.

And one hell of a cock.

CHAPTER
TWENTY-FIVE

Drake

"Did you find all of your clothes?" Gianna asks, pulling a tank over her head. The tight top mixed with her baggy sweat-pants is quite possibly hotter than her miniskirts and heels.

"I thought one sock was a goner, but it was under a cookie tin."

"For the buttons," she nods as if this makes sense.

"Yup. For the buttons."

After our two-hour bath and a blow job, I searched for the clothes we'd discarded in the foyer. Gianna stayed behind, finding clean clothes of her own, and it gave me a moment to take in her personal space. It was both exactly as I envisioned and utterly different from what I expected.

There are pieces of projects lying everywhere. A massive canvas in the living room. Buttons all over the floor. Scrapbooks piled so high in one corner that I'm shocked they didn't fall over during our rendezvous in the foyer. I expected as much. What surprised me was how much it felt like a home.

There are personal touches everywhere—pictures, trinkets, little succulents lining the windowsill in the kitchen. Throw blankets on every chair. It feels lived-in and comfortable, and if the walls could talk, I'm sure they'd tell stories for days.

"So what happens now? Do you leave?" She pauses. "Do you stay?" Her tone shifts higher, as if this option is her favorite. But quickly her brows tug together. "Hey, where is my phone?"

I laugh. "I have no fucking idea."

"Did you bring it in?"

I plant a wet, loud kiss on her lips. "All I remember is that you opened the door wearing basically nothing." I shrug. "Where's your phone? Is my car still running? Did we shut the front door? Hell if I know."

Would anyone blame me for blacking out? Gianna Bardot is a siren on a bad day, but dressed—barely—in a red silk kimono? No words were available. My brain shut down of all thoughts except for making her mine.

"Okay, but give me some credit," she says, smiling proudly. "My plan was brilliant."

"Did you have someone call it so it would ring? Or was that a coincidence?"

She snorts. "Of course, I did. Astrid called you repeatedly, so you'd come right back. In the meantime, I was rushing around here trying to look cute, smell cute, and be as irresistible as I could."

"Your irresistibility score wasn't what kept this from happening before. You know that, right?"

Her shoulders rise and fall as if it doesn't matter anymore. But it does to me.

"Do you want a snack?" she asks. "I always need a snack after sex."

"Does this mean you want me to stick around?"

She looks at me over her shoulder, leading me out of her bedroom. "You're not going anywhere until we have at least one more round."

How is this real?

She flips a light on in the hallway, something I did not do

earlier, and it illuminates the space. The walls on the left are dotted with gold frames of all sizes. Inside them are pictures of people whom I don't know, but who look happy.

"Those are my friends, mostly," she says. "There are some of Lucia." Her gaze sweeps across the images until it lands on one in the top left corner. "That's my mom and dad."

I step closer to get a good look at the couple who raised my girl. They're attractive and very well put together. Her mother's smile is bright but practiced, and her father reminds me of the kind of guy who everyone loves but never quite gets to know.

"How do you feel when you look at that picture?" I ask, wrapping my arm around her waist.

She studies it for a while. "Honestly? Sad."

I pull her closer to me.

"I'm sad they're gone," she says. "I'm sad we didn't have more chances to really understand each other. I'm sorry for the life they could've lived but chose not to, you know? I wonder a lot if they regretted anything in their last moments. If they could've been saved, would they have changed anything?" She looks up at me with doe eyes. "I'll never know."

"You're right," I say carefully, trying to find words that don't try to fix her pain, nor steal her grief. "You won't know. But that doesn't mean the questions aren't worth asking."

She nuzzles into my side.

"Want to know what I know?" I ask softly, remembering the things she's told me about her parents.

She nods against my chest.

"I know that you're a brilliant, strong, motivated, creative, thoughtful, beautiful woman," I say, before kissing the top of her head. "A little stubborn and a little chaotic, but that's what makes you special."

She laughs quietly, squeezing me tighter.

"They created their lives," I say, stroking her back. "And you're creating yours. Look at your home. Look at your job— second-highest-rated show at Canoodle behind a very popular sports show." I chuckle as she pretends to squirm away. "You have friends who will call your phone *sixteen times*."

And you have me.

This was inevitable. There was no way I wasn't going to fall for Gianna Bardot. I knew it when I dared her to date me, pretending like six weeks would get her out of my system. It was a farce, a joke—and now I'm in far too deep to save myself.

She's going to crush me.

And I'm going to let her, so at least I'll know what it was like to have her in my arms.

Gianna pulls away, taking my hand and locking our fingers together. I try not to read too much into it. I try not to acknowledge the lump in my throat as she leads me through the house. But whether it was purposeful or instinctual, she still did it. She opened up to me and allowed me to comfort her.

She trusted me.

"What are you painting over there?" I ask as we go through the living room.

"I'm not sure. I was going to do this mixed-media thing, but it didn't work out. Now it just sits there and mocks me."

I chuckle. "Is painting your favorite thing to do? Or do prefer … collecting buttons?"

"Those aren't just any buttons. They were Mom's and Grandma's. And I was trying to find a way to do something with them, so they didn't get lost." She giggles as we enter the kitchen. "Mom would hate the mess, but I have to think that Grandma would've appreciated them getting kicked over while being carried to my room by a tall, dark, and handsome kind—just her type."

"There are the tetanus cans." I snort. "These are interesting. They do look like butterflies."

"Did you doubt my artistic abilities?"

"No." I watch her rummage in the cabinets out of the corner of my eye. "It was more your sanity that I was concerned about."

She groans. "I have no food except for Matilda. And we can't eat Matilda in her current form."

What is this woman talking about?

"Want to order something?" she asks.

I have so many questions, but I don't know where to start. So I avoid them all and deal with the snack issue. "Do you have crackers?"

"Yeah."

"Butter?" I ask.

"Yeah."

I motion for her to give them to me. "Have you ever eaten butter and crackers?"

"I have not. I'm not sure why you would." She sets a box and a butter bell on the table. Then she grabs a knife. "Figured you'd need this."

"When I was growing up, we'd have this sometimes with our dinner," I say, opening a package of crackers. Memories flood my mind of big bowls of chili and a stack of buttered saltines beside it. "These crackers are a little fancy, but they'll work. You need the thin square ones for this to be exactly right."

She hops on the counter, letting her legs swing while she watches me.

I've never spent time here before. This is my first time in this kitchen—in this house, no less—yet I feel so comfortable. It would be nothing to open a cabinet in search of a glass or open the fridge for a drink. *How surreal.*

"We'd have this with soup a lot in the fall and winter." I smear a glob of butter on a cracker. "Sometimes with roast beef. My dad would crush crackers up and drop them in milk for a snack."

"Ew."

I laugh, offering her the cracker. "I'm with you on this one. Now, open."

"That's the second time you've said that to me today, and I prefer it in the first context." She parts her lips, and I place the snack on her tongue. The first bite crunches as she susses out the flavors and textures. She chews for a moment and then swallows. "*Okay.* That's actually … kinda good."

"See?" I make myself one. "You'll never starve as long as you have crackers and butter."

She opens her mouth again, and I give her the one I made for me. I'd give her almost anything she wants at this point. I'm a sucker for a strong, funny, beautiful woman. Or, maybe, just this one.

"How did you become a pro athlete eating this?" She makes a face like the idea is bizarre. "Aren't you supposed to be eating steak and spaghetti or something?"

"I said I ate it growing up, not when I was training."

"Do you miss it? Playing football, I mean."

Slathering butter on another cracker, I consider this. "No. Not really. I miss the team aspect of it. The camaraderie. But I don't miss practice. I don't miss the travel. The pain. I definitely don't miss that."

"Does it really hurt when you get smashed by another guy on the football field, or do the pads protect you?"

I hand her the cracker. "It hurts like a motherfucker. You usually have some adrenaline in your system, so you don't necessarily feel it right then—although sometimes you do. But the next day? It hurts to breathe."

She starts to eat, but rests her hand on her lap instead. A cloud covers her face, and she stares off into the distance. I'm curious about what she's thinking, but instead of asking her, I choose to give her some space to work through it.

Finally, she turns her attention to me. "Can I say something without it being awkward?"

"Probably not." I grin at her. "Of course. What's on your mind?"

"I don't know if I'm any good at this," she says slowly.

"What do you mean? Good at what?"

She sighs, fidgeting with the edge of her shirt. "You were

right when you said you'd give me a different experience in dating because I've never dated like this before."

"Like what?" I set the knife down and move to her, placing one palm on either side of her. "What are you getting at?"

"What I'm trying to say, I guess, is that you've put so much effort into this thing between us. You've chosen restaurants that you think I'll like for reasons other than I might like the burgers. And glassblowing? That was really, really sweet. You even managed to get me a flower that doesn't smell."

I chuckle, pressing a soft kiss to the center of her lips.

"It's been great, Drake." Her eyes sparkle. "It's been a lot of fun. And I don't know if I've said thank you. But … thank you."

Her words nail me in the chest. She should never have to thank someone for treating her right. *Has she dated complete chumps?* Good for me, but *damn.*

"It's not over, you know," I say, resting my forehead against hers. "There are more surprises up my sleeve."

My phone buzzes in my pocket, making me jump. I forgot it was in there. I push away from Gianna and pull the device out. *That's weird.*

"Hey," I say, my finger hovering over the button. "This is my mom, and it's really late for her to be calling and—"

"Get it."

I flash her a smile and then answer. "Hey, Mom. What's up?"

"I'm sorry for calling you so late, sweetheart. I'm just …"

A cold chill races down my spine. "Is everything okay?"

"There's no emergency." I exhale in relief. "But it's been a night with your father, and I just …"

She cries quietly into the phone, and my heart shatters with each sob. My mind races, trying to put together pieces of a puzzle that I don't have. All I know is that if my mom is calling me at this hour and crying, for fuck's sake, something is wrong.

"What happened?" I ask.

"He wanted to go to work. Couldn't find his keys. Couldn't find his boots. He kept yelling for you, thinking you'd taken

them or hidden them or something. I don't know. And I just …
I'm tired, Drake. I'm drained."

I pull the screen back and look at the time. Then I glance up
at Gianna. She's watching me, a worried look on her pretty
face.

The last thing I want to do is leave—especially tonight. But I
can hear the exhaustion in my mom's voice and … I don't know
what to do.

"I'm not bothering you, am I?" Mom asks.

"No. I'm at my girlfriend's house. Just got back from a date."

Gianna grins.

"Mom? Can you hang on?" I ask.

"Sure, honey."

I mute her. "I know we had plans, but—"

"Go." She nods her head. "You gotta go. If I had a mom like
yours, I'd go."

A wild idea pops into my head, and I probably shouldn't
even bring it up, but the thought of leaving Gianna behind
tonight isn't one that I can stomach. I must try, at least.

"Would you be interested in going with me?" I ask.

Her eyes fly open.

"It's not a big deal," I say. "It's about a forty-five-minute
drive out of the city. We can grab a terrible drive-thru sandwich,
and you can control the radio. I know it might be a little uncomfortable, so if you don't want to, I understand. But Mom just
needs someone to hang out with her for a while and I think we'd
be a good distraction."

She shifts on the counter. "If she's sad, would it be a good
idea to bring me? I mean, I don't like to be sad in front of
anyone, least of all someone I'm meeting for the first time."

"I get that. But when it comes to my mom, if she sees her kids
happy, she's happy. And you, my little pyromaniac, are making
me very happy lately."

Her eyes twinkle as she looks into my eyes. The shield that
used to be there, at least partially, is almost gone. That alone—

even if she doesn't accompany me tonight—makes me so damn happy.

"You really want me to go?" she asks curiously.

"I wouldn't have asked you if I didn't."

She takes a deep breath, then smiles from ear to ear. "Then yes. I will go with you. But I control the radio. No takebacks."

I pull Gianna into a hug as I unmute my mother. "Mom, I'll be there in a bit … with my girlfriend."

Who I think I just fell in love with.

CHAPTER
TWENTY-SIX

GIANNA

"We're here," Drake says, making a right turn onto a gravel driveway. Tall pine trees line the road, shielding the house beyond it from the noise and nosiness of traffic. "This is home."

A two-story white house comes into view. Whiskey barrels and a swing adorn the front porch, the swing swaying in the gentle night breeze. I can imagine curling up there on lazy weekend mornings with a cup of coffee and a book. It's so peaceful.

Drake and I talked all the way here. We ate trash burgers from a drive-thru and traded stories about our lives. He's lived such a life full of people, places, and memories. I could listen to him share things for hours. It's fascinating because most of it, I can't relate to. We didn't have family dinners or homemade chicken noodle soup when we were sick, and my dad certainly didn't teach me to drive on backroads heading to the fishing hole when I was twelve.

But now we're here, and the confidence I had when we left my house an hour ago must've fallen out of the car a few miles back. Because all I can think of now is that I'm way in over my head.

"Should I stay in the car?" I ask, a ball of nerves bouncing around in my stomach. "That would be fine with me."

"Why would you want to do that?"

"I mean, your mom might want some alone time with you. If your dad's still upset, my presence could make it worse. Did we think about that?"

He pulls the SUV next to a white truck and parks. Then he turns to me. I wonder if he can hear my heart racing.

"You'll be a good distraction for Mom, and there's a chance that I get in there and Dad doesn't know me either." He reaches for my hand. "And I'd really like you to come with me. But it's up to you. I want you to be comfortable."

His eyes are bright and clear, searching mine through the darkness. He squeezes my hand before pulling back, and I can sense the tension begin to settle over him. *This must be so hard … and I don't want to add to it.*

"I'll go," I say, sounding way more certain than I feel.

He grins. "Thank you."

I wait for him to open my door and then step out into the cool night. Crickets chirp in the distance. An owl hoots as if it's warning the others in the trees surrounding us that there are visitors. The sky is so dark, lit by a million stars and a bright moon, and I've never felt a place so serene.

Bracing myself for the unknown, wishing I'd worn something a little more respectable, I step through the front door with Drake behind me. A woman, unmistakably Drake's mother, looks up from a small table in the kitchen. Her eyes have bags, and exhaustion streaks her features, but she's beautiful, nonetheless. *And when she sees Drake?* Her whole face lights up.

She stands, holding her arms out for her son. "Oh, you sweet boy. Thank you for coming."

"Of course." He wraps her in one of his warm hugs. I know

how transformative those are and understand why she needed one tonight. "Are you okay?"

I peer around the kitchen, sure that I can hear echoes of laughter and happy birthday songs and silverware clattering against plates. The air is warm and spicy, reminding me of cinnamon. A cookie jar is by a bay window, undoubtedly filled with homemade treats.

"Mom," Drake says, turning to me. "This is Gianna. Gianna, this is Barb Bennett, my mother."

Her gaze shifts to me as a broad smile stretches across her face. "I'm a hugger," she warns, coming to me with the same open arms she had for Drake.

"*Oh.*"

Drake chuckles at my reaction as Barb pulls me against her. My eyes go wide as if to say, *What the fuck is going on?* But it only amuses him more.

"It's nice to meet you, Mrs. Bennett," I say as she leans away. "I hope it's okay that I'm here tonight."

"It's Barb. And you just put the first smile I've had on my face all week." She pats my cheek lovingly. I freeze at the gesture despite the rivers of warmth cascading through me. "Can I get you a drink? Tea? Coke? Water?"

"I'm fine," I say, not wanting her to worry about me. "Just pretend I'm not here."

"Nonsense. I want you to make yourself at home." She points at a cabinet by the sink. "There are cups in there and bowls and plates in the one beside it. The pantry is over there. Have what you want out of the fridge, honey." She clasps her hands at her chest. "I'm just happy you're here."

"Oh, well, I … I'm happy to be here," I say, fumbling over my words.

Drake's brows pull together for a split second before he stands by my side. His palm nestles in the small of my back while he speaks with his mom. The contact helps calm my jitteriness.

"Let's go into the living room," Barb says. "I've sat in this kitchen all night and the chair is killing my back. Are you sure you two don't want anything? I have some leftover meatloaf in the fridge."

"If we'd known we were coming, we wouldn't have eaten," Drake says, winking at me. "How's Dad? Is he asleep?"

Barb sighs, her shoulders drooping. "Yes. Finally. I'm going to see if the doctor can give him something stronger to help settle him at night when he's like this. It's like having a toddler again, only this toddler says some pretty cruel things, drives a car, and uses a chainsaw. This makes Evie as a toddler seem like a teddy bear."

Oh, Barb. No wonder she's exhausted.

We move through a passway filled with pictures of Drake and two blond girls who heavily resemble him. There are shelves with trophies and plaques—newspaper articles framed and preserved. I'd love to go through them someday and read all about his accomplishments.

I bet his parents are so proud of him.

"I'm sorry that I bothered you," Barb says as we all take a seat. Drake and I sit by the window, and Barb takes a floral print chair by a brown recliner. "I just … I didn't know who to call. If I call your sisters, I get Evie thinking the world is going to stop spinning and Elodie thinking she needs to take over everything. There's no one to vent to that won't cause me a bigger headache at the end."

"It's not a big deal. You know I'm always here to help."

I gaze at his profile as he looks at his mother.

Drake is unlike any man I've ever known. He's beautiful in a masculine way, with a strong jaw and sharp cheekbones. He'll stop what he's doing to take care of those he loves. He's sturdy and reliable, sweet and kind. I understand precisely why Barb called her son. If I had the option when something was wrong, I'd call him, too.

The room shifts as that thought filters through my brain. I've never felt like I could count on anyone before. Every person in my life, aside from Astrid and Audrey—and Lucia since our parents passed—has spectacularly failed me or not given a shit when I needed them to at one point or another. But my first, automatic thought about Drake was that I trusted him.

Holy shit.

"I know it's not going to get any easier," Barb says as I tune back into their conversation. "The scary part is that I don't know what it's going to look like. It's still so new, and the unknown is terrifying."

"But you're not alone, Mom. Elodie, Evie, and I are here. We want to help you. We just don't know the best way to do that."

"There's nothing you can do other than answer the phone when I call." Her grin wobbles when footsteps come down the stairs behind her. She takes a ragged breath and looks over her shoulder, clenching the armrests of her chair. "I thought you were in bed, Edward."

"I could've sworn I heard Drake." He rubs the top of his head as he rounds the corner. The moment his eyes land on his son, his entire being changes. "Drake. Hey. What are you doing here? Is it morning?"

"No, no, Dad. It's not." Drake gets to his feet, crossing the room to hug his father. "I just came by to talk to Mom. You doing okay?"

He takes in the room like he's recalibrating his surroundings. "Yeah. I'm good. A little confused. But it's always nice to see you."

Edward shuffles to the brown recliner, his slippers swishing across the hardwood as he moves. He's a burly guy, every bit as tall as Drake but much heavier. His hands are thick and scarred. I bet one day, not too many years ago, Edward was a handful. I can't imagine what it's like for little Barb to manage him now.

Drake returns to his seat beside me, and that's when his father's gaze turns to me.

"Who are you?" he asks, cocking his head.

"Dad, this is my girlfriend, Gianna. Gianna, this is my dad, Edward."

"It's nice to meet you," I say.

"A girlfriend, huh?" He narrows his eyes, assessing me. "How come I ain't ever seen you before?"

"We just started dating a couple of weeks ago," I reply, because the question was directed at me. "And Drake's always talking about his dad and how great he is, so I had to see for myself."

Edward puffs up, proud. "He was, was he?"

"I think you're a little smaller than he let on. Otherwise, you check out so far."

He lets out a loud, roaring chuckle. His burly chest shakes with amusement. Drake and Barb exchange a surprised, but pleased glance as Edward seems to come alive.

"Don't let him talk shit about his old man," Edward says, teasing Drake. "He knows I'll still whip his ass."

Drake tries not to laugh. "I'd hate to have you prove that tonight."

Barb watches their interaction silently but tears well up in her eyes. *What is she thinking, and how does this feel for her?* But the love in her eyes is unmistakable.

I bet she is a terrific mother. The way she embraced Drake, then me—a woman she just met. She made me feel more welcome here than I ever did with my own parents. *How is that possible?*

Who are these people? I didn't think people like this existed in the real world.

"What do you do?" Edward asks me. "For a livin', I mean."

"I'm a podcaster."

"All right. What's your show about?"

Drake subtly reaches for my hand and folds our fingers together.

"It's about a little of this, a little of that," I say. "Mostly, it has to do with relationships. People call me for advice."

"So you're a modern-day … what did they call that, Barb? That thing in the newspapers?"

"Dear Abby?" she offers.

"Yes. You're a modern-day Dear Abby," he says.

I laugh, not sure that comparison is fair for Abby. "I think she was probably a little more proper in her responses than I am. I just … say stuff."

Drake cuts in. "Don't let her fool you. She has one of the highest-rated podcasts in the world."

"What's your podcast called?" Barb asks. "I'll have to tune in."

Please. Don't. The thought of Drake's mom listening to me talk about men and sex is enough to make me never want to sit in front of the mic again. *"Gianna Knows Things."*

"Evie is a huge fan," Drake tells his mother. "She'll be pissed that you got to meet Gianna before she did."

"Well, Gianna, what do you know?" Edward asks. "Tell us something."

"Dad …"

"No, it's fine," I say. "What do you want to know?"

He thinks for a moment. "Who's going to win the baseball championship this year? Can ya tell me that?"

Drake smirks, waiting patiently for my answer. He's probably wondering how I'm going to talk my way out of this one. I feel his gaze on my face but ignore it. Instead, I nod as if I'm really into this conversation with his dad.

"I'll tell you who it's not going to be, and that's the Bobcats," I say, hoping to hell that's right.

Drake recoils in shock. "How do you know who the Bobcats are?"

"The Bobcats have two pitchers, and no one can get on base. I doubt they make it to the postseason. My money would be on the Oilers, but they're going to have to fix that hole in their batting lineup, or they'll get exposed."

The words roll off my tongue, but I have no idea if they make sense. It's a piecemeal of comments I recall hearing, and I'm surprised I remember any of this.

"What the fuck are you talking about?" Drake asks, laughing. "How do you know who the Bobcats and Oilers are? What's happening right now?"

"I'm an athlete, remember? Volleyball?" I smirk. "Or maybe I recall a certain guy going over it on a podcast. Because I listen."

His jaw hangs open, but I can tell he's impressed. "Who is the armchair quarterback now?"

I giggle, remembering when I called him that.

"You are something else," he says, his eyes promising me round two as soon as we get back home. My core tightens at the thought.

"Barb, we got any tea?" Edward asks. "I'll go get it if we do."

She stands, ten times more relaxed than when we arrived, and runs her hands down her joggers. "I'll get it. Drake, there's a little meat-and-cheese tray in the fridge. Why don't you come get that and a package of Hawaiian rolls out of the pantry so we can have a little snack?"

At this hour? Granted, it's not late-late, but it's later than I'd imagine most people have a snack in that form. No judgment. If they're snacky, they might be my kind of people, after all.

"That sounds great," Edward says.

"Gianna," Barb says. "You don't have any allergies or anything that I need to be aware of, do you, honey? I can whip up something safe for you if you need it."

How sweet. "No. I can eat anything but shellfish, but not because I'm allergic. I just don't like them."

"Perfect. I don't like them either."

"Do you want to come with me, or stay here? Either is fine," Drake says softly.

A part of me thinks Barb needs a moment alone with her son. After all, that's why we're here—so he can offer whatever support they need. That's important to him, so it's important to me.

"I'm good," I say. "I'll hang with Big Ed."

Drake snort laughs, rolling his eyes. "Big Ed, huh? Lord, help us." He follows his mother out of the room.

I sit back against the soft cushions and breathe a sigh of relief. *Everything is going so well.* Barb and Big Ed seem to like me well enough, and Big Ed looks relaxed and happy—and not only did he remember Drake, I think Drake is what brought him around. The way his face lit up when he saw him was incredible.

My heart aches as I watch Big Ed fiddle with the remote control. It's easy to see what kind of man he once was. Hard-working, honest, capable. *A lot like this son.*

"That boy of mine …" He nods his head. "He's a good one. But you probably know that."

"I had an inkling that was the case."

"My girls are my pride and joy," he says. "But that Drake. He's a one of a kind. Not a boy in the world who made his father more proud."

A lump lodges in my throat, and a burning sensation bridges my nose. The sincerity in his words wraps around my heart. It's clear to see why Drake is the way he is. His family is amazing.

"You must be one helluva girl to have him bring you home. He doesn't do that. I was telling him the other day to pick a woman like his mom and not to settle for anything less—then you show up. That says a lot about you."

I take a shaky breath. "Well, I hope that's true. Barb seems like a wonderful person."

"Wonderful?" He pfft's me. "God broke the mold when he made that woman. She's a damn saint. The best mother. Hell of a wife." He sighs. "She's my best friend, and as proud as I am that Drake's my son, I'm even more proud that I'm her husband."

Big Ed stretches back in his recliner, a sad, haunting look settling over his face. The lump grows as I watch him shift in front of me. His gaze turns to mine.

"Gianna?" He licks his lips. "I'm getting confused a lot lately.

Even when I'm not, I don't really feel like myself. Can I count on you to do me a favor?"

"Sure. What do you need?"

His eyes fill with unshed tears. "When my brain can't think anymore, or I'm gone for good, will you please remind my wife how much I love her? And that I only spoke well of her when she wasn't around? The only thing that I'm afraid of is that she'll forget that."

Tears slide down the apples of my cheeks.

Damn you, Big Ed.

Damn you.

CHAPTER
TWENTY-SEVEN

Gianna

"Hi, Claudia. Welcome to *Gianna Knows Things*. What do *you* need to know?" I ask, pulling the microphone closer to me. "Let me remind you that I'm not answering any questions about Drake until the end of the show. Please don't ask about him and make it weird."

Because she will ask, and she will make it weird. They all will. And so far, they all have.

I woke up this morning to headlines that Drake was cheating on me with a model from Argentina. His face is plastered everywhere alongside a beautiful woman with a body capable of stopping traffic. He saw it before I was out of bed and called me to explain that he knew her once upon a time and hadn't talked to her in years. *Even if he had, he hasn't spoken to her since he met me, so how is it any of my business?*

Unfortunately, the world thinks it's their business, and I can't log on to Social without seeing post after post speculating on my emotional downfall. Fun times.

"Thanks for taking my call, Gianna. And for what it's worth, I'm Team Gianna. Real girls stick together."

I close my eyes. *Lord help me.*

"But what I need to know is who to trust," Claudia says. "My friends or my heart?"

"I'm gonna need a little context, if you don't mind."

"Sure. So I've been dating this guy for about five months now. I'm in love with him. He checks all the boxes, and I gave him a thorough interview before we even started dating to make sure that I wasn't wasting my time. He had potential, so we started seeing each other, and I fell madly in love with him. The problem is that my friends hate him."

"Ouch. Do we know why?"

"Not really. One says he has bad vibes, which—what does that even mean, right? The other says he's controlling, and that I've changed since we started dating, which I don't understand. But we're supposed to grow up and learn and evolve, aren't we? So even if I have changed, that's growth."

Claudia already knows the answer. Her boyfriend needs to go. She's just hoping that by some miracle, I'll agree with her, and she can use that as justification when her friendships fall apart.

Francine gets one less Christmas present for putting this call through.

I take a deep breath. "Let's start with your friends. How long have you known them?"

"I've known both since middle school. I'm twenty-three now."

"Are they in relationships?"

"Yes, they both have boyfriends."

"What are their relationships like?"

"Good," she says. "One just got engaged, and the other is seeing a guy. It's pretty new, but she seems happy."

"All right. Tell me about your guy. What's he like? What do you do together?"

"He's gorgeous," she says, her voice loaded with excitement.

"He's from a nice family. He loves dogs and has two rescues, Tequila and Sunrise."

My brows pull together. For being so in love with someone, the best thing you can come up with is that he's from a nice family and has two rescues … with those names? Not that he tells her that she's pretty, that he's nice, or that he loves her and takes her on trips to see the actual sun rise?

Not a good start.

"What is he like *to you*?" I ask.

"Oh, he's great. We hang out in his shop a lot because he works so much. He's a mechanic and owns a shop with his best friend. He takes me to Zeroes every Friday for date night," she says, as if taking her to a biker bar is the sweetest thing in the world. "He had this big party planned for my birthday, but he got sick the night before, so he had to cancel. I was so touched that he took the time to do that for me. Guys don't do that."

Apparently, he doesn't do that either, Claudia.

This is as bad as I figured it would be, and the only good thing about it is that it proves my intuitions are correct. None of this passes the vibe check. Her friends are undoubtedly seeing the big red flags waving in the air—the same ones that I see all the way over here—because they're not looking at it through an emotional lens.

Claudia's guy is in this for himself. Every choice from where they hang out to where they go on dates—it all benefits him. Maybe he has good qualities, but she's not sharing them with me. *And canceling her party because* he *can't go?*

Drake would never.

"I have two best friends—shoutout Astrid and Audrey— and because they're my best friends, I value their opinions. I believe they want what's best for me. If I didn't, they wouldn't be my best friends. So if they were telling me that they noticed a change in me for the worse, I'd think about that. If they had concerns for my happiness, I'd listen. Because who wants more for me than my girls? Real girls stick together. Isn't that what you told me?"

Claudia sighs. "Yes, and you're right. I do listen and trust them. But if they were really my best friends, wouldn't they try to like him? Because they're not giving him a chance."

"Is that true? Or did they give him a chance, and he blew it? I don't know the answer, but you do."

She groans in a way that tells me that she knows the answer. I'm right, and he's a dickhead. *It's all in a day's work.*

"You have two choices," I say. "You can listen to your friends and consider their opinions, or you can say screw it and do what you want. But before you decide, think about a few things. Imagine the dates you'll go on and the people you'll hang out with. What will late nights look like? Will he take care of you when you're sick or become interested in the things you love so he can talk to you about them?"

A soft grin kisses my lips as I think about Drake searching out the restaurants in Nashville that he thinks I'll like best and how he asks me about my art projects. It's kind of annoying how great he is.

"I'll think about it. Thanks, Gianna."

"No problem. Thanks for calling in." Francine gives me the sign that the final caller of the day is waiting. "Next on the line we have … Justin," I say, reading off the computer screen. "Hey, Justin. We're not talking about Drake, so please don't bring him up. Other than that, what do you need to know?"

"Hey, Gianna. I really, really need your wisdom right now."

"That's what I'm here for."

He takes a shaky breath that grabs my attention. "I've been seeing this guy for a while. Seven months and four days, to be exact."

I smile at the exactness of the relationship.

"And he's great. Or I'm pretty sure he's great." He pauses. "He was great before last weekend—that I know for sure. I think."

"I take it something happened last weekend."

He sighs, and his stress is palpable. Unlike a lot of my callers, he's not jumping to his significant other's defense right out of the gate, making them seem guilty from the start. I'm curious about where this is headed.

"Last Friday, he told me that he was going to see his sister for the weekend in Kentucky because she just had a baby. I couldn't go because my boss thinks I need to show up for a full 40-hour workweek every damn week."

I hear a smile in his voice, and I instantly like Justin. If his man is playing games with him, I might seek revenge myself.

"So he leaves Friday morning, and I pack him a cute little lunch for the road, and off he goes. I know he was there Friday and Saturday because he sent me pics of him with his niece, who, might I add, is the cutest baby in the world. And thanks to the trial between a pirate actor and blond actress a few years back, I know how to tell when a photograph was taken."

"That's where I learned that trick, too."

"It was truly a public service. Anyway, fast-forward to Sunday when I'm out brunching with a bestie, and who is sitting across the room with another man? *Him.*"

Justin's voice sounds calm, but I can hear the heartbreak just below the surface. Despite having never met Justin a day in my life, I'd fight someone for him. I trust my intuition, and it tells me that Justin is one of the good ones.

"Did he offer an explanation?" I ask.

"No, because I went home, packed my shit, and left."

I lean forward, resting my arms on the table. This is complicated. His reaction—packing his stuff and leaving—is my normal suggestion. Don't waste time on unworthy men. But something feels off to me about this, and I can't put my finger on it.

"He's blowing up my phone," Justin says. "He showed up at my work last Monday but got my shifts wrong, and I wasn't there. My inbox on every platform is loaded with messages from him, but I can't get myself to read them."

"Why?"

He hiccups a breath. "Because I know he'll want to talk to me and I'm afraid I'll either forgive him too easily or have my heart broken. It's easier to live in the gray than plunge into the darkness, if that makes sense."

Francine watches me intently from the sound booth. Curiosity is painted all over her face. The fact that I haven't suggested a rebound fuck and we've been on the phone beyond the five-minute mark might be a record, and she's clearly noticed.

I have, too, for that matter.

My entire platform is built on the premise that love is a choice and that too many of us make bad choices. Life's too short to be unhappy, and it's definitely too short to entertain bad people. *So why does a part of me want to suggest that Justin hear him out?*

The businessperson in me knows that I need to stay on brand. Branding is such a massive part of marketing, and the execs haven't filled the Thursday slot yet—something I've avoided thinking about lately. Now that I've gotten a taste of life when people know your name, it's terrifying. There's no privacy. You become gossip fodder. Everyone has something to say, whether they know anything about it or not, and the thing I used to love most—social media and chatting with people—is the thing that gives me the most anxiety now.

Despite it being off brand to suggest that Justin hear his man out, it would also be very un-me not to be honest. Honesty is always the best policy.

"I usually am on the side of *fuck around and find out*," I say, shifting in my seat. "But maybe let's ... I don't know, *feel around and find out* this time."

"What do you mean?"

"Do you love this guy?" I ask.

"Yes."

"Does he love you?"

"Yes." He sucks in a breath. "I've never doubted it. He's great with me, he's amazing to my mom, and he loves my cats even though he's allergic."

I smile softly as his voice starts to break.

"I'm scared, Gianna, and I don't know if I'm strong enough to know what's real and what's not if I talk to him again."

"Just hear him out," I say, and Francine's eyes go wide. *Yeah, I'm surprised, too.* "I know that's a very un-Gianna-like thing to say. But maybe there are a few guys out there who aren't complete turds."

My attention shifts from the computer screen to the window overlooking the hallway … and the *very* sexy man standing at it, watching me. Our gazes connect, and it's like a wash of happiness hits me in the face.

Drake smiles, the corner of his mouth tipping toward the ceiling. I return his grin and wish I were done with this show so we could get gelato and prepare for the fantasy football draft he talked me into joining. I have so much to learn.

"What if he lies to me?" Justin asks. "And I believe him?"

"And what if he tells you the truth and you don't? Or, even worse, what if you don't ask and are needlessly miserable forever?"

Drake's smile widens, and I roll my eyes at him. I can't hear him, but I know he's laughing.

"Thanks, Gianna," Justin says. "You're right. I'll give him a call."

"You're very welcome. Good luck, Justin. Thanks for calling."

My phone buzzes beside me, and I glance at it as a ten-second advertisement plays.

Drake: Look at you, you little dream maker.

I look up at him and giggle before typing out a quick reply.

Me: I'll show you a dream maker tonight. 😈

Drake: Promise?

Me: 💋

Scott from IT approaches him just as the advertisement ends. They move down the hall, looking at Scott's phone, as Francine gives me the go-ahead.

I clear my throat, not wanting to address my relationship with Drake but having no choice. Francine doesn't understand why I feel so strongly about making a statement. Drake posted on his Social account about the rumors, but I can't do that because I'm not opening my app. I'm not into reading that I'm not good enough for Drake, and that I'm overweight, ugly, and a terrible podcaster. Things have gotten nasty online, and I'm not sure why.

But as much as I don't want to say anything, I feel like I must. I don't like the trolls thinking that I'm hiding from them. And if I keep quiet, they'll say that it validates the rumors, and another contingent will wind up trashing Drake.

This was supposed to be fun and entertaining. *Why did people have to ruin it?*

"Welcome back," I say, ignoring the tightness in my stomach. "Drake and I updated you on our Monday live that things between us are going great. As a quick recap, we've been spending a lot of time together, and it's so different from anything that I've experienced before. He's a really great guy, and I'm not used to spending time with that kind of man." I lean closer to the mic. "And if I've dated you before, yes, that was a candid shot at you."

Francine shakes her head. Another lecture about liability is for sure on the horizon.

"But I also want to say that I saw the headlines this morning," I admit. "They're ... predictable. Uninspired. Work a little harder tomorrow and, for the love of God, pair me up with someone for once. Why is it always the guy with a hot model behind the girl's back? Pair me up with a single, hot football player with a juicy storyline. If you need help coming up with something, email me."

Francine laughs as the outro music begins to play.

"And that's it for this week's episode of *Gianna Knows Things*," I say. "Tune in next week for more hot takes and cold truths. Bye, everyone."

My mic is cut, and I sit back, breathing a sigh of relief.

Things like this would usually get my blood pressure soaring, and I'd call Astrid and vent for an hour. Instead, it's amusing to me that people care. Mostly because I don't.

Sure, I don't like reading the comments, and I can't fathom why people think it's necessary to be so mean. And it does bother me enough that I wanted to say something. But I wanted to speak out more than anything because my relationship with Drake isn't a joke that should be used as hurtful fodder for the world.

And what about the model? Is she in a relationship? Is throwing her into this harming her? If so, that's bullshit, too.

I'm proud of what Drake and I have in a weird way that I don't quite understand. We may not be serious or in love, but we do have respect for each other and a friendship that's deeper than any that I've ever had with a guy. That feels like something worth defending.

I glance at the clock and get to my feet, a smile on my lips.

It's time to find Drake and get the heck out of here.

CHAPTER
TWENTY-EIGHT

GIANNA

Painting in the dark is my favorite. There's something romantic and moody about the dark sky, muted light, and a canvas waiting to be touched. On clear nights with bright stars, I like to create outdoors. It's the only thing I enjoy doing outdoors, come to think of it.

My shoulders carry the tension of the day. Francine expected a word from the top floor about who will take the true crime spot on Thursdays. Drake must have heard the same thing because he seemed a bit on edge during lunch.

We haven't discussed the elephant in the room. At first, I figured that this thing between us would've fizzled out by the time the decision was made, and it wouldn't matter. But the fizzling has turned to sizzling, and now I'm afraid the news will be a bucket of cold water on the fire. We'll have to leave this little bubble we've created and face reality. And I'd like to prevent that from happening for as long as possible.

At the very least, I was promised six weeks with Drake. I want to get that full experience.

My phone buzzes on the step stool beside me, and I glance at the screen. *Francine? On a Thursday evening?*

I place my egg carton of paint on the coffee table and wipe my hands with a towel. Then I pick up my phone and read her text.

Francine: Just got out of a meeting. Do you have a few minutes to talk?

Me: Sure.

Before I can worry or wonder what she might be calling about, the phone rings.

"That was quick," I say, answering and immediately putting her on speakerphone. "Hey, Francine."

"Hi, Gianna. How are you?"

"Good. You?"

"Harried. I have a few things to run by you, starting with an email that I sent this morning. There is a list of podcasts that want to feature you in the coming six weeks or so, along with a few national magazines looking for interviews. I need to know how you feel about these as soon as possible. Personally, I think a lot of them are a good call. There are a few that probably aren't a good use of your time, but it's ultimately up to you. Let me know if you want my opinion on any of them."

National magazines? What the hell? "Is this about me, or the show, or Drake?"

"It's a mixed bag. There are notes in the email."

My stomach knots. "Okay. Great. Thanks."

"Mercy Malone is back on the books. She'll be in the States over the holidays and will stop by the week before Christmas. I don't know that date off the top of my head, but I'll add it to the calendar when I get back to my office."

"That's great news," I say, smiling. "Very exciting. I saw online that she bought a Murat painting in Amsterdam last week. I hope she's getting into her art era because that would be so much fun."

She laughs. "That would make an interesting segment for sure. Next ... I don't know where to start with this." The levity in her tone disappears. "Tomorrow marks one month of this dating thing with you and Drake."

I'm well aware of that.

It's been on my mind a lot for the past few days. I've tried to gauge whether he's thinking about it, too, but I really have no idea. He goes through each day like the one before.

The uncertainty of what happens once the six-week period finishes scares me. And the fact that I'm scared terrifies me. I'm not like this. I cut the tie and move on because no one checks all the boxes anyway.

But Drake? He kind of does.

"Not only has this thing stirred up so much interest in your show, but it's also done big things for Drake's," Francine continues. "He's seen exponential growth, especially with females, which isn't hard to figure out. All Canoodle's shows have benefited from this, and the execs want to capitalize on it."

"Of course, they do."

Francine clears her throat. "I'm just going to put this out there. Drake will likely be moved to Thursdays."

"*Oh.*" I move backward until the edge of the couch hits the back of my legs, then I sit. "Okay."

I stare at the stack of scrapbooks in the corner and give myself a moment to decide how I feel. *Sad? Angry? Disappointed?* Instead, I'm ... numb. It's probably a delayed reaction, and I'll be heartbroken in an hour. That would be very Pisces of me.

"Are you okay?" Francine asks.

"Well, I mean, it really sucks," I say, grasping for something inside me to cling to. "I've always known that this was a possibility and that Drake had a great shot at it—and he's deserving, of course. I'm happy for him."

I smile, although it's not quite full and bright. I *am* happy for Drake. He will kill it, and he works so hard and is so great at what he does. If it can't be me, I wouldn't want it to be anyone other than him. *And celebrating him will be so much fun.*

But I just wish it could've been me.

"I know it sucks, and I battled for you long and hard up there today. I want you to know that," she says.

That only makes me feel worse. "Thank you. I know you did, and I appreciate you. You can't always strongarm your way into everything you want—although you are pretty good at it."

We share a chuckle, and I wish I could've been good enough to win this for us. Francine deserves it. I hope she doesn't think she's wasted her energy on me.

"I'm sorry," I say, my bottom lip quivering, which pisses me off. "I know this is disappointing to you, too, and—"

"Stop it right there. This is business. You win some, and you lose some. I'm proud of what we've put together. This isn't the end for us. It just isn't the door that we're supposed to go through, if that makes sense." She sighs softly. "By the way, please don't share this with Drake. It's not, by any means, a done deal. They're taking their slow-ass time making a final decision, and I don't want to get his hopes up if it goes another way."

"Understood."

"Now that the bad news is out of the way," she says, a door shutting in the background of the phone. "I have some potentially great news."

"Okay ..."

"Canoodle is very impressed with you, and the success of your show—especially in the last few weeks—is creating a halo effect. The perception of the whole Canoodle brand is shifting, and the late teens to late twenties age group is flocking to you."

I grin. "I do love it when people flock to me."

"They want to talk with you about rethinking *Gianna Knows*

Things and really making it a platform brand within the Canoodle family."

What? "Speak to me in English, Francine."

"Right. Sorry." She laughs. "They basically want to create a network of spinoffs surrounding GKT, which is what they're calling your brand. Think dating style shows, blind dates, shows focused on second chances, and fake dating—which is a direct tie to you."

I get to my feet and pace the living room, trying to grasp what she's saying. It sounds like a great option, but my hackles are raised. The people I trust least in the world are corporate executives, and to hear that those very people have ideas about *my brand*—that they're already rebranding in their heads—has me worried.

"What happens to *Gianna Knows Things*?" I ask.

"More attention. A better studio. Tons of branded merch. They want you out there as the face of the platform because people know you and love you. So your job would be promoting the new line of shows. As far as content, they want more of your personal life—that sells. Maybe include your followers on your dating quests when this one with Drake ends."

I stop moving as my chest trembles. *"When this one with Drake ends."*

I don't want to do either of those things—end things with Drake or talk about dating other people—and I *definitely* don't want to do them with the world watching. My show is about entertaining people and giving them advice that they might not get from their friends. It's not supposed to be about *me*.

When I dreamed of a big-time show, I wanted my name to be attached to a talking point. I didn't want to *be* the talking point. I don't want people judging me and talking about my love life like it's a freak show. This past month has made that abundantly clear.

And I *absolutely* don't want to be a corporate sell-out. I don't want my voice used to spout whatever bullshit line that a bunch of men in suits somewhere on the top floor want me to say.

That'll happen over my dead body. *Haven't they listened to my podcast?* They'd know that if they had.

Each breath is a struggle, fighting against an invisible band stretched across my chest. There are so many interconnected moving parts that it's hard to find one to focus on. So many pieces of my life, parts that I love, might be coming to a complete stop.

That makes me want to puke.

"How do you feel about this?" Francine asks.

The excitement in her tone is undeniable, and I feel like an asshole that I'm not equally jacked about the developments.

"It's a lot to take in," I say, sounding as happy as I can. "Thank you for going to battle for me."

"Any time, any place. You know how much I think of you, Gianna. But I do need to get going because I have a stack of things to take care of before I go home. I'll recap all of this in an email, but give me a few hours to get it all together. As you said, it's a lot to take in."

"No rush. Thank you again."

"Of course. Talk soon."

"Goodbye."

Tears well up in my eyes as I try to focus on the positives in this because there are many. This could be bigger than the Thursday slot. *This might be a massive opportunity.*

My parents would've loved that for me.

But as I look around at my house, my paint, and my buttons, I can't ignore the pain in my chest. *How much will I have to give up to be a success? And if I don't, what will that cost Francine?*

I open my text app without thinking, and my thumbs fly over the keys. There is only one place that I want to be—one place where I know I'll feel like everything will be okay.

Me: Bored?

Drake texts me back immediately.

Drake: Just got home from playing basketball with Jory.

Me: What I'm hearing is that you're about to be wet and naked.

Drake: What I heard is you saying wet and naked, and now I need you to come over.

Me: It took you long enough to say that.

Drake: I didn't know I had to. I thought it was implied that I want you here whenever you want to be here ... and when you don't, too.

I re-read his words and feel the stress of Canoodle decisions float away. It's Drake's superpower, among other things.

Me: I'm on my way.

Drake: Have you eaten?

Me: No.

Drake: Any requests besides yourself? 😈

I laugh.

Me: Pizza?

Drake: It'll be here when you get here.

Me: You're the best. 🖤

Drake: Only for you.

I dump my purse on the couch, fish out my keys and wallet, and head to the door.

CHAPTER
TWENTY-NINE

"I decided not to apply for the job in North Carolina," Elodie says through my speakerphone, catching me by surprise. "I figure you might've forgotten about it since I haven't brought it up since the day at the lake. But in case it was rolling around in the back of your brain, you don't have to worry about it anymore."

"Why? What happened?"

"Well, I'd like to say it's because I can't leave you guys behind. But the real reason is that I offhandedly mentioned it to my boss on Monday, and she went to the big boss and got me a hefty raise that takes effect next week."

I nod approvingly. "I like that."

"Me, too." She laughs. "So what are you up to?"

"Right now, I'm lighting a candle in the kitchen because Gianna is on her way over."

It sounds like such a flex as it comes out of my mouth. *Gianna Bardot is on her way to me.* What a lucky fuck I am.

I take a quick look around the kitchen to ensure I didn't miss anything. The counters are clean, and the floor is swept. The bathroom has been straightened, and I changed the sheets on my bed. The flowers we made at Blow Me were delivered today. They sit on the counter for her to take home.

"How are things going with Gianna?" Elodie asks.

"I hate to jinx myself, but they're going great. It's just so easy with her, El. It's only been a few weeks, but I can't remember what my life was like without her." I chuckle. "That sounds like a crock of shit, doesn't it?"

She laughs. "Not necessarily, but it is funny hearing you talk like this. I love it, though. I love that you found someone who makes you this happy, because I can hear it in your voice."

Gianna does make me happy. I've been thinking about that a lot lately. I'm happier than I've ever been in my life.

"Hey, she's here," I say as my doorbell rings. "Can I call you tomorrow?"

"If you want, but I didn't have anything else to say. I just wanted to tell you that Raleigh is off the table."

"Glad to hear it." *Also glad that we don't have to tell Mom.* "Love you."

"Love you. Bye."

I slide my phone on the counter on my way to the door. I yank it open and find Gianna standing on the other side. She looks me up and down … with a frown.

"What's wrong?" I say, when I see the disappointed look on her face.

She pouts. "You promised that you would be naked and wet, and you're very clothed and very dry—*ah!*" She giggles as I wrap my hand around the back of her neck, bringing our lips together in a hard, deliberate kiss. My tongue sweeps across hers, and she moans into my mouth, her body melting against me.

I pull away, dragging in a ragged rush of air and resting my forehead against hers. "Hey."

"Hey," she says breathlessly.

"What's getting eaten first—the pizza or your pussy?"

She reaches between us and palms my already hard cock, grinning mischievously. "Me. The answer is always me."

"You're damn right that the answer is always you."

"It feels like the answer should be *you*." She cups her hand around my length through the soft fabric of my sweatpants and runs it up and down. The friction is just enough—the constriction just tight enough, to make me shiver. "I'm going to ride the fuck out of you tonight."

What am I supposed to say to that? I grin. *Could she be any more perfect?*

Every muscle in my body flexes as I imagine her straddling me—her perfect tits bouncing and her fire pussy pulsing on my cock. Her giggles. Her moans. The way she says my name mid-orgasm is something dreams are made of.

I take her hand, wait for her to kick her slides off by the door, and lead her into the apartment.

"Let's get you naked," I say, entering the kitchen. "I'm assuming you're already wet for me."

"You would assume right. I've had a stressful evening, and I need to get off, please."

I spin her around and pull her arms over her head. "You have come to the right place." I press a hasty kiss to her lips before I yank her shirt over her head. "Is there anything you want to talk about?"

"Yeah … but no." She sighs, playing with my hair as I remove her pants and panties. "Just being here helps."

My hands stall for a moment as that hits me. *Being here helps.* My heart thunders as I stand again and smile at her. Her cheeks blush, but she doesn't say anything. I don't mention it either. She said it. I heard it. That's enough.

I reach around her, pressing her chest to mine, and unfasten her bra. As I step back, it falls to the floor, and my hands immediately go to her tits. The feel of them in my palms—full, heavy, and perfectly shaped—short-circuits my brain. If I didn't want to taste her so much and give her the release she needs, I'd spend an hour on them alone.

Instead, I grip her by the waist and sit her on the stone countertop. "Lie back."

She puts her elbows down and then reclines until she's flat against the quartz. "I love how I can come here and order sexual favors à la carte."

"Babe, I offer a delivery service if it's more convenient."

She giggles as I help her scoot her juicy ass to the edge.

"Open up for me," I say, guiding her knees up and out. "There you go."

I love to play with her, build her up until she's ready to scream. Show her that she's worth all the time and energy in the world. But tonight, she explicitly told me she needed this to help with stress, and if she needs to come, I will oblige.

"You are beautiful," I say, grazing my finger up her slit. She trembles from the contact. "Your pussy is soaked. Do you know how hard that makes me?"

Her head falls to the side, and her eyes flutter closed as I gently slide my finger through her folds.

"Do you want me to be gentle?" I ask, going a bit deep between her lips. "Or are you wanting it hard? Tell me how to make you happy."

"I love it like this," she says, softly. "But this time, I just need to come fast and hard. I need the relief."

"Say less."

I dip one, then two fingers into her body. She groans, writhing against my hand as I push deeper into her flesh. "That's exactly what I need."

"That's two fingers. Do you want another one?"

"Yes," she hisses, her lashes splayed on her cheeks as if she's relishing my touch.

I add a third, stroking them in and out until I find an easy rhythm she enjoys. She sucks in a breath, her lips forming an *o* as she breathes, and exhales it in a sexy rush that I can feel in my cock.

She's so wet, so hot—ready for my dick. But if she wants to come on my face, then so be it.

It's not like it's a hardship to lick her pussy dry.

"Remember," I say, blowing across her swollen clit. "I want to hear you."

"Okay," she whispers.

I drag my tongue along her seam, flicking the tip of it against her bud. She moans as her back comes off the counter and arches toward my face. Her body is so responsive. She's so receptive to me.

"You're so fucking gorgeous," I say, grinding my teeth together to keep from coming in my pants. "My God, Gianna. Seeing you spread out like this in my kitchen, just for me ..."

I pick up the pace with my fingers, working her hole harder. She rocks against me, pushing harder against my hand, desperate for the relief she seeks.

I spread her pussy open with my free hand and drag my tongue across her clit. She screams, thrashing against the counter as I lick her. Her hand flies to the side, knocking over a vase holding a million Sharpies. They fly across the counter and roll to the floor in a cascade of color.

"Fuck, Drake!" she yells, the word capped by a cry over the marker waterfall. "Do that. *Please.*"

My stomach clenches as my balls tighten so painfully hard.

I suck her bud into my mouth. She reaches for my head, wrapping her fingers through my hair and pushing me closer to her. I keep my face glued to her pussy—licking, sucking, nipping until her legs begin to tremble.

Her exhale is shaky, but I can hear the relief in it. Being able to do this to her, for her, makes me feel more powerful than any tackle or touchdown I've ever made.

"Don't stop," she begs, drawing in a breath mixed with a sob. "Don't stop. I need this."

My fingers pound into her, and she meets me thrust for thrust. As she shakes and her muscles pulse around my hand, she lets out a cry that pierces the air. She tries to wiggle away from me, but I refuse to let her move—refuse to let her escape the pleasure she told me she needed. I plant a hand on her abdomen and press hard enough to hold her in place.

Her cries begin to fade, and I ease my assault slowly but surely, helping her return to her baseline as gently as possible. Her body softens as she whispers a satisfied sigh, and a slight smile ghosts her lips.

I ease my fingers from her, planting a kiss on her stomach before leaning away.

When I look up, she's staring at me. The look in her eyes is layered, and I can't quite decide what it means. "Thank you."

"*Never* thank me for that." I grab a towel out of a drawer and wipe my face with it. "That's a privilege."

She snorts, taking my hand and sitting up. "Right."

I take her chin in my hand and make her look me in the eye. "I'm not joking. Being allowed access to you like that? *It's a fucking privilege.*" I don't look away until I'm sure she heard me.

She hops off the counter with a devilish grin on her face. "You. Follow me. Now."

"Yes, ma'am."

———

GIANNA

It's his turn.

His bedroom is warm as we enter, and a bedside lamp gives

it a sexy glow. Music plays softly from his television, but the screen is dark. The beat amplifies the energy between us as I undress my man.

I shove his gray sweatpants over his hips, and he makes quick work of kicking them to the side. They land with a swoosh by the door, but his cock, thick and *so damn hard*, stands at attention. *Begging for me.* He lost his shirt somewhere on the way to his room, and I can't help but run my hands along his granite abs.

"This is almost unreal," I say, exploring every ridge and valley of his muscles with the tips of my fingers. My heart pumps faster as his gaze softens in appreciation—*of me or my words?* I don't know.

My touch slides up his smooth skin until it lands on his pecs. The muscles flex beneath my palms as I gently shove him toward the bed. Drake smirks, playing along like I could push him hard enough to move him—because we both know that's impossible. He falls back onto the navy comforter covering his king-sized bed.

He scoots back to the headboard, leaning against the pillow as I climb onto the bed, too. His eyes are glued to mine as I position myself between his legs and take his cock in my hand.

"You made me feel so fucking good," I say, running my tongue up and down his shaft. He's so hard that the veins in his cock are swollen, bulging from the velvety skin. "Now it's my turn to repay the favor."

My tongue darts out, sweeping the precum leaking from the tip. He shivers, hissing a breath as I suck gently on the head. Feeling him, watching him react to me like this is so fucking powerful.

"I love the taste of your cum," I say, stacking my hands around his length and pumping him slowly. More fluid appears at the tip. I grin at him as I take the crown between my lips and swirl my tongue around it.

"Fucking hell, Gianna," he growls.

I giggle as he pops free. "Do you like this?"

"What the fuck do you think?"

I stroke him from root to tip and shrug. "It looks like it." I reach between his legs and massage his balls. "As much as I'd love for you to spray your cum down my throat—"

"*Good God.*"

"What I really want is to ride you," I say, smirking. "Do you have any objections?"

"Oh, please no," he mocks, laughing. "Please don't sit on my cock and put those big titties in my face."

I laugh, too, climbing over his legs. My feet on the bed, one on either side of him, I reach backward and palm him. Then I position the tip at my entrance.

Drake's breaths are fast and shallow as his hands cinch down on my hips. "You've ruined me. It gets no better than this."

"We'll see about that." I drop smoothly down his shaft until I feel his balls touch my ass. "Getting better?"

He groans, shivering as his fingers dig into my skin. His hands tuck beneath my ass, assisting me as I lift and fall once again.

"Motherfucker," he says, tilting his head back against the headboard. "You're gonna kill me."

I giggle. "Don't die yet. I want to feel you come in me from this angle."

He growls, making me giggle harder.

I stroke him with my pussy, bouncing on his cock, watching him fight for his life beneath me. It's so heady, so intoxicating that I feel myself ready to bust all over him again.

Dropping to my knees, I smirk as he licks his lips and reaches for my tits. My hips roll in slow circles as his fingers do the same to my nipples. My blood sears through my veins as I absorb the stimulation, both physically and visually.

His eyes are sapphires, dark and hooded. His neck is strained. A day's worth of stubble dots his jaw as he clenches it in anticipation of unloading inside me.

I pick up my pace, grinding harder against him, the precipice of another orgasm growing closer by the second. Leaning back, I slide a hand between us and press my throbbing clit.

"Fuck," I hiss, the stickiness of my cum coating my fingers.

"Take me in as deep as you can. I want to fill every fucking inch of you." He squeezes my waist and pulls me down as if I could fit another centimeter of him inside me. But the added pressure is fucking delicious, anyway. I buck harder against him, working my clit faster. "That's it. Ride me, baby. Do you feel how much I want you? Can you feel how hard my cock is for you?"

I suck in a breath, the beginning flashes of my climax flirting with my vision. "I'm going to come."

He pounds into me from below. The duality of the motion is too much, and I topple over the edge wildly. Frantically. *Passionately.*

"Fuck!" I scream, the waves of pleasure ripping through me. I ride him fast and hard, listening to him growl through his own orgasm. The sounds coming from his throat are like shots of energy, extending my orgasm long after it should've been over. "So good, Drake. *So good.*"

He shakes violently, his eyes rolling back in his head. I fall forward, catching myself with my palms on his chest. He shivers, wrapping his arms around my back and pulling me down on top of him.

Our breathing is ragged, and our hearts race. He presses a kiss to the top of my head as I nuzzle into the bend of his neck.

"Feel better?" he asks, chuckling softly. "Did that release your stress?"

I smile against his shoulder. "For now."

"Want to get in the bath, and I'll bring you pizza?"

That's it. He's perfect.

He brushes my hair out of my face, his eyes twinkling.

I can't deny the warmth that spreads through me or how

satisfied and safe I feel with him. But I also don't want to talk about it. Not now.

"Sounds great, as long as you bring a bottle of wine and join me," I say.

He leans up and kisses my shoulder. "Anything for you."

For the first time in my life, I just might believe that.

CHAPTER
THIRTY

Moonlight streams through Drake's bedroom windows, creating a peaceful ambiance as we lie together. His bedside lamp provides enough light for us to flip through Mercy Malone's tour pictures. Drake points out little details that I would never notice—things like faces in the crowd, inconsistencies across venues in the stage design, and the subtle interactions between the dancers and the band. His perspective is fascinating. I have to wonder if it's because he's used to reading plays and picking up on cracks in defenses and player habits.

My habits are more of the *let's meet a random person at a laundromat and buy a few thousand plastic spoons that were headed for the landfill* variety. Not super helpful in any situation outside of, well, my life. Even then, sometimes my propensities are less helpful and more enthusiastic, well-intentioned calamities.

I glance up at my man, the black framed glasses he wears at night giving his features a smart, sophisticated aura. It's my favorite look of his, and the first time I saw him wearing his glasses, I made him wear them while I sucked his dick.

Drake's foot crosses mine beneath the sheets, and his toes

wiggle against mine every few minutes as if to remind him I'm still here. A shy grin pulls at the corner of his lips every time, and I don't think he notices. But I do.

His phone rings, breaking the silence of the night. "Who the hell is calling me this late?" He grabs the device and groans. "It's my sister Evie."

"Take it if you need to. It won't bother me."

He kisses me quickly before answering it, immediately putting the call on speakerphone and pulling me closer to his side. Men don't usually do this in front of me—talk so openly to a random call in the middle of the night. *Probably because they're on bullshit.* It's just another thing about Drake that I love.

"Hey, Eves," he says.

"Hey, so, Elodie told me that she was thinking about moving to Raleigh, and you knew it, and neither of you told me."

He chuckles softly, as if he expected this conversation to happen. "True."

"What the fuck, Drake?"

"She hadn't made up her mind yet and asked me not to say anything, so I didn't."

She gasps. "Where is your loyalty?"

"Well, at that moment, it was with Elodie." He chuckles louder. "She's not going, so it doesn't matter. Relax."

"I'm like the blond-headed baby child of this family, and no one takes me seriously."

I cover my mouth with my hand to suppress my giggle. Drake rolls his eyes.

"I wonder why no one takes you seriously, Evie," he says. "Is that all you called me for? Because I'm busy."

"Doing what?"

He lifts his brows, looking over his shoulder at me with a curious look.

I shrug. "I don't care," I whisper, knowing he's asking for permission to tell her that I'm here. It's not like the world isn't already in our business.

"Oh, I'm not doing much," he says, a taunt in his tone. "Just lying here with Gianna."

Evie shrieks. "*No, you are not.*"

"Yes, I really am." He presses a kiss to my forehead. "I love that you say it like you're surprised that she'd be with me, you little shit."

"Did you tell her I'm a fan? That I'm obsessed with her? That my entire office listens to her every week—*oh!* Tell her she needs merch! Do you know how many sweatshirts, hats, and hoodies people would buy? A fuckton. I have design ideas, if she needs them."

"More attention. Tons of branded merch."

Evie's suggestion brings back my conversation with Francine today, and I can feel the stress of it building in my shoulders once again—only more this time. Because if people are going to be wearing stuff with my name on it, I need to control what it says. And something tells me that if I let Canoodle rebrand me, that won't be the case.

"I'll let her know," Drake says, unaware that my thoughts strayed. "She's listening if you want to say anything to her."

"What? Drake! Why didn't you warn me that she could hear me?" She groans. "You really do hate me, don't you?"

I lean closer to the phone. "Hey, Evie."

She squeals. "Hey, Gianna. This is not how I thought we'd meet because, obviously, this is not my best look. But this is me with my brother and not me in the street. The me in the street is much cooler than the me with Drake. And please don't judge me based on this conversation or anything that he might've told you about me. And if he's still listening," she says louder, "I know things about him that I could share, too."

I laugh, stroking my fingertips over Drake's abs. "It's fine. I have a sister, so I understand."

"Thank God."

Drake yawns. "Okay, that's all you get of my girl tonight. We're going to bed."

My girl. I burrow my face against his side so he can't see me beam.

"Fine," she says. "I just wanted to yell at you for not telling me about Elodie. Now I'm pissed at you for this, too, you fuckhead."

"Love you, too," Drake says, laughing through another yawn.

"Ugh. Love you, too. It was so nice to meet you, Gianna!"

I laugh. "It was nice to meet you, too, Evie."

Drake ends the call before Evie can carry on, then plops the phone on the nightstand. "Do you need anything before I turn this light off?"

"Nope." I wait for him to roll back over, facing me, before I get situated at his side. One arm draped over his middle, I sigh. "Evie sounds fun."

"She's a giant pain in my ass."

I chuckle.

Drake rests his chin on the top of my head and exhales softly. His shoulders sink into the pillows while his chest rises and falls in slow, even movements. I close my eyes and absorb his peace.

This is nice.

I've always been a night owl, mainly because my brain seems to turn on when the sun turns off. The nighttime hours are when I generally feel most creative, and I get my best inspiration sometime after midnight. But over the last couple of weeks, since I started spending nights with Drake, that's begun to shift.

Drake is disciplined when it comes to rest. He says it's a vital part of being an athlete, even more important than the work at times. Without downtime and sleep, the *go hours*, as he calls them, aren't as successful. So it's ingrained in him at this point to slow down in the evenings and be asleep by the time I'm usually just hitting the gas.

It's been an interesting change to be in his world of routine. He never expects me to follow his schedule, but I've found a rhythm to it that I enjoy. Or maybe it's just being with him that I love.

"Mario called me this evening before you got here," he says softly. "He said that he expects them to decide who's taking the true crime slot next week."

I force a swallow, remembering that I promised Francine that I wouldn't share with him what she told me—just in case she's wrong. "I heard something like that, too."

"We haven't talked about that," he says quietly.

I shrug, knowing we need to talk about this before it happens, but wishing it wasn't right now. I haven't sorted my feelings about it. We don't even know for sure what the decision will be. Hopefully, we get a heads-up before it happens so it's not awkward.

It's not every day that you go head-to-head with your boyfriend for the biggest promotion at your company—and everyone you know, plus thousands of others, are watching.

"No, we haven't," I say. "But I think if we open that door, there are other things that we might have to discuss, too." *Like what will happen between us when this is over.*

He hums sleepily. "Yeah. We have time," he says, the words drifting off as he falls asleep.

I try to sleep, too, but can't. My mind has been activated, and when it moves this quickly, there's no stopping it. Not even with Drake.

I've been trying to live in the moment and not think too much about what happens when our experiment is complete. This last month has been the greatest few weeks of my life—and that's a problem. It's so great with Drake. It exceeds any dream I ever could've imagined. He's all the things from handsome to intelligent to protective in a way that still lets me breathe.

He lets me be me.

But the problem with that is … I'm me.

I love who I am, and I like myself as a person, which I think matters a whole hell of a lot in the grand scheme of things. But I know from personal experience with people who were required to love me, who were genetically designed to have affection toward me, that I'm not lovable long-term. I'm too quirky. Too honest. I don't always value the same things as everyone else, and that's often a dealbreaker.

So even though Drake seems amused by my dumpster diving and ketchup-stained shirts, I must keep my expectations realistic. I'm fun, but I'm probably not forever.

"It's a part of the fun of this whole thing. I have a window to say all the things I want to say before I have to go back to being your coworker."

His words from our date at Hess sear into my brain.

"You and I would never be together under normal circumstances. I want to fall in love and have a family."

My chest constricts so tightly that I can barely breathe. It caught me off guard when he said it before, but thinking about it now, it hits differently. Those are his words, his confession—our truth, and nothing has changed.

He's control, and I'm chaos. He's disciplined, and I'm a disaster. He wants devotion, and I'm a disappointment, and there's no way I can be anything different.

It's only natural that Drake will want a wife who can be as warm and nurturing as Barb. I killed Matilda. He's a slightly smaller version of Big Ed, and it makes sense that he wants a big family, a dog, and tea ready in the kitchen. I can't even get to my kitchen table, thanks to the aluminum-can butterflies.

There was a bird bath in the Bennett's front yard. There's a urinal in mine, for fuck's sake.

Drake groans, rolling over and onto his back. His forehead wrinkles as if he's deep in thought or pain.

"Hey, are you okay?" I ask, propping up on one elbow.

A smile ghosts his lips, and the wrinkling of his brow eases before my eyes. "Yeah. I love you."

He mumbles something incoherent, still deep asleep, and I stare at him in disbelief.

Tears fill my eyes, clouding my vision. His hand brushes against mine, and he instinctively pulls me against him and holds me tightly. I don't have the heart, nor the want, to extract myself from his arms.

My chest tightens, filling with a warmth so hot that it almost burns my ribs. A lump the size of Ohio seals my throat as I memorize the heat of his body, the sound of his breath, the smell of his skin. *The feel of this moment.*

Because I might have been wrong all along. Maybe love is a chemical reaction that you can't control. But that doesn't mean it's smart to succumb to it … even if you want to.

I snuggle deeper against him, kissing his shoulder and squeezing my eyes shut.

"I love you, too," I whisper, and try to fall asleep.

CHAPTER
THIRTY-ONE

> Drake: First thing Dad asked when I walked in the door was if you were coming. Guess you made quite the impression.

I smile at his text, pulling my visor down to shield my face from the early afternoon sun.

Audrey bops along to a song on the radio from the driver's seat. She borrowed her dad's truck for our trip to Pearl's, so I didn't object to her choice of music. Since I didn't say anything inappropriate to her brother, who showed up unexpectedly, she didn't choose bubble gum pop.

> Me: What can I say? I'm an impressive girl.

> Drake: There are many impressive qualities about you. If you'd like, I can name them off one by one tonight while you have my dick in your mouth.

> Me: You sure know how to make a girl happy.

My core clenches at the thought of being on my knees in front of Drake. I've always loved giving blow jobs—there's something innately powerful about making a man, no matter how alpha he thinks he is, lose control. But it's become something more with Drake, something beyond knowing I can make him come undone with the flick of my tongue.

It's not so much about the control of his pleasure. It's kind of about giving up control of mine.

> Drake: I try. 🩶

I know you do.

"Is that Drake?" Audrey asks, turning down the radio.

"Yeah."

A twinge tugs at my heart, a sensation that's new to me. It started last night after Drake's sleep-talking episode. It's a feeling of overwhelming gratitude mixed with the anticipation of incomprehensible loss rolled into one with a timer shoved in the top. The only time the pressure subsides is when I'm in his arms.

Talk about inconvenient.

Me: Want to come over tonight?

My brain tries to stop my thumbs from pressing the letters on the keypad, but fails to prevent them from sending the text. It's tricky because I'm stressed, so I want to be with him. He has a way of making me feel better. *Well, many ways, really.* But I'm stressed because I know I can't keep being with him.

That it will come to an end.

How do you manage that? You don't. You grab a flare, hold your breath, and ride the sinking ship until the very last minute.

Drake: Absolutely. You can show me your fancy new coat tree.

Me: It's SO GOOD. Just wait until you see it.

Drake: I'm excited to see what you do with it.
It'll be amazing, I'm sure.

I frown, wishing he'd just be mean or something. *Can't he be an asshole? Doesn't he have it in him?*

Make this easy for me, Drake.

I look up just in time. "Make a right here," I say, pointing at a road beside a church sign.

"That's not what the navigation says."

"I know, but Pearl told me that the navigation gets wonky out here and to turn beside the church sign with yellow letters."

Audrey shrugs. "Whatever you say."

Me: We're close to Pearl's. Have fun with your parents, and I'll see you tonight.

Drake: Can't wait. Be safe, babe.

"I can't with this guy," I say, huffing in frustration—more at myself than anything.

"Why?"

"Because, Auddie, he's literally perfect. He opens the car doors in public and then fucks my face in private."

She winces, but I ignore her.

"He's kind. He loves my art, and he never tells me that I'm being too loud or that my house is a mess, which you know is always the case. And I just ..." I sigh, dejected. "And it doesn't matter."

Audrey licks her lips before nibbling on the bottom one. "Why wouldn't it? I don't understand."

"He told me he loved me," I say, the words falling out of my mouth like a lead balloon. Audrey's eyes go wide. "He doesn't know he told me. Turns out that Drake is a sleep-talker."

She grips the steering wheel tightly, trying—and failing—not to look surprised. "So what are you going to do?" she asks gently.

"Fuck if I know. I figure that I have less than two weeks left in this science experiment of ours, so I'm going to enjoy it. Maybe he'll get sick of me before that, or he'll realize that I'm a good time, not a long time. That'll solve my problem."

Or, maybe this thing with the podcast will come to a head, and he'll realize that I'm not the brilliant businesswoman that he thinks that I am, and that'll turn him off.

We drive along the country road quietly for a few miles. Houses are sprinkled among the fields, and nearly all of them have a barn and chickens running in the yard. I lean my head back and sigh.

"What are you thinking about?" Audrey asks.

"Orgies."

"You are not." She rolls her eyes. "Listen, I know this is very complicated for you, and I understand why. But maybe this feels so uncomfortable and scary because you're shedding your skin. You're growing."

I turn my face to hers. "Don't bring your PhD into this friendship."

She giggles. "I'm just trying to help. You've been so happy lately and—I don't mean in a mean way—but calm. Content. And I love that for you."

"Yeah, well, I love that for me, too, Auddie. But I couldn't be this happy forever. I wouldn't know what to do with myself." *But I bet I could figure it out.*

Her face grows serious, and I know that damn PhD is about to come for me. I should change the subject or pivot to something less, well, about me. But something inside me wants to hear what she has to say. Because if Audrey doesn't believe something, she won't say it. She's not like Astrid, who will say things to shut you up, or like me, who sometimes says things just to get a reaction.

"You say that you're not someone to love for a long time, but you do realize that isn't logical, right?" she asks softly. "You're just afraid, and this is the way you protect yourself. It's a self-fulfilling prophecy."

Damn.

"You don't earn love, Gianna. It's not a performance review."

Tears well up in my eyes, and I refuse to look at her. "Yeah, well …" I look up and see a moss-green house with black shutters, just like Pearl described. *Oh thank God.* "That's it."

Audrey pulls the truck up the driveway and parks it next to a red Cadillac. We hop out of the truck, I open my own door for once while drying my unshed tears and head up the walkway. Before we get to the steps, a tiny woman comes out of the house.

"Gianna?" she asks.

"Pearl?"

She beams. "I'm glad you found me all the way out here."

"That church sign was a good tip. Auddie would've blown right by it."

Audrey blushes.

"Hi, Auddie," Pearl says. "Any friend of Gianna's is a friend of mine. Come on in, girls."

Audrey looks at me wide-eyed, and I shrug. I didn't know that Pearl and I were that close, either.

Pearl steps gingerly through the door. She can't be five feet tall, and her hair is a shade of blond orange that I'm absolutely sure comes from a do-it-yourself bottle of dye. I respect that, even if the color is atrocious.

The air smells like an apple-cinnamon air freshener used in abundance to cover what might be mildew. The wallpaper peels up in the seams, and the carpet has seen better days ... like in the nineteen eighties. And the light fixture above us has one out of three bulbs lit.

"Here she is," Pearl says, gazing fondly at the piece of mahogany I purchased for way too much money. "This was my father's. It sat just inside his front door for as long as I can remember. No one used this one but Daddy. His coats and hats were always covered in coal residue from the mines."

That explains why it's so important to her.

She sniffles. "But, yes, this is it. I can help you load it in your truck, if you want."

Audrey smiles at her.

"I think we can take care of it, but thank you," I say.

"Would you girls like a glass of tea?" Pearl asks, her eyes lighting up. "I just made some fresh this morning."

I glance at Audrey, but already know her answer. Sure enough, her soft eyes tell me that her little empath antennae are on duty.

"Sure," I say.

Pearl clasps her hands at her chest. "Really? Great. Follow me into the kitchen."

"Gianna told me that you're taking a cruise," Audrey says as we take a seat at the small wooden table beside the stove. "Where are you thinking about going?"

"Ah, I don't know. Anywhere, really. I'm just trying to blow all my cash before I croak."

Audrey coughs, trying to hide a laugh.

"I know you girls probably wonder what cash I'm talking about, considering the state of this place," she says, pouring three glasses of tea. "But this isn't where I live. I live up the road a ways." She hands each of us a glass and then joins us at the table. "I grew up in this house. This was my mama and daddy's place. I've never been able to sell it. My brother lived here after his divorce until he passed away a few years back. It's sat empty ever since."

That's a relief.

The tea is perfectly sweet and crisp, reminding me of my grandma's tea from my childhood. Even the glasses remind me of her. They're heavy-bottomed with a brownish-gold design that looks like stars.

"Did you ever get Lover Boy to bend you over the bed?" Pearl asks.

Audrey snorts, tea shooting out of her nostrils. I giggle before it turns into a full-blown belly laugh. Pearl hands her a napkin, laughing, too. Audrey's eyes water as she tries to get herself under control.

"I apologize for her," I say to Pearl. "Audrey is a good girl, and we love that about her."

"Hell, yes, we do," Pearl says. "There's nothing wrong with that, Auddie. You are who you are. People these days are too afraid to embrace how they really feel. That's why there are so many unhappy souls walking the earth."

She's probably right.

"But, back to your man," Pearl says, turning to me. "Are you having sex yet or not?"

Audrey's flabbergasted. Bewildered. If she had Pearl pegged to be a sweet old lady, which I think is the case, she's understandably shocked.

"I'm having great sex," I say. "It took some finagling, but I finally got the dick."

"Good for you. I was remembering you in my prayers in the evenings."

I laugh. "You were praying for my sex life? Pearl. *Baby.* You're a great friend."

"Oh, hell. God created sex," Pearl says. "How can it be a bad thing? It's only dirty because humans made it that way. If you're not hurting anyone, I say enjoy it."

We sip our tea as Audrey and Pearl get into a surprising conversation about traveling. It seems Pearl was quite the jetsetter back in her day. Audrey goes all over the place with her family. As I listen to them debate what's the better island— Grand Cayman or St. Thomas, my thoughts float to Drake.

I imagine him in his parents' living room, sitting across from Big Ed. I wonder if his sisters are there and if his mom is making something delicious in the kitchen. Drake said she would be doing that today. After all, it is Sunday, and Sunday dinners are a big deal in the Bennett household.

My shoulders pull forward as a hollow warmth settles in my gut. Not being with him feels like such a loss, like a bruise that only I can see. I should've gone, too. I wanted to. It just seemed ridiculous to dig myself in deeper with those sweet people. There's no need to create a bond with Barb and Big Ed, or Evie and Elodie. The fewer complications, the better.

My throat thickens, and I try to wash it out with another drink of tea.

"Well, Pearl, we'd better get going," I say, once her and Audrey's travel tales end. "I have a big week coming up, and my house is a disaster."

"Sure, honey. I understand."

Audrey rinses our glasses out, and Pearl places them in the dishwasher. I wipe down the table and push in our chairs. Then we return to the entryway and the infamous coat tree.

"It was nice to do business with you, Pearl," I say.

She cackles. "You know that's a damn lie."

I laugh, too. "Have fun on your cruise."

"I'll call you with a report." She turns to Audrey. "It was nice to meet you, young lady."

"It was nice to meet you, Pearl."

Audrey and I lift the coat tree, which is inexplicably heavier than I would've imagined. We nearly trip going down the walkway. We manage to get it into the truck bed without damaging either the wood or the metal, then climb into the cab.

Pearl waves as we back out of the driveway.

Audrey takes a call from her brother as I gaze out of the window, wishing that I were with Drake. Because there will come a day, sooner than later, I fear, that I won't have the choice.

And that's going to really, *really* suck.

CHAPTER
THIRTY-TWO

Drake

"Hey, gorgeous," I say, wrapping my arm around Gianna and hauling her into me. "I missed you."

She smiles up at me. "I missed you, too."

I close the door before taking her face in my hands and pressing a kiss to her lips. Her body relaxes the moment we touch, and I can almost see the stress of her day melt away. I love that I can do that to her.

"Where's the coat tree?" I ask after pulling back. "I need to see this thing."

"It's in the living room. Audrey helped me clean it off outside because it had about thirty years of grime on it. It's not looking too bad now."

She leads me into the house, our hands locked together.

"Auddie, this is Drake," Gianna says, stepping to the side. "Drake, this is one of my best friends Audrey."

A pretty woman with light blond hair and the shyest smile nods. "Hey, Drake."

"Hi. It's nice to meet you." I smile back, hoping it makes her more comfortable. "I take it that's your truck out there?"

"My dad's. We took it to get Vern."

I glance at Gianna. "Vern?"

"That's what we named the coat tree," she says, as if naming inanimate objects is typical. *God, I love this quirky woman.* "Doesn't it look like a Vern?"

"Sure," I say.

I take a look at the dark-colored pole with hooks protruding from the top. It's seen better days, probably in the last century, but it does have a uniqueness about it. Character. Whatever Gianna decides to do with it will be incredible.

Audrey laughs at my reaction. "Vern is the name of Pearl's dad. We thought it only made sense to name it after him."

Gianna nods along as if this conversation is sensical.

"Was there another choice?" I ask, playing along. "It had to be Vern."

Audrey's eyes sparkle. There's an innocence in them, an unsullied, potentially naive air about her that raises my curiosity. She seems opposite of Gianna in every way. They're an interesting pair.

"I'm going to go," Audrey says, picking up her keys from the coffee table. "Call me later."

"For sure," Gianna says.

Audrey tucks her chin, cheeks flushed and leaves quietly. Once the door snaps closed, I exhale—glad to have my girl all to myself.

"You were missed at dinner," I say, venturing over to her easel. She's made progress on the painting she's been working on since I've known her. Every time I see it, there's an adjustment. I don't know what she's creating, and I'm not sure she knows either. But the process of watching her make something out of nothing is better than any final product. "Evie was pissed at me for not bringing you along."

"Did you tell her you invited me?"

"I did. She did not care. In Evie's world, Evie makes the rules, and all logic and common sense are useless."

She smiles. "How's Big Ed?"

I take a deep breath and exhale slowly, hoping it keeps my blood pressure steady.

After dinner, we sat outside while Dad napped and had a long talk about the future. It was hard, and I don't think any of us wanted to do it, but it was necessary. We had to get on the same page.

Mom admitted she needed help—or would soon. Elodie explained that we were worried about her and that she needed to prioritize seeing her friends and getting manicures. Whatever made her happy. Evie offered to move back in, which was met with a resounding no and a lot of laughs. I offered to move my schedule around to help with the doctor's appointments and house maintenance. Mom reluctantly agreed.

"He had a bad day," I say, sitting on the couch. Gianna curls up next to me, resting her head on my shoulder. "He asked about Bingo a bunch for some reason. Bingo was Elodie's dog when we were growing up. He hasn't been alive for probably twenty years."

She stretches an arm across my middle, touching her lips against my bicep.

"We did get Mom to agree to having more help, though," I say. "Elodie is taking the reins because she's your prototypical oldest daughter. Everything and everyone is her responsibility, although she doesn't say it like that." I slide my arm around Gianna's back and hold her close. "I think this is her way of feeling like she has some control over the situation. She'll make her lists and monitor everyone's emotions, and that'll help her sleep at night."

Gianna grins. "Do you think if she came over and helped me get organized that she would sleep even better?"

I chuckle. "What would you do if everything were organized around here?"

"Get itchy, probably." She laughs, too. "I think I'm the opposite of Elodie. Chaos feels like control to me. I've never realized that until now." She pauses, lost in her thoughts. "Mayhem makes it harder to be surveilled. You can't fail if you don't play, so to speak."

That's interesting, but knowing what I know about her family, it makes sense.

"I'd love to get you and Elodie in a room together," I say, stoking my fingers down her arm. "Aside from the organizational part, I think the two of you would really get along."

"Why?"

"Well, you're both brilliant and creative, although in different ways. You're a brilliant artist, and Elodie is more innovative when it comes to working through a problem. She's never taken no for an answer like someone else I know."

Gianna kisses my arm again, and I think I feel her smile against my shoulder.

"What about Evie?" she asks. "Would we get along?"

I hum while I think about that. "Yeah, you would. I mean, of course, you would. But she's kind of all over the place. She could call me from a prison in Thailand tomorrow, and I wouldn't be all that surprised."

Gianna giggles. "Really?"

"Really. She gets an idea, and she does it. She doesn't think it through, contemplate the ramifications, or perform a risk assessment. She jumps in with both feet … probably in heels, to really grab headlines."

"She sounds fun."

"Depends on who you are to her," I say. "If you're her friend and can ignore her calls, she's probably a barrel of fun. If you're her brother? Not so much."

"I bet Lucia says that about me."

We sit quietly together, neither of us forcing a conversation. There's no need with Gianna to fill every moment with something for the sake of it. It's one of my favorite things about being with her. I can just *be with her*. And that's enough.

"Is Lucia married?" I ask. "Or does she have kids?"

"Nope, although she'd be happy to get married if she met the right guy, and I can see her being a mother someday. I could see her adopt a baby if she doesn't meet the right guy. She's just maternal, I guess."

"Elodie goes back and forth about adoption. She's thirty-six and thinks she's too old to have kids—especially with no husband in sight."

"I think it's a nice idea to adopt," Gianna says.

Oh. "Is that something you'd like to do someday?"

We haven't talked about having a family since I brought it up on our first date. She balked, and I chalked it up to something she didn't want to discuss right off the rip—which, understandable. I've never brought it up again.

But things have changed. The way I feel about her has changed. We're almost five weeks into this relationship, and I can see myself settling down with her. She fits into my life like a glove, and I think I fit into hers just as easily. If I had my way, I'd consider myself permanently taken. But if we're talking about or thinking about a long-term relationship, we'll have to discuss it at some point.

Gianna shifts, pulling away from me slightly. "I haven't given it a lot of thought personally. I just meant theoretically."

"Do you want kids at all?"

She breathes heavily, avoiding eye contact, which is unusual.

"What's going on?" I ask, confused.

The silence surrounding us is pregnant with tension. Clearly, I led us here but I don't know how or why. Gianna bites her lip as her breathing grows strained. If I've ever seen her in discomfort or saw her anxious, it's now.

It takes her a full minute of fighting herself over whatever is bothering her before she makes a decision. I hold my breath, curious but also on edge. I don't like the look on her face. Not at all.

She gasps a shaky breath and shrugs. "We probably need to have this conversation now and get it over with."

"Um, what conversation?"

She shifts in her seat, gripping the edge of the sofa like she might take off running at any minute. "When we started this whole fake real dating, it was supposed to be fun for six weeks—"

"*Gianna.*"

"—and it has been fun. It's been amazing. *You're amazing.* But you said it best on our first date." She drags her eyes to mine as if she's about to take a bullet. "Under normal circumstances, we'd never be together."

I flinch. *What the fuck is going on?* "What are you talking about?"

"Drake—"

"I said that weeks ago when we were first getting to know each other," I say, panic rising in my throat. "Hell, I probably said it so that you didn't bolt." I narrow my gaze, so utterly confused. "Where are you going with this?"

She stands up and moves across the room. Her eyes are wild, her chest rising and falling like she's struggling for air. She doesn't want to say this—she doesn't go wherever she's headed. But I don't know where that is and I can't stop her.

"We have fun together," she says, her lips quivering. "But we aren't supposed *to be* together."

I snort. "I absolutely disagree."

Her head whips to mine, and for the briefest moment, I see a flash of hope in her eyes.

"Did I do something wrong? Did I hurt you or offend you somehow?" I ask.

"No." She licks her lips. "But you did tell me that you loved me in your sleep last night."

Oh. The air stops moving around us. *That's what's going on.*

My heart pounds as the blanket is jerked off the baby. It all makes sense.

I might've been sleeping, but for Gianna, love is a choice.

And I added to the pressure, essentially making her feel like I took her choice away.

Her eyes fill with unshed tears. But like the fighter she is, she holds them back. I want to grab her, hold her, and kiss this ridiculous fear out of her. But if I do that, she'll push back. She'll feel more cornered than she already does.

Still, I do love her, and it's not wrong that she knows it. She's just going to need time to accept it.

"I didn't mean to tell you that way," I say gently. "I didn't plan on telling you anytime soon because I knew you'd do this. So, I'm sorry I said it how I said it, but I'm not sorry that you know the truth—something you probably knew anyway."

Gianna ignores this. "You and I are such different people. Sure, we can fuck and have a good time. But this isn't something that goes on forever." She draws in a shaky breath. "You're from this big, wonderful family, and you'll naturally want one of your own. And I just … I don't fit in that world."

"According to who? Don't I get a say in who fits into my world?"

"Sure, you do. But you've already told me who that is, and that profile *isn't me*."

She laughs sadly, and the sound is clogged with emotion. It smashes my heart into a million pieces. Each shard slices as it hits, and I feel the burn in my chest.

"You aren't seeing this for what it is. It's been almost five weeks, Drake. You haven't had time to think about what this would mean in the long term. I will disappoint you. I promise."

My sweet girl. Fuck your parents for doing this to you.

"This was always the ending, and you know it," she says softly. "You told me that. And it's just time we accept it, I think. This is as good a time as any to get this in the air. We're just getting deeper, which will make the inevitable just that much harder."

"Maybe it's time for you to accept that I'm not going anywhere. *Ever.* I've always known that there was a perfect woman out there for me, and that one day I'd turn a corner and there she would be." I grin. "I just didn't expect the ketchup on your shirt part."

Tears roll down her cheeks. Still, I don't go to her.

"If it makes you feel any better, I've known this was going to happen since the moment I asked you to try me," I say. "You'd have your finger on the eject button as soon as things got serious."

"That's not what's happening. It's not like that."

"No, it *is* like that. *It's just like that.*"

Seeing her cry just feet away from me and not being able to go to her is the worst form of torture. She's stubborn and headstrong, and she must choose to come to me. She must pick me of her own free will. She's scared to do that now. In her version of what love is, she thinks I'll eventually uncheck a box and go on about my day.

She's about to learn that's not how it works. *Because I love her.* Every quirky, hardheaded, beautiful piece of her.

"We should just end it now," she says through her tears. "There's no need to prolong this."

"I agree. There's no point in any of this."

She nods as if I'm agreeing with her and walking away. It takes everything I have not to chuckle.

"So I'll go home and give you space because I think that's what you want," I say slowly. "When you decide it's okay to love me back, I'll be waiting."

"Drake …"

"I love you, Gianna."

She hiccups a sob, and I clench my fist at my side to keep from pulling her into me. Walking away from her is going to be the hardest thing that I've ever done. But if I want to keep my girl, then I must. As much as it tears me up inside, it's the only thing to do.

And the sooner I go, the sooner she can realize this is nonsense.

I start toward the door, but stop by the cookie tin of buttons. "By the way," I say, holding her gaze for dear life. "You can't disappoint someone when you never had anything to prove."

I commit every detail of her to memory. The shine of her hair, the shape of her lips. The sweet curve of her hip. Then I give her a soft, reassuring smile and leave.

Luckily, my tears wait until I get in the SUV before they fall.

CHAPTER
THIRTY-THREE

Drake

Sunday night

Me: Just wanted to tell you good night. I love you.

She might as well get used to hearing it.
It takes her twenty minutes to respond.

Gianna: Good night.

———

Monday morning

> Me: Mondays suck ass.

> Me: It's the only thing I can think of that I dislike that involves sucking.

> Gianna: I can vouch for that.

It takes all the self-restraint that I can muster not to respond.

———

Tuesday afternoon

> Me: Catch. 🏈

> Gianna: 👀 Don't throw it so hard. 🏈

> Me: 😏 I can be gentle. 🏈

> Gianna: 😊 I know. 🏈

> Me: 😘 I love you. 🏈

> Gianna: 🙈 🖤

"That's better than nothing."

———

Wednesday morning

Me: Taking Big Ed for a doctor's appointment today.

Gianna: Is he okay?

Me: I just volunteered so that Mom can take care of a few things.

Gianna: I've been thinking a lot.

Me: I hope that's good for me.

Gianna: This isn't about you. It's about me. I know that sounds cliché.

Me: It also sounds true.

Gianna:

Me: I'm here when you're ready.

Gianna: Why are you so great?

Me: Genetics.

Gianna: Thank Big Ed for me today.

Me: I will. Love you.

Gianna: xo

CHAPTER
THIRTY-FOUR

Drake

"Thanks, Dr. Howser," I say, as Dad and I get to our feet. The doctor shakes my hand, then Dad's. "Will your office schedule the scans, or do we need to do it?"

"We'll do it. Your mom will get a phone call from the lab, and they'll set it up." He opens the exam room door. "If you all need anything else, don't hesitate to call." He turns to Dad as we enter the hallway. "Ed, it was good to see you. Let me know if I can do anything for you, all right?"

"Yeah, yeah. All right," Dad says, sliding his hand over his hair—or what's left of it, anyway. "Thanks, Doc."

Dr. Howser and I exchange a smile.

My father and I leave the office and step into the cool afternoon. The sun is out, but partially covered in clouds, and a murder of crows flies above our heads. Dad puts his hat on as soon as his feet hit the sidewalk, and he exhales.

"How are you feeling?" I ask him.

"Where's your mother again?"

I smile. "She's at the dentist. She'll be home when we get there."

He scoffs as he reaches the passenger door. "I don't know why in the hell she thinks that I can't drive myself to the damn doctor. I wiped your ass, and now she thinks you need to wipe mine."

"Hey, Dad, no offense, but I'm not wiping your ass whether Mom says to or not."

The irritation on his face shifts into humor, and he chuckles.

We get buckled in and back on the road without discussing Mom's dental appointment again. It would only be the five-thousandth time. I can see why Mom is so tired. Just the mental load of this is exhausting, but I'm so grateful to be able to do it.

I took a ton of notes on my phone during the appointment and asked all the questions Mom wrote down for me. The doctor is adjusting Dad's medication to help with his evening agitation and helped me better understand what the future might look like. It's different with every case. But I do feel like I have a better grasp of what kind of support my parents might need.

"What day is it?" Dad asks, flipping his visor down.

"It's Wednesday morning."

"Don't you have school today?"

I pause and think about my answer. The doctor said it's best not to correct him if it will lead to more confusion or distress. We're supposed only to correct him if it's for his safety or if it'll reduce his anxiety. He called it "compassionate redirection," which sounded a lot easier in the office than in practice.

"I have to go in later today," I say, leaving out the fact that it's to work and not to class.

"Oh."

"Do you want to stop somewhere and get some lunch?" I ask.

"Nah, I just want to go home and see your mother."

I bite my lip to keep from getting emotional.

Dad was always the beast, the man who could do and fix anything. To see him almost childlike, yet still in his huge body, is sad. And weird. But Mom is clearly his safe space. I'm glad he has her.

I grasp the steering wheel harder as my brain drifts to Gianna. This is what I want to be for her—her safe space, her rock when things get hard. She deserves someone to love her like I will. *Like I do.*

"Don't you have a girlfriend now?" Dad pulls his brows together. I'm afraid to answer because I don't know what decade he's living in right now. "What's her name?"

Damn. How do I compassionately redirect this? "She was busy today."

"That dark-haired girl. What's her name?"

"Gianna?"

"Gianna. Yes. That's her. Where is she at today?"

"She's working. She said to tell you hi."

His smile reaches both ears, and he rests back in his seat. It might be the first time I've seen him relax all day. He turns to me, ready to speak, but then his forehead wrinkles again.

"What's wrong?" I ask.

"You're not in high school anymore."

"No, I'm not. I'm fifty pounds heavier than I was back then."

He chuckles. "I noticed that but didn't want to mention it."

"I'm still in great shape, old man. Check this out." I take my right hand off the wheel and flex. "See that?"

He lifts the sleeve of his shirt on his left arm and flexes it. The amount of muscle he still carries around is mind-boggling. He might not remember where he parked his car, but I bet he could damn near bench press it.

"Talk to me when you're my age," he says, thoroughly enjoying himself. "Of course, I'll be dead by then."

"What the fuck?" I ask, laughing.

"What? I will be. There is no sense in pretending I'm going to last forever. You know you're going to die too someday, right?"

What's happening here? "Yeah, but I'm not sitting around thinking about it."

"Oh, to be young and dumb again."

I throw up my hands and try to fight another laugh. I'm not

sure whether to banter with him like we always have, or if that will make him more argumentative. The last thing I want to do is bring him back to Mom, ready to spit nails.

We drive for a few minutes in silence. Dad eventually dozes off, snoring lightly beside me. The sound reminds me of the way Gianna sounds when she finally falls asleep around two in the morning.

I miss her. I miss her giggles, kisses, and the random shit she gets herself into. I miss her love of food, her attempts to learn football, and her blow jobs. I miss holding her, walking by her office to drop off a drink, and coming up with new ways to make her smile.

And I've warred with myself a million times since Sunday on what to do about it.

Do I go to her and plead my case again?

Do I give her the space she needs and hope it doesn't take years for her to realize I'm the one for her?

Do I try to be her friend like I was pre-date and see if I can win her trust like that?

I've always believed that the universe would put the woman for me in my path. Surely, if Gianna is truly the love of my life, the universe will put us back together.

I hope. God, I hope.

———

GIANNA

Clouds roll across the sky, covering the sun and cooling the air. The weather report said rain, but I didn't have an umbrella at the office and didn't want to run home to get one. *If I were truly prepared, would I be me?*

Besides, if it pours on me while I'm out here, at least my parents will recognize me and know that I haven't changed.

The thought puts a sad smile on my face.

The cemetery lawn is soft, and I had to take my heels off so they wouldn't tear up the ground. Also, so I didn't break my neck.

Their headstone is in the back, a shiny black stone with their picture etched in the front. It was Lucia's idea, and I went along with it. I think it gives her peace somehow to see them memorialized in granite as a happy couple for eternity.

Pretty red flowers fill the grave vases on either side of the stone. They look nice. Watching the plastic petals flutter in the wind causes my chest to tighten.

I squat in front of it and dust off the ledge. I don't know why I'm here; I never come here. But today it just felt necessary.

The bridge of my nose burns as the wind picks up, and my bottom lip trembles. I haven't cried over my parents since the day of their funeral. *Why am I crying now?*

"Hey," I say. The word triggers a sob to escape my throat—one I didn't realize was waiting in the wings. In an instant, tears fill my eyes, and I find myself unable to see anything around me.

"I don't know what to say to you." I feel much less silly than I expected. It's like they're here—like they can hear me. And that's more comforting than I ever imagined it would be. "Dammit, why did you have to die?"

Tears stream down my cheeks, snot reaching my top lip. My chest shakes violently, and I chastise myself for not bringing a tissue. But I didn't expect to cry.

I wait until the sobs turn to sniffles and my cheeks are hot to the touch. Then I try again.

"I met a guy," I say, laughing through the tears. "He's fantastic. I think even you two would have to approve."

It's satisfying to know they can't argue with me about it, or point out a flaw, or tell me I'm wrong. That alone is worth the drive to the cemetery.

"His name is Drake, and he told me he loved me a few days ago," I say. "And I freaked out. I blame it on you, just to be clear.

I don't really know if that's fair. I wonder sometimes how distorted my memories of you guys might be. I lost you at nineteen—in the throes of teenage rebellion. Would we have managed to find common ground as adults? Would I have understood you better? Would you have understood me? Because I'm the same girl. I still love art, and chaos, and I have a filthy mouth that you certainly would disapprove of."

I wipe my face with the bottom of my shirt. Mascara mars the pale purple fabric, but there's nothing I can do about it now. *Looks like I'm going home before going back to the office.*

"So here's the thing," I say. "My freak-out was because of you. Let's go with that. But if that's the case, it's because that's all I know. I only know what you showed me growing up, and, let's face it, that wasn't someone telling me they love me for funsies on a Saturday night."

I blow out a breath as the tears begin to slow.

"Audrey says I think of love as something to be earned and as a form of self-protection. It sounded a little whackadoodle at first, but when I thought about it, I realized she's right. But as I lay in bed last night, missing Drake and wondering how I could un-fuck this situation, I started to wonder—why were you the way you were? Did you two have trauma as children? What caused you to be so cold? To care so much about what everyone thought? Why did you think it was okay to prioritize everything above Lucia and me?"

I wipe my face again and then stand tall. My chest doesn't shake, and my eyes are dry. The band that's squeezed my chest for days is finally loosening, and I can breathe.

"Whatever the reason was, it's no excuse. Your family, your little girls—me and Lucia—should've been everything to you." I take a breath. "But I forgive you. Maybe your decisions were like mine when I screwed up my life, and you were only doing what you know how to do. I have to forgive you. If I don't, I'm going to be as miserable as the two of you were, and I deserve more than that."

I watch as a crow lands on a tree branch on the edge of the cemetery. It studies me, its little head cocked to the side, and I wonder how many people it's watched do the same thing I'm doing.

"Drake and I will have a life together filled with hugs and children and buttons on the floor and hopefully tea in the fridge." I blink back another round of tears—happy ones, this time. "And if you're watching from wherever you are, I hope you're proud of me." I grin. "If not, that's okay. I'm proud of myself."

I press a kiss to the headstone and let my palm linger on the top of it for a few moments. Then I turn on my bare foot, heels dangling from my fingers, and leave.

CHAPTER
THIRTY-FIVE

"Are you ready?" Francine asks from my office doorway.

Nope.

I avoid eye contact because I know they're swollen from crying at the cemetery, and rummage around my desk, presumably to find a notepad and a pen. "Sure. Let me just grab a couple of things."

Meeting with the Canoodle execs an hour after I cried my eyes out to my dead parents wasn't how this day was supposed to go. But nothing in these past six weeks went how I thought it would. So I don't know why I'm surprised.

At least I swung by the house and changed clothes. Going into this meeting with snot on my shirt would've been worse.

I find a pad of paper and a pen, then take a quick, hopeful glance at my phone. It's dark. Drake hasn't called or texted since this morning, when he told me he was taking Big Ed to the doctor. I know it's routine, or it sounded that way, but I would still love an update.

Even though I don't deserve one.

I struggle to breathe as I rise from my chair. I'm still buzzed from the adrenaline of the afternoon and the anticipation of finding Drake. I simultaneously want to beg him for forgiveness and throw up at the realization that I fucking love him. Of course, he won't hold my behavior against me, but he deserves an apology. I've made peace with my parents, talked to Lucia on my way home, and now I need to talk to Drake, and all will be well in my personal life.

I hope.

Now onto my work life, and I have no idea where it's about to be headed.

"Are you okay?" Francine asks as we move down the hallway.

"Sure. Why?"

She peers at me out of the corner of her eye. "You just look a little tired. That's all."

I shrug because I don't know what else to say.

Drake's office is dark as we pass. Juni said he took a personal day and might be in this afternoon. I want so badly to check on him, to hear his voice, and make sure everything is okay with Big Ed.

No, what I really want to do is run out of this building and fly to his apartment and jump into his arms with the biggest apology the world has ever seen.

Francine leaves me to my thoughts on the elevator ride to the top floor. I stare straight ahead, not trusting myself to make eye contact with her. I don't need her judgment or want her pity. And I definitely don't want to be compelled to explain.

I open the conference room door and let Francine enter first. She breaks the ice with the suits, allowing me to duck behind her with a quick hello and an even quicker wave.

"Thank you for joining us," Mr. Brevard says from his place at the head of the table. He's a big guy with no muscle tone and soft hands—a discount version of Big Ed.

No, Gianna. Focus.

"Of course," I say, relieved that my voice doesn't crack. "I'm happy to be here."

Mr. Johnson, Mr. Brevard's sidekick for all I can gather, leans back in his chair, smoothing his tie down his chest. "Shall we get started?"

"We're ready," Francine says, side-eyeing me.

"Let's go ahead," Mr. Brevard says. "They said they might not make it."

Before I can consider who they're talking about, the door swings open. Mario enters, followed by Drake.

Our gazes collide, and I'm sure the others in the room can feel the zing. His eyes narrow as he takes me in with my swollen eyes and puffy lips. I tried to hide it with makeup, but clearly failed. Francine and Drake have both noticed.

I give him a soft smile, trying to let him know that I'm okay. It doesn't suffice. The vein on the side of his throat throbs as if he's pissed.

Is he angry with me?

My palms start to sweat as I realize that maybe I don't know what's going to happen. Maybe Drake is getting screwed over and thinks I'm the reason, although I don't think that's true. Or, perhaps he's upset that I'm upset and didn't call him. *He didn't give me time.*

The truth is, I don't know the answer because I was a fool. That plummets my spirits even farther.

"There they are," Mr. Brevard says. "I'm happy we could all meet and get this taken care of in one swoop."

"We're glad to be here," Mario says.

Drake's eyes bore into me from across the table. I can't look at him anymore, or I'll cry again. Somehow, over the past few days, I've become a crybaby. I hate it.

"I'm going to get right to it, if that's okay," Mr. Johnson says, not waiting to see if it is, in fact, okay. "I'm sure you know that we've been discussing who might be the best fit to replace the true crime podcast on Thursdays."

"We're aware," Francine says, as Mario mutters a version of the same.

"We've been very impressed with both of you, Drake and Gianna, especially over the past couple of months," Mr. Johnson says. "You're both quick on your feet. Creative. You have a knack for marketing. People, especially in your target demographic, Gianna, have flocked to Canoodle Media this quarter, and we have the two of you to thank."

Mr. Brevard turns to Drake. "We think that *Sports Take* is the better fit for Thursdays."

Francine pats my hand beneath the table as if I need consoling.

I don't know what to feel about this. My gaze lifts to Drake's. He's not smiling or blinking—just staring at me. Mario is doing the talking, thanking them for choosing their podcast and for believing in them. But my insides are a tangled mess of emotions anyway. I'm not sure that I can process anything else today.

"We'll meet with you two separately on Monday about moving forward," Mr. Brevard says. "I'm going out of town tomorrow for the weekend and wanted to get this part behind us before I leave."

"Gianna, we want to talk with you and Francine, however, about doing something a little different with the *Gianna Knows Things* brand," Mr. Johnson says, leaning forward and clasping his hands in front of him. "How would you like to help us develop your GKT brand into something new? Something bigger."

I take a deep breath and tear my attention away from Drake. As distracted as I am, this is important. I've worked for this opportunity for far too long, and I owe it to myself to advocate on my behalf.

"That would depend, Mr. Johnson," I say. "I've worked very hard to create the GKT brand." *Why are we calling it that?* I'm too tired to care. It's a *pick your battle day*, and this isn't one I'm willing to fight. "What are you proposing?"

Francine nods. "I agree. GKT is Gianna's baby, and I think we need to wade into these waters very carefully."

I give her a quick smile, grateful for the support.

"We're thinking of taking it to the next level," Mr. Johnson says with a fake enthusiasm that annoys the hell out of me. "New format—from live podcast to an actual online show. Daily episodes that are pre-recorded. Think reality show meets daytime talk show, only scripted."

I should've drunk more coffee today because this man makes no sense. "And who writes the script?"

"We'll hire a team of writers. Don't worry about that."

"Don't worry about that?" I ask incredulously. "With all due respect, what makes *Gianna Knows Things* special and different is, well, what Gianna knows. If someone else is writing the script, wouldn't it be like every other show out there?"

Mr. Brevard holds a hand out like he's cautioning me to stay in my lane. That makes me want to jump three lanes and blow a donut. *They didn't talk to Drake like this. Fuckers.*

"There is a formula that works, and we know what that is," he says. "That's the difference between a show like GKT and a household name. Bigger audiences have expectations."

"Would I have control over the script—or a say at all?" I ask.

"Sure, you could give us your notes, but it'll be up to the team to make the final call," Mr. Johnson says. "This is what we do, Gianna. You have to trust us."

I close my eyes and try not to laugh. If I do, if one little rumble of a chuckle manages its way from my chest to the outside world, it's going to be ugly. It's going to look delirious, like a meltdown in epic fashion. While that will be cathartic, it won't be helpful.

Francine glances at me and then steps in. "You mentioned last week about spinoff shows. Can you talk to Gianna about that?"

"Sure," Mr. Brevard says. "Ultimately, what we want to do is create a whole Canoodle family of shows built around GKT.

We'll court the late teens to early thirties demographic. You'll be the face of the brand. Francine shared with us the list of requests already pouring in for you to appear on podcasts and in magazines nationwide." He folds his hands in front of him. "The potential here is limitless."

Mr. Johnson engages Francine about the technical aspects that mean nothing to me.

I sit back and watch them go back and forth about my work. And as I watch the discussions happen about me, but without me, I realize what will happen if I agree to this move. I'll be used to make these fat cats even richer. They'll parade me around like a dog on a leash, telling me what to say and where to go.

It's the antithesis of what my show stands for.

I've spent months telling my listeners to follow their gut and use their voice. I've built a following by being honest. Thousands of people trust me to tell them the raw, unfiltered truth. *How can I sell out now?*

A flood of nervous energy spreads through me in a gentle but steady wave. This isn't what I want. I don't need to be a household name or fancy GKT branding. I wanted those things before because I needed to be accepted. I wanted validation. I wanted to belong to something bigger than myself in a way that didn't feel personal so that it couldn't hurt me.

But this isn't what I needed.

I glance over at Drake. His bottom lip is between his teeth, and his fingers clutch the armrests on his chair. He looks like he's two seconds from leaping up, and, really, so am I. Because I see things clearly now.

I didn't need acceptance and validation from others. I needed someone to come in and help me tear down my walls and give me space to find a new path.

What I really needed was a sprinkle of magic fairy love dust.

"Excuse me, Mr. Brevard," I say in a lull in the conversation. "I am not sure that this transition you're proposing makes a lot of sense, and I don't know that it's in my best interests."

He exchanges a curious look with Mr. Johnson.

"I think you misunderstand what we're saying, Miss Bardot," Mr. Johnson says.

"Apparently so."

Mr. Brevard sighs. "As we advance, GKT will be transitioned to the format of our choosing. That's in your contract. You have no say in it."

"What if I refuse?"

"You have every right to walk away from Canoodle at the end of your contract," Francine says over the top of Mr. Johnson's reply. "You own the rights to your brand. We ensured that we negotiated that in the deal when we signed on here. They can make decisions on how to publish your show while you're here—but only while you're here."

"If you refuse," Mr. Johnson says, "we will invoke Article Ten of your contract. You'll wrap your current season, which ends this week, and we'll part ways."

"And I keep all rights to *Gianna Knows Things*?" I ask.

Mr. Brevard nods. "You do."

I look at Francine, and she nods subtly, urging me to turn this down. So I take a long, deep breath and blow it out slowly before I speak. I give myself time to regret the decision, but the longer I sit with it, the more it makes sense.

"I'm sorry," I say. "You'll have to invoke Article Ten because I can't agree to this. I've sacrificed a lot in my life because of who I am and what I love. If I don't embrace it now, what was the point?"

The suits look at each other and implement a predetermined plan.

"You'll need to clean out your office immediately," Mr. Johnson says. "You can return for your show on Friday, but you will need to leave the premises right after. May we also remind you that you cannot disparage Canoodle Media or any of its associates on air or otherwise."

"I would never."

"Great." Mr. Johnson stands and shakes my hand, then Francine's. "It was nice working with you ladies. I'll have security usher you out, Gianna."

Francine and I get to our feet. But, as we rise, so do Drake and Mario.

I shiver as I watch Drake gather his things. *What's he doing?*

"Mr. Bennett?" Mr. Brevard says, apparently unsure what's happening as well.

He bites the inside of his cheek as he lifts his gaze to Mr. Brevard. "I'm going with her."

"*What?*" I say before I can stop myself. "Drake …"

"I'm not working for a company that would talk to a woman like that," he says calmly, as if he doesn't give a shit what Mr. Brevard says. "You tried to steamroll her into doing what you want so you could essentially steal her brand." He looks at me and smiles proudly. "She's too smart to let that happen."

Fucking tears again.

"We're ready and willing to renegotiate your contract next week," Mr. Johnson says. "You'll be properly compensated in accordance with the move."

Drake chuckles, shaking his head. "Money is not an issue for me. Have you ever looked up my contracts from when I played pro ball?"

My jaw drops. I haven't thought of that. *How much money does he have?*

Drake laughs at the look on my face.

"I'm tendering my resignation, effective immediately," he says. "You can send any communications for either of us, me or Miss Bardot, to my attorney."

I drop my pen and paper and race around the table. Drake catches me as I fling myself into his arms in front of everyone. He's never held me tighter.

"I'm sorry," I say, whispering in his ear. "You have no idea how sorry I am."

He presses a kiss to the side of my face. "You have nothing to be sorry for. Just promise it's out of your system because I can't do this again."

I half laugh, half sob as I hold his face in my hands. I stare into his beautiful blue eyes. "I love you, Drake."

He presses a soft kiss to my lips, then smiles. "I know."

Our fingers lace together as the security team from downstairs arrives to lead us out of the building.

CHAPTER
THIRTY-SIX

Gianna

"You can't expect tea in the kitchen all the time," I say as Drake slides his SUV into my driveway. "And I'm not a good housekeeper. And my art is everywhere and—"

"And you need to stop apologizing."

A warmth that I haven't felt in days spreads through me like a river. Watching Drake jump out of the vehicle like it's on fire and jog to my door feels like Christmas. Climbing out and into his arms is … *right*.

"I've missed this," I say, tucking into his side as we walk into my house.

Drake snorts, then starts laughing at the sight of my foyer. "And I've missed this."

Disarray doesn't begin to describe the scene in front of us. It's reminiscent of the aftermath of a burglary or if a bunch of raccoons were locked in a house for three days.

"Not my proudest moment," I say over his laughter. "But, also, I was heartbroken, okay? Sure, I did it to myself, but a broken heart doesn't care who did the breaking."

"All you had to do was call me, and I would have been here to fix it."

Our lips crash together. My body goes limp against his. He's intoxicating and amazing … and mine.

Finally, I pull away and gaze into his eyes. "You really quit Canoodle? That just happened, right?"

"Fuck 'em."

"Drake," I say, laughing. "That was your job."

He puts his mouth against mine and whispers, "I'm rich, you know."

"No, I didn't know." I shove him away, giggling. "And I don't wanna know."

"Why not?"

"It's awkward."

He chuckles. "It's hard to be with me for my money since you didn't know I had any." His chuckle turns into laughter, and his eyes sparkle happily. "Did you think I played football for free? Or did you think I was terrible at managing money?"

"I didn't think about it, actually." I shrug. "Why were you working at Canoodle if you don't need the money?"

"Idle hands are the devil's playthings."

My grin turns mischievous as I pull my shirt off and fling it into the kitchen. Drake smiles, amused, as he removes his, too.

"I feel like I need a tetanus shot to be in here," he says, removing his pants as I shove mine down my legs.

"Shut up and kiss me."

He grabs the back of my neck and yanks me into him. The feeling of his body against mine puts back all the pieces of my broken heart.

"How do you want to do this?" he asks, licking his lips.

"You choose this time, and I'll pick next. I just want you inside me."

He grins. "While I love the way you think, I was thinking more like *us*. How do you want to do *us*?"

I play with the back of his hair while he kisses down the side of my neck. "I don't know. But my art stuff won't fit into your apartment and—hey," I say, pulling back. "Why do you live in an apartment if you're so rich?"

He chuckles against my shoulder.

"*Anyway*," I say, not really needing an answer. It just proves my point that he wasn't exactly flashing signs of extreme wealth in my face. "I don't want to spend another night without you, so you're welcome to move into the Goal House if you want." I snicker. "Good thing you're rich. You can hire a housekeeper."

He laughs, picking me up and carrying me into the living room.

We stop next to my easel. He takes in the angry blacks, blues, and greens with swirls of pink and light blue. Something about it makes him smile.

"What?" I ask.

He shakes his head. "Think you could teach me to paint?"

My eyes light up, and I know my smile touches the corners of them. "Teach you to paint? Really?"

"Really."

"Yes. I'd love that," I say, beaming. "You taught me fantasy football, after all."

"Your team sucks, by the way."

"What?" I shriek as he nips my bottom lip, carrying me down the hall. "How do I suck? All my players are cute."

He smacks my ass, making me giggle. He smacks it again before tossing me on the bed. I barely stop moving before he's on top of me.

I stare into his eyes.

For the first time in my life, *I'm happy*. Accepted. Seen. Protected.

Chosen.

Loved.

I guess there might be something to that magic fairy love dust, after all.

EPILOGUE

GIANNA

One week later ...

"Are we celebrating something tonight?" Kim asks, surveying the number of people at the table that typically holds me, Audrey, and Astrid.

"So there's this guy," I say, grinning at my friends across the table.

Astrid laughs as Audrey states a random six-digit number.

"Oh, come on," I say. "That's not true."

"Doesn't matter," Astrid says, grinning. "That game is over."

It really is. I lean my head on Drake's shoulder and sigh happily.

My friends used to count how many times I started a story with that phrase, because each time meant I'd met another guy. Now, that phrase is officially retired. There's only one guy, and he's here forever.

"What's that mean?" Gray says, his arm stretched around Astrid's chair.

"Fuck if I know," Drake says. "I've already learned to just roll with the punches. I don't ask questions."

"We're celebrating our unemployment," I tell Kim. "Drake and I quit our jobs last week."

She smiles. "This might be the first time I've ever heard that one, but I'm here for it. What can I get you all to drink?"

We rattle off our favorites even though the girls and I don't need to tell her.

"I'll be right back." Kim heads to the kitchen.

Stupey's is dead for a Saturday night. The rain didn't help. We would've stayed in, too, if Astrid, Gray, and his brother Hartley hadn't come to town.

"So what are you going to do now that you're unemployed?" Hartley asks.

Drake squeezes my thigh under the table. "We've been throwing ideas around. We might start a podcast of our own."

"We might get chickens," I say.

Astrid snorts. "I'd love to see that."

"Or we might just hibernate for the winter and figure it out in the spring." Drake shrugs.

I jam a thumb his way. "Apparently, my boyfriend is loaded, so we don't worry about it."

The table laughs because I'm the only one who didn't realize this.

The guys get into a conversation about baseball and the Bobcats not making the playoffs. I start to chime in when my phone buzzes. I flip it over and see Juni's name on top.

Juni: Hey, Gianna!

I pick up the device and type a response.

Me: Hey, Juni! How are you?

Juni: Great. I won the office pool. I'm two hundred bucks richer because of you. So thanks. Haha

Me: What was your guess?

Juni: I guessed you'd be together until forever. Everyone else had an end date within the last week, so I won. Yay!

Her messages make me smile. I love Juni so much.

Me: Meet me for lunch sometime?

Juni: Say when.

Me: I'll text you next week.

Juni: Perfect. Tell Drake I said hi.

Me: Will do. 

"We need to set Juni up with someone," I say, setting my phone down. "She's so cute and sweet. That was her. She won the office pool."

Drake grins.

"Set her up with Jory," Gray says. "Juni and Jory. Could get confusing, but he's single."

"Hey," Drake says, nodding. "I like that. Maybe we can set them up—"

"And send them to Hess," I say. "Yes. Let's do it."

Our friends banter again, the sound loud and chaotic … and perfect. I sit back with my fingers locked with Drake's and feel so unbelievably grateful. I have the best boyfriend, the best friends, and a wider group of friends and acquaintances that are nothing short of amazing.

And a sister.

I grab my phone again, feeling sentimental.

> Me: I love you.

> Lucia: Are you okay?

> Me: Yeah. Why?

> Lucia: The last time you texted me out of the blue, I had to come to the hospital and pick you up. Stitches from falling off a bar table, if I remember correctly.

Oh, I forgot about that.

> Me: You'll be happy to know that I'm at Stupey's with my friends. Safe and sound.

> Me: Thanks, Lucia, for being a good sister.

> Lucia: Have you been poisoned?

> Me: You're a jerk.

> Lucia: Ah, there she is. Love you. I'm at a concert. Can't type.

> Me: Have fun.

"Did Auddie tell you that she's going to stay at our cabin for a while this winter?" Astrid asks.

"No, she did not." I make a face at Audrey. "I talk to you every day, and this hasn't come up?"

"It just happened. I was talking to Hartley on the way over, because we all rode together, about the ranch, and I think it might be good for me to get away from here for a while."

I lift a brow at Hartley. He's handsome and seems like a good guy, but it never hurts for my friends' guys to know they're on my radar.

"You don't need a taser, Gianna," Gray says, grinning.

I wink at the bastard.

"When we come to Nashville for the season, she's going to stay at the ranch," Astrid says. "Fun, huh?"

I sneak another look at Hartley. *Tall, dark, sweet but a little brooding?* "Yeah, fun."

Drake elbows me in the side, making me laugh.

Kim brings our drinks, and everyone orders their entrées. I lean against Drake, my real boyfriend, and relax.

After repeating my mantra for years, I finally believe it.

I am enough for this moment. And all of those other moments led me here.

To them.

I look up at Drake and catch him watching me with a soft, sweet smile.

And to him.

Thank you for reading TRY ME. I hope you enjoyed it and will consider leaving a review.

If you haven't read Astrid's book, PLAY ME, it's available now on Amazon, Audible, and in Kindle Unlimited.

Chapter One is next for your convenience and reading pleasure.

UP NEXT: PLAY ME

Synopsis

He's supposed to be playing rugby—not playing *me*.

I didn't think it was possible to hate someone. Like utterly despise another human. Then **I was hired to babysit the Royals' newest star** and found out just how wrong I was.

My job should've been easy. Keep the hotshot on time and

out of trouble. But that's hard to do when I dream of smothering him with his jersey.

Every day delivers a new reason to detest Gray Adler. His truck is the size of a whale, and he uses the horn like a weapon. *And, no, that's not a euphemism.* He can't manage a sentence without being rude. And the universe, in its cruelest joke, gave that tattooed, walking red flag the body of a Greek god.

Just when I finally get used to hating him, things take a turn.

A **scalding-hot, mind-blowing** *I can't do this with a man I work with* sort of turn.

Suddenly, those rough hands make my skin sizzle. His sinful smirks fade into grins just for me. And our banter shifts into something much more profound than it should.

But Gray Adler is hiding something. And when those secrets collide with my vulnerable heart, I ask myself an important question.

Is he finally telling me the truth, or am I still getting played?

CHAPTER ONE
Astrid

"Can you still track me?"

"That doesn't make me sound creepy at all," I say, watching dollar bills flow from my bank account into my gas tank. My compact car may not be flashy, but what it lacks in style, it makes up for in gas mileage. *Thank God.* "But, yes, I can see where you are unless you removed yourself from our friend circle in the app. Why?"

Gianna sighs. "Because I'm about to meet a guy in front of a defunct carpet store, and all I can think about is a scene in a horror movie where the killer asks the girl to help him load a rug. You can guess how that ends."

"I'd rather not." I release the trigger, let the residual drips of gas fall into my tank—*gotta get every penny's worth in this economy*—and return the dispenser to the pump.

The late morning is unseasonably warm for spring. Birds perch along the power lines, forming neat little rows overhead. The sky is cloudless, allowing the sun's bright rays to heat my face as I duck back into my car.

"Okay," I say, giving my friend all my attention once I'm settled in my seat. "Do you know this guy you're meeting?"

"Nope. Met him on Social last night."

"And why are you meeting him?"

She groans. "To buy a urinal."

"As one does."

"Don't be a smart-ass, Astrid."

I laugh. "I just wish this surprised me a little more. That's all."

I start the engine and wait for my phone to reconnect to Bluetooth.

Gianna and I have been friends since we were kids. A classmate put gum in her hair in first grade, so I dumped my juice on his crotch and made it look like he peed his pants. Turns out that juice on your pants is a much bigger travesty than gum in your hair in elementary school.

It also creates the best friendships, even if her dreamy Pisces tendencies occasionally drive my goal-oriented brain bananas.

"Finding a urinal has been on my bucket list for a long time," she says. "You'd be surprised how hard they are to find. And they're not cheap."

"At least tell me it's a new one." My response is met with silence. I rest my head against the seat and take a long breath. "Let me get this straight. You're meeting a stranger in an abandoned parking lot to buy a used urinal you found on the black market?"

"Don't say it like that."

"Why? Because it sounds utterly ridiculous?" I sigh,

fastening my seat belt. "I love your love for art, but I really need you to implement more stranger-danger protocols—like not meeting strange men in strange places for strange items." I glance at the clock. "If you can wait an hour, I can go with you. I just have to take care of a few returns for my boss's wife, and then I can get away for a little while."

"Can't. I'm meeting him in fifteen minutes."

Oh, for the love of Pete.

I stare out my windshield and wonder if this is what parenting feels like. You watch someone you love toddle into the world, hoping they don't kill themselves. Over a urinal.

It's amazing humans still exist, especially ones like Gianna Bardot. That she's survived for the past twenty-seven years amazes me.

I grab my phone and find the app our friend group uses to share our locations.

"You're logged in," I say, watching her designated car emoji travel south out of the city. "I'm watching you now."

"Good. Okay. If you don't hear from me in twenty minutes, I've probably been stuffed in the back of a van. Literally, not figuratively, unfortunately."

I snort, glancing in the rearview mirror as a large black truck pulls in behind me. The engine rumbles, creating a low vibration that I feel in my bones. I narrow my eyes to see who's sitting in the driver's seat, but the window tint's too dark.

"What are you doing for dinner?" Gianna asks, pulling my attention back to our conversation.

I drop my phone in the cup holder. "No clue. I just finished breakfast."

"Just now? I've been up working since six thirty."

"I didn't say I just woke up." I've already done a load of laundry, loaded the dishwasher, and cleaned out two closets today. "Not only have I finished my chores and completed nearly all my tasks for Renn and Blakely for the day but I've also spent a couple of hours looking for a new side hustle."

"Your last side hustle just ended. Can't you take a few weeks off and relax for once?"

I wish. "No. If I have time on my hands, I need to pay down this debt faster. The interest is killing me."

Gianna sighs. "That means you don't read enough. If you read more books, you wouldn't have time to worry about your debt."

"That's a responsible take on things." I laugh. "Besides, I can't sit still long enough to read a book for fun."

"Audiobooks were made for a reason, Astrid."

"So were books about personal safety, but you ignore those."

She laughs. "Sometimes you have to risk things for art."

Her joy over this urinal and the sense of adventure she feels about the process brings a smile to my face.

If there were one thing, one habit, that I would adopt from someone else, it's Gianna's *passion*. She throws herself into random art pieces, recipes, and side quests she unearths as a wildly successful advice columnist. It's something I could never do. The lack of structure makes me itchy, and I feel the overwhelming need to put it all on a calendar … and take the fun out of it.

"Want to meet at Stupey's for overpriced sandwiches?" Gianna asks. "My treat since you bought last time. I think Audrey's going to be around this weekend. The three of us haven't been all together for two whole weeks."

"Sure." I glance back at the truck again. It's still behind me despite nearly every other pump available. *Weird.* I consider pointing out how aware I am of my surroundings and suggesting that Gianna do the same. But she's too fixated on the urinal to listen now. "I'll drop it in the chat, and we'll work it out."

"Sounds like a plan."

My boss's name flashes across my infotainment center. At the same time, the black truck revs its engine. *Is he revving that thing at me?*

"Hey, Renn's calling me," I say, glaring at the truck. "Text me when you secure the toilet and you're on your way home."

"Urinal, Astrid. *Ur-in-al*."

I laugh. "Bye."

"Bye, friend."

I tap the button to accept Renn's call, push in the brake, and then move my hand to the gear shifter. But as soon as I touch the knob, the truck revs again—and that stops me in my tracks. *He's definitely revving his engine at me.*

"Hey, Renn," I say, watching the behemoth behind me. Irritation snakes its way down my spine. "What's up?"

"It's been a hell of a morning. I didn't catch you in the middle of anything, did I?"

"Nothing much. Just waiting out some guy who's overcompensating for something by having an extra-large truck."

Renn pauses. "Waiting him out? For what?"

"He pulled in right behind me even though every other pump but one is open. I'm at the gas station, by the way. And because I haven't rushed to get out of his way, he's revving his engine at me."

"*Oh.*"

"What can I do for you?"

"Don't get arrested? That would be great."

The engine roars again—louder this time.

"Can you hear that?" I ask, my fingers gripping the steering wheel.

"Yeah, I can. Are you able to leave?"

"Sure, I could. And I would if he hadn't tried to bully me." I roll my window down and hold my hand out, palm-side up. "Now, I'm going to sit here until he leaves."

"*Astrid.*"

A large, thick forearm sticks out of the driver's side window, mimicking my gesture. *Fucker.*

"Why did you say you called?" I ask, annoyance stinging my cheeks.

Renn sighs as if he doesn't know what to say. It's like a part of him wants to continue persuading me to leave, but the rest of him knows it's pointless—and that side is right. I'll gladly back down from a skirmish if I'm wrong. I'll even apologize. *But in this case?* I'm not. So I won't.

"I have a proposition to discuss with you," he says.

"That sounds vaguely interesting."

"*Will you move?*" a voice shouts from the truck.

I mute Renn. "*Yeah. When I'm ready!*" I yell back before unmuting my boss. "Do you want to discuss it now or later?"

"Do you think you can swing by my office this afternoon?" Renn asks.

"Some of us have things to do today!" he shouts again.

I hit mute and then stick my head out the window. "Then pick another pump!" I settle back in my seat and huff before unmuting Renn again. "Sure. I have a couple of errands to run for Blakely, and then I'll be free."

"That works."

A horn blasts out of nowhere, the sound echoing thanks to the awning covering the gas station. I jump, anger prickling my scalp, and unbuckle myself. *He did not just do that.* "I'll see you then."

"What's going on?" Renn asks.

"I gotta go."

"Astrid, what's happening?"

I pop the handle, and my door swings open. "This asshole just honked at me."

"Let it go."

"Thanks for the advice, Elsa," I say, my finger hovering over the button to end the call. "I'll let you know when I'm on my way. Talk soon."

I drop my fingertip against the red button, then fling my legs out of the car, slamming the door behind me. I storm toward the truck, my anger singeing the edges of my restraint.

My tennis shoes pound against the asphalt with more force

than is probably necessary, but I can't help it. If there's one thing I hate more than anything, it's men who audaciously think that their penis gives them a free pass to act like a chump. It's like they believe that their five-incher has magical powers. In my twenty-eight years of life, I've never met a woman who claims a penis gave her more than a headache and, on the rare occasion, a semi-satisfying orgasm.

Heat billows from the front of the truck, blasting me as I march by. The top of the tires are waist-high, and I can't fathom why anyone driving in the city needs tires this big. It's obnoxious … kind of like the driver.

"Do you have a problem?" I yell over the sound coming from beneath the hood. The scent of gasoline and grease fills the air, stinging my nostrils. It crosses my mind for one quick, fleeting moment that this may not be significantly different from Gianna's meetup for the urinal.

I'll just have to be a hypocrite today.

I round the side mirror jutting out and come face-to-face with my nemesis. He stares down at me from his perch in the cab of the truck with a sardonic expression that sends my temper soaring.

He arches a thick brow, pinning me to the spot with deep, walnut-colored eyes. "Yeah, I do have a problem. You're blocking the pump."

"There are literally …" I peel my gaze from his and quickly count the vacant pumps. *All of them are open.* Every. Last. One. "You have nine different options. Pick another one."

"I want this one."

"You can't always get what you want."

His lips twitch. "True, because I'd also like to take that stick out of your ass, but that's probably off the table, too, huh?"

I gasp, startled by his crudeness. Surprise siphons the blood from my face. Words wedge themselves in my throat from the shock of the moment.

"You're a fucking asshole."

"I've been called worse," he says with a nonchalant shrug. "Will you move now?"

"I would've happily moved out of your way if you'd asked nicely. But you didn't," I say, pointing a finger at him. "Instead, you rolled up here in this ridiculous truck and revved your engine at me like some kind of threat."

He makes the cockiest face—quirked brow, subtle smirk—like I'm acting irrational, and he thinks it's funny.

"Then you honked your horn at me, which is unacceptable anywhere except maybe to avoid a collision." I'm fighting to stay calm. "You are rude and disrespectful, and I have a personal rule that I don't acquiesce to men who try to bully me."

"Wow." He grins, displaying a set of dimples. "Bully you? *Okay*. You realize that you were sitting in your little car, taking up real estate while you had social hour, right?"

"Not that it's any of your business, but I was talking to my boss."

The lively twinkle in his eye is like throwing fuel on my simmering fury. "Do it in the office, sweetheart. Not here."

"*Sweetheart*?" I bark, my eyes widening. "You will *never* get the pleasure of knowing me well enough to call me sweetheart."

"Thank God for small favors." The chuckle he only half-heartedly tries to suppress proves otherwise. "Know what I find interesting?" he asks, rolling his tongue along his bottom lip. "I find it interesting that you claim to be some kind of manners police when you're the one blocking the damn pump."

My hands go to my hips as I bite back the first thought that comes to mind because, unfortunately, I know he's *technically* right. It *is* bad manners to block a pump. But they say the devil is in the details, and I try to avoid the devil at all costs.

I take a breath, then wear the biggest, most facetious smile I can manage. "I'll leave when you ask nicely, *sweetheart*."

He rests one massive forearm along the window and gives me the most blasé look ever. I pointedly ignore his pouty bottom lip and the perfect amount of scruff peppering a rock-hard jawline. Instead, I remember his insolence.

"I should sit here all day just because you're a jerk," I say, unblinking.

He turns off his truck without breaking eye contact. "Fine by me. I have time today."

Before I can think of something quick-witted to say—*didn't he just say he has somewhere to be?*— an older sedan pulls up to the pump beside us, nearly clipping the bollards protecting the equipment. A small, older lady gets out, oblivious to the standoff happening feet from her, and waddles around the back of the car in her Velcro-strapped shoes. She fiddles with the pump, groaning as she tries to lift the nozzle from the machine. Whiffs of grandma perfume float in the air, and I suddenly crave snickerdoodles.

I fold my arms over my chest, unable to argue with this guy in front of somebody's grandma.

He sighs. "Move," he says more softly this time, bringing my attention to him once again.

I take a step back as the truck door swings open. He doesn't bother with the step rail but instead hops down with a natural ease. He doesn't bother to look my way either.

He's taller than average, which surprises me. Broad shoulders fill out a plain black T-shirt, and thick thighs stretch the denim covering them. Dark hair is cut close to his head. He carries himself with a confidence that's universally accepted as attractive—and it's such a shame.

Why waste a package like this on a guy with such a bad attitude?

"Are you doing okay over here?" he asks the woman like he wasn't just being awful to me five seconds ago. "These pumps can get a little tricky."

"Yes, they can." She sighs, clutching her pocketbook in her free hand. "I have a heck of a time wrangling these things. My arthritis is something awful. My John used to pump my gas for me, but he's been gone for twenty-three years now. Feels like yesterday sometimes."

"I'm not John, but I'd be happy to pump your gas for you today."

Oh, please.

I shuffle a bit closer so I can hear more clearly.

She coos, clearly smitten with him and his thoughtfulness. And, although she's getting played by Truck Boy, I can't blame her. He must seem genuinely sweet from her perspective. There's no way for her to know he's a fox in sheep's clothing.

"You don't mind?" she asks. "I don't want to take up too much of your time."

He glances at me out of the corner of his eye, his dimple shining in his cheek. "Not at all, ma'am. I'm going to be here a while anyway."

I glare at him.

"Oh, you're such a good boy. So many young men don't want to bother with an old woman like me." She loops her arm through his elbow, and they slowly move to the driver's side. "When you get to be my age, you feel like you don't belong in the world anymore. You can barely work the new gadgets, and everyone's so impatient with you. It's terrible."

"I'm sorry you feel that way," he says as he opens her car door.

I stand beside his truck and watch them, trying to make sense of this encounter. He flipped from prick to prince in five seconds flat. My mind spins in bewilderment.

"Wait just a second," the lady says, dropping into her seat with a huff. "I forgot to put my card in to pay."

"It's on me today," he says.

I roll my eyes so hard it hurts.

He comes back to the pump, his gaze leveling with mine. A smug grin is all it takes to send me back into a free fall. But, before I can get a word out, he steps to the left and out of sight.

My first instinct is to stand my ground and wait for him to

finish. If I move, he wins. But with each second that passes without him in my line of sight, I think more clearly. And a glance around reminds me that I'm standing at a gas station, arguing with a stranger over a pump.

It's like a bucket of cold water being tossed on my head.

So what if he wants to be a child about this? I have errands to run … and I'm getting off schedule.

"If you want to play games, Truck Boy, you'll have to find someone else to play with you," I say.

I throw my hair over my shoulder in a final act of defiance and march my way back to my car.

Take a deep breath, Astrid. Get out of fight or flight. It's over.

I fill my lungs again and slowly exhale.

At least my asshole quota has been met for the day, and it can only get better from here.

Thank God for that.

If you haven't read Astrid's book, PLAY ME, it's available now on Amazon, Audible, and in Kindle Unlimited.

MORE FROM ADRIANA LOCKE

Chapter One
Brooke

WANTED: A SITUATION-SHIP

I'm a single female who's tired of relationships ruining my life. However, there are times when a date would be helpful. If you're a single man, preferably mid-twenties to late-thirties, and are in a similar situation, we might be a match.

Candidate must be handsome, charming, and willing to

pretend to have feelings for me (on a sliding scale, as the event requires). Ability to discuss a wide variety of topics is a plus. Must have your own transportation and a (legal) job.

This will be a symbiotic agreement. In exchange for your time, I will give you mine. Need someone to flirt with you at a football party? Go, team! Want a woman to make you look good in front of your boss? Let me find my heels. Would you love for someone to be obsessed with you in front of your ex? I'm applying my red lipstick now.

If interested, please email me. Time is of the essence.

My best friend, Jovie, points at my computer screen. The glitter on her pink fingernail sparkles in the light. "You can't post that."

I fold my arms across my chest. "And why not?"

Instead of answering me, she takes another bite of her chicken wrap. A dribble of mayonnaise dots the corner of her mouth.

"A lot of help you are," I mutter, rereading the post I drafted instead of pricing light fixtures for work. The words are written in a pretty font on Social, my go-to social media platform.

Country music from the nineties mixes with the laughter of locals sitting around us in Smokey's, my favorite beachside café. Along the far wall, a map of the state of Florida made of wine corks sways gently in the ocean breeze coming through the open windows.

"Would you two like anything else?" Rebecca, our usual lunchtime server, pauses by the table. "I think we have some Key lime pie left."

"I'm too irritable for pie today," I say.

"*You* don't want *pie*? That's a first," she teases me.

Jovie giggles.

"I know," I say, releasing a sigh. "That's the state of my life right now. I don't even want pie."

"Wow. Okay. This sounds serious. What's up? Maybe I can help," Rebecca says.

Jovie wipes her mouth with a napkin. "Let me cut in here real quick before she tries to snowball you into thinking her hare-brained idea is a good one."

I roll my eyes. "It *is* a good one."

"I'll give you the CliffsNotes version," Jovie says, side-eyeing me. "Brooke got an invitation to her grandma's birthday party, and instead of just not going—"

"I can't *not go.*"

"Or showing up as the badass single chick she is," Jovie continues, silencing me with a look, "she wrote a post for Social that's basically an ad for a fake boyfriend."

"Correction—it *is* an ad for a fake boyfriend."

Rebecca rests a hand on her hip. "I don't see the problem."

"*Thank you,*" I say, staring at Jovie. "I'm glad someone understands me here."

Jovie throws her hands in the air, sending a napkin flying right along with them.

Satisfaction is written all over my face as I sit back in my chair with a smug smile. The more I think about having a *situation-ship* with a guy—a word I read in a magazine at the salon while waiting two decades for my color to process—the more it makes sense.

Instead of having relations with a man, have situations. Done.

What's not to love about that?

"But, before I tell you to dive into this whole thing, why can't you just go alone, Brooke?" Rebecca asks.

"Oh, *I can* go alone. I just generally prefer to avoid torture whenever possible."

"I still don't understand why you need a date to your grandma's birthday party."

"Because this isn't *just* a birthday party," I say. "It's labeled that to cover up the fact that my mom and her sister, my aunt Kim, are having a daughter-of-the-year showdown. They're using my poor grandma Honey's eighty-fifth birthday as a dog and pony show—and my cousin Aria and I are the ponies."

"*Okay*." Rebecca looks at me dubiously before switching her attention to Jovie. "And why are you against this whole thing?"

Jovie takes enough cash to cover our lunch plus the tip and hands it to Rebecca. *Perks of ordering the same lunch most days.* Then she gathers her things.

"I'm not against it in *theory*," Jovie says. "I'm against it in *practice*. I understand the perks of having a guy around to be arm candy when needed. But I'm not supporting this decision … this *mayhem* … for two reasons." She looks at me. "For one, your family will see any post you make on Social. You don't think they'll use it as ammunition against you?"

This is probably true.

"Second," Jovie continues. "I hate, hate, *hate* your aunt Kim, and I loathe the fact that your mom makes you feel like you have to do anything more than be your amazing self to win her favor. Screw them both."

My heart swells as I take in my best friend.

Jovie Reynolds was my first friend in Kismet Beach when I moved here two and a half years ago. We reached for the same can of pineapple rings, knocking over an entire display in Publix. As we picked up the mess, we traded recipes—hers for a vodka cocktail and mine for air fryer pineapple.

We hung out that evening—with her cocktail and my air fryer creations—and have been inseparable since.

"My mom is not a bad person," I say in her defense, even though I'm not so sure that's true from time to time. "She's just …"

"A bad person," Jovie says.

I laugh. "*No.* I just … nothing I can do is good enough for her. She hated Geoff when I married him at twenty and said I was too young. But was she happy when that ended in a divorce? Nope. According to *her*, I didn't try hard enough."

Rebecca frowns.

"And then Geoff started banging Kim and—"

"*What*?" Rebecca yelps, her eyes going wide.

"Exactly. Bad people," Jovie says, shaking her head.

"So your ex-husband will be at your grandma's party with your aunt? Is that what you're saying?" Rebecca asks.

I nod. "Yup."

She stacks our plates on top of one another. The ceramic clinks through the air. "On that note, why can't you just not go? Avoid it altogether?"

"Because my grandma Honey is looking forward to this, and she called me to make sure I was coming. I couldn't tell her no." My heart tightens when I think of the woman I love more than any other. "And, you know, my mom has made it abundantly clear that if I miss this, I will probably break Honey's heart, and she'll die, and it'll be my fault."

"Wow. That's a freight train of guilt to throw around," Rebecca says, wincing.

I glance down at my computer. The post is still there, sitting on the screen and waiting for my final decision. Although it is a genius idea, if I do say so myself—Jovie is probably right. It'll just cause more problems than it's worth.

I close the laptop and shove it into my bag. Then I hoist it on my shoulder. "It's complicated. I want to go and celebrate with my grandma but seeing my aunt with my ex-husband ..." I wince. "Also, there will be my mother's usual diatribe and comparisons to Aria, proving that I'm a failure in everything that I do."

"But if you had a boyfriend to accompany you, you'd save face with the enemy and have a buffer against your mother. Is that what you're thinking?" Rebecca asks.

"Yeah. I don't know how else to survive it. I can't walk in there alone, or even with Jovie, and deal with all of that mess. If I just had someone hot and a little handsy—make me look irresistible—it would kill all of my birds with one hopefully *hard* stone."

I wink at my friends.

Rebecca laughs. "Okay. I'm Team Fake Boyfriend. Sorry, Jovie."

Jovie sighs. "I'm sorry for me too because I have to go back to work. And if I avoid the stoplights, I can make it to the office with thirty seconds to spare." She air-kisses Rebecca. "Thanks for the extra mayo."

I laugh. "See you tomorrow, Rebecca."

"Bye, girls."

Jovie and I walk single-file through Smokey's until we reach the exit. Immediately, we reach for the sunglasses perched on top of our heads and slide them over our eyes.

The sun is bright, nearly blinding in a cloudless sky. I readjust my bag so that the thin layer of sweat starting to coat my skin doesn't coax the leather strap down my arm.

"Call me tonight," Jovie says, heading to her car.

"I will."

"Rehearsal for the play got canceled tonight, so I might go to Charlie's. If I don't, I may swing by your house."

"How's the thing with Charlie going? I didn't realize you were still talking to him."

She laughs. "I wasn't. He pissed me off. But he came groveling back last night, and I gave in." She shrugs. "What can I say? I'm a sucker for a good grovel."

"I think it's the theater girl in you. You love the dramatics of it all."

"That I do. It's a problem."

"Well, I'll see you when I see you then," I say.

"Bye, Brooke."

I give her a little wave and make my way up Beachfront Boulevard.

The sidewalk is fairly vacant with a light dusting of sand. In another month, tourists will fill the street that leads from the ocean to the shops filled with trinkets and ice cream in the heart of Kismet Beach. For now, it's a relaxing and hot walk back to the office.

My mind shifts from the heat back to the email reminder I received during lunch. *To Honey's party.* It takes all of one second for my stomach to cramp.

"I shouldn't have eaten all of those fries," I groan.

But it's not lunch that's making me unwell.

A mixture of emotions rolls through me. I don't know which one to land on. There's a chord of excitement about the event—at seeing Honey and her wonderful life be celebrated, catching up with Aria and the rest of my family, and the general concept of *going home.* But there's so much apprehension right alongside those things that it drowns out the good.

Kim and Geoff together make me ill. It's not that I miss my ex-husband; I'm the one who filed for divorce. But they will be there, making things super awkward for me in front of everyone we know.

Not to mention what it will do to my mother.

Geoff hooking up with Kim is my ultimate failure, according to Mom. Somehow, it embarrasses *her,* and that's unforgivable.

"For just once, I'd like to see her and not be judged," I mumble as I sidestep a melting glob of blue ice cream.

Nothing I have ever done has been good enough for Catherine Bailey. Marrying Geoff was an atrocity at only twenty years old. My dream to work in interior architecture wasn't deemed serious enough as a life path. *"You're wasting your time and our money, Brooke."* And when I told her I was hired at Laguna Homes as a lead designer for one of their three renovation teams? I could hear her eyes rolling.

The office comes into view, and my spirits lift immediately. I shove all thoughts of the party out of my brain and let my mind settle back into happier territory. *Work.* The one thing I love.

I step under the shade of an adorable crape myrtle tree and then turn up a cobblestone walkway to my office.

The small white building is tucked away from the sidewalk.

It sits between a row of shops with apartments above them and an Italian restaurant only open in the evenings. The word *Laguna Homes* is printed in seafoam green above a black awning.

My shoes tap against the wooden steps as I make my way to the door. A rush of cool air, kissed by the scent of eucalyptus essential oil, greets me as I step inside.

"How was lunch?" Kix asks, standing in the doorway of his corner office. My boss's smile is kind and genuine, just like everything else about him. "Let me guess—you met Jovie for lunch at Smokey's?"

I laugh. "It's like you know me or something."

He chuckles.

Kix and Damaris Carmichael are two of my favorite people in the world. When I met Damaris at a trade show three years ago, and we struck up a conversation about tile, I knew she was special. Then I met her husband and discovered he had the same soft yet sturdy energy. All six of their children possess similar qualities—even Moss, the superintendent on my renovation team. Although I'd never admit that to him.

"I swung by Parasol Place this afternoon," Kix says. "It's looking great. You were right about taking out the wall between the living room and dining room. I love it. It makes the whole house feel bigger."

I blush under the weight of his compliment. "Thanks."

"Did Moss tell you about the property I'm looking at for your team next?" Kix asks.

"No. Moss doesn't tell me anything."

Kix grins. "I'm sure he tells you all kinds of things you don't need to know."

"You say that like you have experience with him," I say, laughing.

"Only a few years." He laughs too. "It's another home from the sixties. I got a lead on it this morning and am on my way to look at it now."

"Take pictures. You know I love that era, and if you get it, I want to be able to start envisioning things right away."

"You and your visions." He shakes his head. "Gina is in the back making copies. I told her we'd keep our eye on the door until she gets back out here, so it would be great if you could do that."

"Absolutely," I say, walking backward toward my office. "Be safe. *And take pictures.*"

"I will. Enjoy the rest of your day, Brooke."

"You, too."

I reach behind me to find my office door open. I take another step back and then turn toward my desk. Someone moves beside my filing cabinet just as I flip on the light.

"Ah!" I shriek, clutching my chest.

My heart pounds out of control until I get my bearings and focus on the man looking back at me.

I set my bag down on a chair and blow out a shaky breath. "Dammit, Moss!"

He leans against the cabinet and smiles at me cheekily.

"We're going to have to stop meeting like this," he says. "People are going to talk."

Flirt is available on Amazon, Audible, and in Kindle Unlimited.

ACKNOWLEDGMENTS

This book was such a labor of love. I haven't fallen so hard for two characters in a long time. Drake and Gianna stole my heart from the first page, and I hope you loved them, too.

I'd like to thank my Creator before all else. Always.

The hours that I spent writing this book, more than usual, meant a lot of takeout dinners, piled up laundry, and dishes in the sink. (How does that happen when you order takeout? Seems sketchy to me.) But my husband, my biggest cheerleader, jumped in like he always does and kept our home base running. I'm forever grateful. My sons also give me so much energy and inspiration. They become as invested in the process as I do, checking on me, on the plot, and bringing me snacks. They're forever my best work.

I'm surrounded by so many amazing women, and without them, I would write less books, cry a lot more, and know a lot less about a lot of random stuff. My best friend Mandi Beck is my muse for Gianna. They're both spitfires, stubborn, and loyal almost to a fault. There were so many times when I was writing Gianna that I had to stop and laugh because it was *so Mandi*. I'm lucky to call her my bestie.

To my work wife Jessica Prince—we're back baby! Ha! Jess and I had the same deadline (and were equally behind on said deadline). But we sat down, turned on Zoom, and got all the snacks. Many, many hours later, tons of check-ins and sprints, laughs, and a few tears, and we wrapped our projects and celebrated. Love you, Jess.

I start most days with a phone call to S.L. Scott, my emotional support author. We're finally on opposite writing schedules, which makes it easier to bounce ideas off each other. Without her, I would stare at a more blank screens, laugh a lot less, and my office would smell a lot worse. (She sends the best air fresheners!) Here's to more morning business calls!

Author Kenna Rey also happens to be one of my closest and smartest friends. I trust her instincts and storytelling abilities more than nearly anyone else in the world. She just gets me and what I'm trying to do, sometimes before I even realize what I'm doing. Every time she says yes to working with me, I consider myself lucky. Try Me is a thing because of Kenna.

I'd also like to thank my assistants Tiffany Remy and Jenn Hess, the fabulous Jenny Edits, Sarah Hansen with Okay Creations, photographer Michelle Lancaster, the best proofreader and friend Michele Ficht, the fabulous Jenny Sims with Editing 4 Indies, and Marion Archer with Marion Making Manuscripts.

And, as always, thank you to my readers. Thank you for trusting me to tell you a story and spending a little time in my world. I love you. Xo

ABOUT THE AUTHOR

Adriana Locke is a USA Today and Amazon Charts Bestselling author with a knack for writing swoony, unforgettable contemporary romances. At nineteen, she traded her small-town roots for big-city life, only to realize her heart beats for quiet mornings and cozy chaos. These days, she's living her happily-ever-after in Ohio with Mr. Locke—her high school sweetheart—four lively sons, and two hilariously hyper Jack Russell terriers.

When she's not penning love stories that will leave you laughing and sighing, Adriana is battling the epic quest of missing silverware, "gardening" (a.k.a. chatting with her plants), or leaving her grocery list on the counter as she heads to the store. Grab a cup of coffee, settle in, and let her books whisk you away to a world of heartwarming romance and irresistible heroes.

www.adrianalocke.com